Deceiving
Lies

Also by Molly McAdams

Forgiving Lies
Stealing Harper
From Ashes
Taking Chances

Deceiving *Lies*

MOLLY McADAMS

WILLIAM MORROW
An Imprint of HarperCollins*Publishers*

DECEIVING LIES. Copyright © 2014 by Molly Jester. All rights reserved. Printed in the United States of America. No part of this book may be used or reproduced in any manner whatsoever without written permission except in the case of brief quotations embodied in critical articles and reviews. For information address HarperCollins Publishers, 10 East 53rd Street, New York, NY 10022.

HarperCollins books may be purchased for educational, business, or sales promotional use. For information please e-mail the Special Markets Department at SPsales@harpercollins.com.

FIRST EDITION

Library of Congress Cataloging-in-Publication Data has been applied for.

ISBN 978-0-06-229931-4

14 15 16 17 18   OV/RRD   10 9 8 7 6 5 4 3 2 1

For my amazing in-laws. Your support has meant the world to me, welcoming me to this scary, big, unknown world called Texas and being there for me when my family was so far away meant more than you'll ever know. I love you both and know my readers will fall in love with y'all as Kash's parents.

Prologue

Rachel

I NERVOUSLY FLIPPED MY LONG HAIR over my shoulders and smoothed my hands down my shirt a few times as I took deep breaths in and out. My back was to Kash's truck, hiding me from his parents' house while I collected myself, but I was starting to consider taking off running. *Why the hell did I buy and wear heels today?*

"Rach?" He laughed when he came around the truck and caught sight of me. "What are you doing? You look amazing."

I grimaced when I glanced down at my dark, skinny jeans and the electric blue top that I'd gone out to buy today, since I hadn't brought any clothes to Florida that I'd deemed acceptable to wear when meeting his parents. "It's not the clothes."

He grabbed my chin and tilted my head back until I was looking at him, and waited until I stopped fidgeting. "They're going to love you," he assured me as he brushed his lips across mine. "You have nothing to worry about."

"How can you say that? I got engaged to their son without ever meeting them, they hardly know I exist, Kash." *And I got their son shot . . .* I knew it wasn't my fault, my therapy sessions with Dr. Markowitz at the end of last year had helped me realize that. But that didn't mean Kash's and Mason's families would feel the same. "Honestly, at the time I just thought you weren't close with them, it didn't seem weird to me because, well . . . because I didn't have parents for you to meet either. But now—"

"Stop. You're overthinking this, they know everything that happened now, and you have no idea how excited my mom was when I called her this morning to tell her you were here. Right now, they're just happy because they know I've been miserable without you. But, babe, they're going to love you."

I exhaled roughly and nodded my head. "Okay, let's do this."

"That's my girl." He kissed me hard before wrapping his arm around my waist and walking me toward the house. "I mean, honestly, how could they not love you and your bitchy personality?"

"You're such an asshole, Kash," I hissed at the same second the front door opened and his mom stepped out. *Oh good Lord, kill me now. This is where I need to run away.*

Mrs. Ryan's eyebrows shot up to her hairline, and Kash tried to choke back his laugh but failed miserably. It felt like my stomach was simultaneously on fire and dropping. Not a good feeling, I was going to be sick. I was the freaking Queen of First Impressions with the Ryan family. When I'd met Kash at the beginning of last summer, I'd been a bitch to the extreme, and our first three run-ins had gone over about as well as a bale of turtles in a sprinting race. Now there I was, cussing in front of his mom in the first seconds of ever seeing her.

I started feeling light-headed as I held my breath, waiting for Mrs. Ryan to tell me I was not good enough for her son, or to reprimand me. Instead she crossed her arms over her chest and leveled a glare at Kash that impressed even me.

"What on earth did you say to the poor girl?"

He raised his hands in surrender before wrapping his arm around me again. "No clue what you're talking about. And why do you automatically think it had to be something I did?"

"Because I know you, Logan."

"Eh . . . so anyway. Mom, this is Rachel. Rachel, this is my mom."

She brushed back a chunk of black hair that had fallen into her eyes and smiled brightly at me. I still felt like I was frozen and didn't know how to breathe properly. "Rachel, it's so good to meet you, honey!"

I almost blurted out *"But I just called your son an asshole right in front of you!"* Instead I plastered a smile on my face and tried to relax my body as Kash let go of me and she wrapped me in a hug. "It's nice to meet you too. Thank you for having us to dinner."

"Of course"—and then softer, so only I could hear—"he gets the obnoxious, asshole gene from his father. But, unfortunately, it's one of the things I love most about my guys. You just get used to it and become a master at slyly flipping them off with a smile."

My eyes widened and I blinked rapidly as we pulled away from each other. *Is she being serious?*

She smiled at me again and kissed Kash on the cheek before slapping his shoulder. "Be nice to her, she just got here! But always remember this, honey, the minute Richard and Logan stop giving you a hard time, is the minute they stop loving you. So, as long as he's pissing you off, you know he loves you. Now come on, your dad just started the grill and I'm going to make margaritas for Rachel and me. Oh, do you like margaritas?"

I nodded and then had to shake my head to get my mind working properly again. "Uh, yeah. Yeah, I do, I love them."

"Well then, I think we're going to get along just fine. C'mon, now!" She turned and walked into the house, and Kash pulled me into his side, his lips going to my ear.

"Now was that so bad?"

"Aside from the fact that the first time your mom saw me, I was cussing . . . I think I just fell in love with her."

He laughed low as he pulled me into the house. "Just wait 'til you meet my dad."

1

Kash

"RACH, DO YOU REALLY NEED THIS MANY SHOES?" I watched as she unpacked the third box in our closet just inside the bathroom and wondered how any person could ever have a need for that many pairs of shoes.

Her hand stopped midway to the shelf with another pair, and her bright blue glare turned on me. I took a step back.

"Are you actually asking me that right now?"

"Say no," my dad whispered from behind me. "Course he wasn't, Rachel. He's just mad that he won't have anywhere to put his sparkly hooker heels."

Rachel laughed and went back to putting her dozens of shoes away. "No worries about that one, Rich. I put them up already, they even have their own little place away from everything so they don't get ruined."

My mom pushed through Dad and me to get into the closet with an armful of clothes to hang up. "Really, Logan. Give the girl a break. I have more shoes than this."

"Oh, Marcy! I forgot to tell you—"

"Is this gonna be a long story?" Dad drawled, cutting Rachel off.

"Actually, it is," she snapped right back with a playful smirk. "So get comfy!" As soon as she launched into her story about whatever the hell those two always talked excitedly about, my dad turned and gave me a shove into the large bathroom.

"Have I taught you nothing when it comes to women?" he asked softly.

"What? That's a shit ton of shoes!" I hissed and looked back to see her pull more out. I swear to Christ this last box was like Mary Poppins's purse. It was a never-ending pit of shoes.

"Okay, we're gonna do this quick and easy. One, your woman can never have too many shoes, clothes, purses, or jewelry. Two, it doesn't matter if you know you're right—because God knows your mother is wrong about . . . well . . . just about everything—but it doesn't matter. They are *always* right. Just say a simple 'Yes, sweetheart, I'm sorry I'm a dumbass' and you'll be fine. Three, them asking if they look okay is a trick question. Because, let's face it, even if we think it's the ugliest shirt we've ever seen, it's probably in style and we wouldn't know either way. So they always look *amazing,* remember that word."

I laughed. Rachel could wear a sack and I would think she looked amazing. Or she could wear nothing . . . I preferred her in nothing. I cleared my throat and had to look away from Rachel when I started picturing her naked.

"Four, and probably the most important if you want to keep your manhood, do not *ever* ask if she is PMS-ing. No matter what. Might as well dig your own grave if you do that."

Too late. I was always asking Rach if that was why she was in a bad mood. And if I was right, there was no way in hell I was going to tell her I was in the wrong. She could bitch about it if she wanted, but I wasn't going to go easy on her for the sake of getting out of an argument. Arguing with her was one of my favorite things.

Nodding, I slapped my dad's shoulder and smiled. "Thanks, Dad, I'll remember all that."

". . . have to go back and see if they're still there." Mom was excited about something, and from the look of it, Rachel was too.

"Yeah, we do! Anyway, I just had to tell you about that, I knew you'd flip," Rach mumbled as she flattened the last box of shoes. Thank God Mary Poppins's box had officially emptied out.

"That was a *lovely* story"—Dad drawled again—"and you tell it so well, with such *enthusiasm*."

Mom rolled her eyes and shook her head as she smiled, and Rachel just looked at my dad like she was about to let him have it. At the last second, her head jerked back. "Wait. *Forrest Gump* . . . really, Rich? You're using *Forrest Gump* quotes to insult me?"

"You have met your match, honey!" Mom cheered, and Dad just huffed in annoyance toward them, but shot me a wink.

"She doesn't put up with your bullshit or mine. Son, I'm telling you, you better hold on tight to that one."

"I will, Dad. Rach, are you done with the shoes?"

"I'm not sure. If you bring up my shoes again, I could probably sit here and rearrange them, maybe set them up by color, size of the heel, and length of the boot."

"Woman, get out of the damn closet. I have to put this up, and if you coordinate your shoes, I swear to you they will be in a pile on the floor the next time you come in here."

"Logan Kash Ryan!" Mom chided at the same time Rachel swore, "I will gut you."

My little Sour Patch. So fucking cute when she's threatening my life.

"Wait, what are you putting up?" she asked as she walked out of the closet, which was big enough for a car.

"Fake wall."

"Uh. Why?"

"Kind of like a really cheap safe room. Actually, that's a lie. It's just for you to hide behind if someone were to break in or something."

She laughed loudly and kissed my throat. "Kash, really? You're being just a little bit paranoid. We're not putting up a fake wall."

Before she could move away, I wrapped an arm around her and pulled her close. "Babe. I almost lost you once, I'll be working shitty hours and there will be a lot of nights you're here alone. This is for my peace of mind, don't be difficult."

"Nothing is going to—"

"Rachel, stop. We're putting up the wall."

"You're being paranoid!"

I kissed her hard once before pushing her gently away. "I probably am, but I don't care. With all the clothes hung up, you won't even notice it's there. And if something happens, it's there for you to hide behind. I love you, but I'm getting my way on this, okay?"

She rolled her eyes and gave my mom a look that Mom clearly

understood, since she started laughing. "All right, Kash. If you want to put up the fake wall to help you sleep at night—er, to keep you happy when you're away—then have at it."

Rachel

"OH MY WORD, this is a disaster," I whispered as I pulled yet another shirt off my body and threw it on the bed before heading back to the closet.

I'd been in Florida for two weeks, and we'd spent every day with Mason, his family, or Kash's parents; so Kash told me yesterday that he was taking me on a date tonight. I *had* been excited about time with just him . . . but then last night happened.

I'd had my first dream about Blake in over a month, and to make matters worse, Kash had been gone because he'd gotten a call from the police department as we were getting ready for bed and then left minutes later to go help. Apparently word on the street was two gangs were getting ready to have it out. I'd laughed and said it sounded a little *West Side Story*-ish, but when Kash told me there'd already been a lot of bloodshed between the two, and the body count would be high if they didn't prevent it from happening, I'd shut my mouth.

Ever since I'd woken up in a cold sweat at 3:00 A.M., I'd been edgy, terrified to turn a corner in the house, and having flashbacks of everything that had gone down with Blake last year. I was ready for him to be gone from my life. It was ridiculous that even in death, he still found ways to torture me.

Now I was running fifteen minutes late and I still couldn't find something that would cover all my scars. I didn't pay a lot of mind to them now, since they'd faded significantly, but after the dream, it was like they were neon signs on my body screaming, "*Look, look, look, look, looooooook!*"

I grabbed a thin, long-sleeved shirt and threw it on, but the MINE on my chest was flashing its bitchy, bright lights at me; so I grabbed a button-up shirt and pulled it over. Even though the top buttons couldn't button without looking all kinds of messed up because of the size of my chest, the collar still covered the little scar.

There. I'm ready now.

"Rach, what are you wearing? It's hot outside."

Don't care. "It's winter," I reasoned as I caught Kash's gaze in the mirror.

His gray eyes were heating as they trailed over my nonexistent ass, and while I loved that he was appreciating the view, I wasn't in the mood to be checked out right now. I was having a mini freak-out. Tonight was going to be an epic fail if I couldn't stop thinking Blake was going to randomly show up at the movie or restaurant.

Blake's dead. He died in Texas. Blake's dead. He died in Texas, I continued to chant to myself over and over again, but it wasn't helping.

"Yeah, but it's also seventy today." Kash's voice broke through my inner-chanting. "Take off the shirt underneath."

"I'm fine."

Wrapping an arm around my waist, he pulled me so my back was against his chest and brought his lips to the sensitive spot behind my ear. "I know you're fine, but you're gonna be too hot," he whispered, his voice dropping even lower as he began slowly unbuttoning my shirt.

Goose bumps covered my body when the cool metal of his lip

ring brushed against my skin, and I felt myself getting ready to say I would do whatever he asked of me. He was such a cheater. He knew what that piercing did to me.

"Open your eyes, Rachel."

I did as I was told, and found his gunmetal gray eyes looking directly into mine. Even through the reflection of the mirror, I could feel the heat from them and sense the want. His hands trailed over my chest, waist, and stomach; the pressure was so light I almost couldn't feel it, but it was doing insane things to my stomach, and my breathing quickly escalated. I watched as he slowly took my top shirt off, the movement of his hands so calculated and controlled, it felt like we had just entered some form of foreplay.

After he tossed the first shirt onto the bed, his hands did their barely there touches over the swell of my breasts and down my waist again until he hit the hem of the long-sleeved shirt. One hand slipped under, and a breathy whimper of need sounded in the back of my throat when his warm hand caressed my bare skin. He smiled against my neck and nipped on it lightly. I wanted to shut my eyes and enjoy every touch, but everything in me was screaming to watch the most erotic undressing I'd ever witnessed or been a part of.

Like with the button-up, his movements were slow and controlled as he pulled this shirt higher, but now he gave little teases of fingertips being brushed against my skin. By the time it was over my head and he was letting it fall to the ground, my entire body was on fire and I was practically panting with need.

"Rachel." His voice traveled over my bare shoulder like a caress, and I let my bodyweight fall against him.

"Hmm?"

Suddenly he was gone and I stumbled back a step before catching myself. I turned to see where he'd gone, and my button-up shirt hit me in the face.

"What the—"

"Get dressed, we gotta go."

"The hell, Kash? You can't do stuff like that to me and then stop!"

"Have you forgotten what frustration feels like?" he asked huskily. I wanted to punch him in the face.

"I hate you."

His lips curved up into my favorite smirk and he winked. "I love you too, Sour Patch."

Douche.

2

Kash

"Rach, I'm tired. Can we go to sleep?"

"Hmm?"

I looked over at the TV she seemed so transfixed on and smiled. She was such a fucking nerd. "Babe."

"Yeah?"

"Bed. Now."

Her laugh filled the living room, and her blue eyes flashed over to mine. "It'll be over in a little bit, hold on."

Uh, no. I had plans, and she was messing with them. I walked over to where she was lying on the couch and snatched the remote out of her hand to shut the TV off. When she sat up to grab it back, I pulled her close and over my shoulder before standing back up.

"Put me down! I wanted to finish watching that."

"You're recording it, it can wait until tomorrow."

"But it's *Duck Dynasty*," she whined, and I could picture her frowning as I carried her through the hall.

"And it can wait."

She slapped my ass as hard as she could, and I paid it right back. "Jerk! I don't make you stop watching *your* shows."

"But my shows are good."

"*Duck Dynasty* is amazing!"

"Rach, you'll live." I put my hands on her waist and bent over as I pushed her off my shoulder and onto the bed. She jackknifed up and I crawled on top of her and pushed her right back down.

"You're such an—" She cut off quickly and moaned when I gently bit down on her neck and brought her shoving hands above her head and pinned them to the bed.

Making a trail up her neck, I kissed her thoroughly and smiled when she leaned toward me as I backed up. "Such a what?"

"I don't remember," she said against my mouth and pressed our lips together again.

"That's what I thought, Sour Patch."

She growled but was still smiling when I moved both her wrists into one of my hands and let my right hand reach underneath the pillow until I hit what I was looking for. Her lips moved to my jaw and she wrapped her long legs around my back.

Tonight was already going completely differently from how I'd imagined it would, and when she did that, I was ready to put off what I'd planned to do. But I didn't want to wait any longer—Rachel had been here a month, and though that wasn't a long time, I knew she was more than ready for this again.

"Rachel."

"Yeah?" she asked huskily and rolled her hips.

Shit, she's not helping right now. Keeping her hands pinned to the bed, I sat back far enough that she had to unlock her legs, but stayed hovering over her.

"What—"

"I know I messed up before," I began, cutting her off. "I'll never regret asking you to be mine when I did, but I know I should have told you everything first."

Her blue eyes went from narrowed to wide in a second when she realized what I was saying.

"I can't begin to explain to you the physical pain I went through every day knowing that I'd ruined everything and lost you for good. I will never take you or your forgiveness for granted, and I swear I will never tell you another unforgivable lie."

"Kash," she whispered, and I watched as her eyes took me in.

"I want to take care of you, I want to protect you, I want to love you, and I want to fight with you for the rest of my life."

She laughed softly and her mouth parted when her left hand clenched around the ring I'd just placed in her palm.

"Rachel, will you please marry me?"

"Yes!" She crushed her mouth to mine and I sat her body up and brought her closed left fist in between our bodies. She stopped kissing me when I coaxed her hand open and inhaled audibly when she saw the new ring.

"You're not allowed to take this one off."

"I won't," she promised as I slid it onto her ring finger, and before I could tell her that I loved her, she wrapped her arms around my neck and kissed me until we were both falling back onto the bed.

Her hands made quick work of pulling my shirt over my head

then sliding down my torso 'til they hit the top of my workout shorts. She was wearing one of my shirts, and I used it to pull her body off the bed. I helped her out of it before tossing it behind me and helping her rid me of my shorts. My eyes took in her mostly naked body as I climbed back on top of her and bent to pull her nipple into my mouth. She groaned and her back arched off the bed as her hands fisted in my hair.

Leaning onto my forearm, I let my other hand trail down her stomach and slowly pulled her underwear off. The tips of my fingers traced the path back up her long legs, and when I hit her knees, I used the one hand to part her legs and continued my path up her thighs. She inhaled sharply and I smiled against her breast when my fingers teased her opening, and I fucking loved that she was ready for me and pulled my head even closer to her chest. I moved toward her other breast, and just before I reached it, she flipped us so I was on my back and brought her mouth down to mine as she straddled me. She guided me to her and I growled against her lips when she sank down on top of me and began rocking her hips.

Her lips moved to my ear, softly brushing against it as she said, "No teasing, and no frustration. Tonight, I just want you."

She had me. Always.

Rachel

THE BACK OF MY THROAT BEGAN BURNING, and I blinked rapidly to stop the tears that were quickly forming as I looked at myself in the mirror. This was the one. I somehow knew that without a doubt, but something about all of this still felt incredibly wrong.

Turning to smile at Kash's mom, Marcy, and at Mason's sister and mother, Maddie and Mrs. Gates, I noted their expressions and knew they agreed with my assessment. I was so thankful they were here for me today, but as I let the tips of my fingers trail down the soft white, ruched tulle, I couldn't help but wish for someone completely different to be sitting in that chair.

My mom should have been here for this. She was supposed to be here for all of this.

In the three weeks since Kash had proposed for the third—and last—time, Marcy and I had been on a wedding planning kick that didn't show signs of slowing down until we had every last detail in place. As part of that, we'd been dress shopping all morning. I'd put off looking for a dress for myself as we picked out the bridesmaids and mother dresses, but that only worked for so long before the three of them were shoving me into a room with a sales assistant who was getting all up close and personal with my body as she helped me into dress after dress.

After five misses, I found myself in this one. The one dress I didn't want to even look at, but the assistant begged me to "just try." I should have known the evil genius would try and succeed at making me cry.

The strapless dress flowed down to the ground in a sweep train, making me look ethereal, or like I belonged in ancient Greece. But my favorite part was the crisscross bodice that led to an empire waist, and I stared, transfixed, as my fingers trailed across the ruching. It was perfect, Kash would love it—and I knew if my mom were here, she would have loved it too. A few traitorous tears slipped down my cheeks and I made quick work of sweeping them away when the women all made sounds of admiration and sympathy as they saw them.

"You look stunning, Rachel," Marcy choked out and began searching through her purse.

"I was going to ask how you feel in it, but it's all over your face. You're glowing," Mrs. Gates added and rubbed Marcy's shoulder when she started blotting her cheeks with a tissue she'd found in her purse.

Maddie stood up and walked over to me, turning my body so I was facing the mirrors again. "What if we did this," she said mostly to herself as she loosened her hair from a clip, and began gathering up mine.

I watched as she made a messy—yet somehow styled—bun, low on the side of my neck and held it together with the now-hidden clip before stepping away. My next intake of breath was audible, and she smiled.

"Perfect."

I couldn't respond, but I agreed wholeheartedly. Bringing my hands up, I covered the majority of my face, not even bothering with the tears still slowly falling down my hands, and continued to stare at the transformed reflection in the mirror.

"What do you think? Is this the one?" the saleswoman asked softly, and I turned to smile at her.

"Yeah." I stopped to clear my throat and shook my head as I gathered myself. "Yeah, it is. I love it."

She did a happy clap reminding me so much of Candice, and I asked Maddie to grab my phone to take pictures so I could send them to Candice and her mom, Janet. After calls from a squealing Candice, and a crying Janet, I reluctantly went back to the dressing room to change into my clothes.

Once the dresses were bought, and an extra bridesmaid dress ordered for Candice to try on in Texas, the three of us went out for lunch and the wedding planning took off once again. We already had a venue, photographer, and food for June 28; and now that I had the dress, I felt like the rest would fall into place easily. But for the first time in these last three weeks, I wasn't in the mood to plan. I wanted my mom to be here helping, and nothing was going to ease the ache of knowing she couldn't.

"OH, MADDIE! You so shouldn't have brought me here," I whispered as I took in all the dogs whimpering and barking in their kennels at the shelter a few days later.

"Why?" She turned to look at me with worried eyes. "Are you afraid of dogs or something?"

"No, now I want to take one home with me!"

"Ha! They're sweet, and looking at them like this just breaks your heart, doesn't it?"

My eyes latched onto a skin-and-bones pitbull that looked like he was ready to cry. "That's the understatement of the year. How do you work here and not take all of them home with you? I start bawling whenever I'm watching TV and I hear Sarah McLachlan start singing, because I know abused and depressed-looking animals are about to follow."

Maddie threw her hand over her mouth to muffle her laughter as she led me through a maze of dogs. "Oh God, that's so true! It's like you can't find the remote and change the channel fast enough!"

A dog so ugly he was cute smashed himself against the gate next to me, and in my mind I was hearing him beg me to take him home. "We need to go before I adopt all of them. Why did you bring me here?"

"I need to check on my babies. When I came in about a week ago, someone had abandoned a dog and her puppies at the door.

Like, literally left her tied to the handle of the door, and the box of her puppies next to her. They just became available for adoption two days ago, and I hate not seeing them every day, and I just know they'll all be gone by the time I come back in on Saturday."

I want to take you home! And you, oh you're really sad-looking, I need to stop looking at you. This is such a bad idea, I need to get out of— Oh, I want to take you too! "Maddie, I'm not joking, we need—"

"Aww, just you two left?"

My jaw dropped and I stopped walking. "Oh. My. Word."

"Aren't they precious?"

"I'm in puppy love," I whispered as Maddie pulled a little golden retriever puppy out of a smaller kennel.

"This one is such a trip. I swear he's the flirt of the bunch. Indifferent toward males, loves all females."

I took him from her arms and about died in cute-heaven when he wrapped his big paws around my arm like he was hugging it. "You just know you're cute so you use that to your advantage, don't you?" I crooned at him, and snuggled him closer when he plopped his head on my chest. "Such a guy."

Maddie laughed as she held the other one. "I'm sad they're all going to be gone soon."

"Why don't you get one?"

"Right"—she snorted—"and pay the thousand-dollar pet deposit at my apartment? Um, no thank you."

"One thousand dollars? Why? It was like, two-fifty at the place we were at in Texas!"

"I'd like to know the same thing, *and* I would have a monthly 'pet rent.' Isn't that crazy?"

"So that's how you work here and don't adopt them. Got it." I looked down and watched my little flirt gnawing on my thumb, and the second he realized I was looking at him, he tried to jump out of my arms and fully onto my chest. *He has puppy breath!* "Kash is going to be so pissed," I murmured against his nose.

"Maddie, I'm in love."

"I know, they're just so dang cute."

"How much to adopt?"

She gasped and did a weird little dance while holding the other puppy. "Wait! Kash would be pissed!"

"I just told Trip that."

"Who?"

I pointed at the puppy. "You said he was a trip, and I think it's cute. So how much?"

"Oh, I love that! It's only thirty-five dollars. But I really think that maybe you should wait, maybe talk to Kash first?"

"I told you I'm in love! I want him now." Then I looked down at the pup and fake-whispered, "We just aren't going to tell Daddy until he gets home."

Maddie laughed and put the other puppy back in the kennel. "Shit, he's going to be so mad!"

"Don't care. In puppy love."

"Whatever, don't say I didn't warn you."

"Got it, put all the blame on you." Trip gave me little kisses, and I knew the fight coming my way was totally worth it.

Kash

THE SIGHT I WAS MET WITH IN THE KITCHEN was a dead giveaway. Rachel wanted something. She only voluntarily made pancakes when she wanted something, or was showing me her appreciation for something I'd done. And since I'd been gone for thirteen hours at work, I knew it wasn't the latter.

"Hey, babe! How was work? I really missed you and I'm glad you're home. You hungry? You were gone so long today; did you stay over? What time is it? Why don't you go get comfortable and I'll finish up here?"

What in the fuck? My eyes widened as she wrapped her arms around my neck. She was rambling, which means I had been wrong about both. She didn't want something; she'd done something. "What'd you do?"

"What do you mean?"

"You suck at trying to act normal. And you're making pancakes without me asking you to." She just sat there with a plastered smile on her face, and I decided to push it more. "You're really shitty at hiding things from me, you know that?"

"So how many do you want?"

"None. No, wait, that's a lie. I want four. But who the fuck is this Barbie in my kitchen and what did she do with my Rachel? My Rachel would have snapped at me just then and told me to make pancakes myself."

"I just wanted to do something—"

A crash from the back of the house sounded, and Rachel froze but didn't look scared. I pulled out my gun from the holster and maneuvered out of her arms.

"No, Kash! Please put the gun away, I don't want you to shoot or scare him!"

"Him? Who the fuck is in my house, Rachel?!" Without waiting for an answer, I stalked off down the hall and straight toward the shut bedroom door. This wasn't fucking happening, she would never cheat on me. I *knew* she wouldn't. Another loud noise sounded, and I swore I would kill the son of a bitch. Shoot first, ask questions after.

"Kash, wait!"

I flung open the door, and my eyes went to the perfectly made bed and lamp that had been knocked onto the floor. Before I could say anything, I heard a whine coming from the corner of the room and walked slowly toward it.

Huddled into the corner near the other nightstand was a puppy looking up at me like he knew exactly what he had done. Rachel was talking quickly, and I knew she was trying to explain why the dog was here, but I was just trying not to laugh. I holstered my gun and bent down to pick up the shaking puppy.

". . . please don't make me take him back!"

I turned and looked at my beautiful fiancée. I wanted to play with her so bad, but when she was giving me puppy-eyes about as good as the little shit in my arms could, all I could think about was giving her anything in the world that she asked for.

"Did you get him from the shelter where Maddie works?"

"Maybe."

I nodded and scratched behind the pup's ears. "And I'm guessing Maddie was with you?" When Rachel nodded, I continued, "Did she say anything to you about getting the puppy? Like maybe . . . don't?"

"But I'm in puppy love with him! I wanted him so bad, I'm sorry. Please don't be mad at me, I knew you would say no and I couldn't stand the thought of letting him go to someone else!"

Coughing to cover my laugh, I let my eyes fall over her pleading expression and sucked hard on my lip ring so I wouldn't smile. "Maddie feed you a story about the puppies being adopted quickly and she was afraid they'd all be gone by Saturday?"

"Wait, what? How did you know?"

"Because, woman I love whom I want to strangle sometimes, Maddie took you to the shelter to see which of the *two* puppies you liked best. They were officially adoptable, but they were holding both of them because I was going to get one for you."

"You were?"

"Yeah, but obviously you jumped the gun on that one. So, uh, surprise . . . I guess?"

She squealed and launched herself at me, taking the puppy from my arms. "Thank you so much, I love him, you're the best!"

I rolled my eyes and fell onto the bed. "What are we gonna name him?"

"Trip." I knew from her tone there was no room for negotiating that, so I just smiled at her.

"All right, Trip it is. Are you going to make me pancakes now?"

"Make them yourself. I've been freaking out about your reaction all day, and I want to play with him now."

And *that* was more like my Rachel.

3

Rachel

"YOU STILL DOING OKAY?" Kash asked, and kissed my neck softly.

"Yeah, your family is fun. I feel like I don't need to say anything and they'll just continue to provide all the entertainment."

We were at a family dinner with a bunch of his aunts, uncles, and cousins—and though I'd been nervous to meet more of his family, there was no way to stay nervous around this bunch. There were a lot of them, they were loud, and they were a freaking riot. At any one moment at least two people were in an argument, there were cousins tackling or hitting one another, others giving one another a hard time about the game on TV, and even more laughing throughout the house. It felt like I was in a real version of *My Big Fat Greek Wedding*. Except Kash's family wasn't Greek.

I have two cousins, and I'd only met them once when I was really young, so I didn't know what it must have been like for Kash to grow up with this. Out of the nineteen cousins he has, there were only three older than him and they ranged down to the youngest at eight years old. Even through the yelling and fighting, it was apparent this family loved each other and would stick together through anything.

I'd never known any different, so having Candice and her brother, Eli, as my best friends and makeshift family had been all I'd needed growing up. But seeing this—seeing the way Kash interacted with five of his cousins closest in age . . . I found myself wishing I'd had this.

"They're something else," Kash said, laughing, interrupting my thoughts. "That's for sure. I'm gonna get another beer, do you want one?"

"No, but I can get it for you," I offered, but he put a hand on my shoulder to keep me in place. A wry smile crossed his face when I glared at him.

A few of his little second cousins were infatuated with my hair and putting small braids throughout it. There was no way Kash was going to let me get out of this easily.

"I have to go potty," announced one of the little girls, sitting on my lap.

My eyes about bulged out of my head, and Kash burst out laughing as he turned toward the kitchen. "Uh, well then you should go to the bathroom."

"Will you take me?" She started squirming, and I thought I was going to die.

A little kid is about to pee on me! I looked around wildly as the little girl kept doing the potty dance on my leg, and I tried to figure out what I would have to do if I took her to the bathroom. "Um, okay. Just . . . don't go before we get in there."

Just as I started to stand, Ava—the mom—came to my rescue. "Come on, sweetheart. Let's go to the potty." Looking up at me, she mouthed *I'm so sorry,* and turned to look around. "Rachel, I hate to do this to you—but can you hold Shea for me?"

I looked at the chubby infant in her arms, and my mouth popped open but nothing came out. I'd never held a baby before. But Ava had been sweet to me all afternoon, and right now she was saving me from bathroom duty, and I honestly didn't know how I was supposed to say no to her. *No, Ava, I will not hold your baby.* Yeah, I could see that going over so well. I would forever be known as the girl that refused to help out.

"Sh-sure," I spit out, and kind of just put my arms straight in front of me.

"She's tired, just let her lay on your chest."

I sat there frozen as Ava put Shea on my chest so her chubby cheeks were resting on my collarbone, and automatically put my arms around her to keep her there.

"Okay, I'll be right back! Come on, sweetheart, let's go!"

Blowing out a breath I hadn't realized I was holding, I looked down at the baby in my arms and smiled when she kept fisting the collar of my shirt in her little hand. When she caught me looking at her, she lifted her head shakily and smacked her hand against my chin before dropping her head back onto my collarbone. The two girls that had been braiding my hair cooed over the baby for a minute before taking off after some appetizers that were brought into the house . . . and then it was just little Shea and me. I had just been thinking about how much easier this was than I'd thought it would be, when she grabbed a chunk of my hair and pulled as hard as possible.

"What is it with my hair today?" I whispered to her as I went through the painful process of getting every strand out of her little fist and making sure they stayed attached to my head.

She reached again, but I put my index finger out and she immediately wrapped her tiny fingers around it, her little eyes widening as she stared at it.

As soon as Ava was back in the living room, the potty-dance daughter started crying, and Ava turned them right back around and disappeared down the hall. But I didn't mind, I was enjoying having little Shea with me. Her eyes were growing heavy as she continued to watch her fingers wrapped around mine, and by the time Ava was walking back toward us, she was out. Her little lips were slightly open, and my chest and neck were warm from the heat she was emanating.

"She's asleep?"

"Yeah, just happened," I whispered and was getting ready to sit up to hand her back off when I noticed the relieved look on Ava's face. "I can keep holding her . . ."

"Oh my God, would you? I know as soon as she's up I won't be able to eat, I need to grab something now while she's asleep."

"Yeah, go for it." Smiling at her softly, I leaned back into the couch and looked down at the tiny baby sleeping on me. It couldn't be that hard. She was sleeping, and I was just sitting here anyway . . . right?

Looking up, my eyes locked on Kash's expression, and everything in me locked up. His eyebrows were scrunched together and drawn down, like he was trying to figure out the answer to a difficult question, and he was pulling his lip ring into his mouth the way he did when he was mad. Though he was looking directly at me, his eyes were unfocused and I had to wave my free hand to get his attention.

His stormy eyes snapped back to life, and from across the room I watched as he raised one eyebrow and jerked his head up once in question.

I mouthed an *are you okay?* to him and felt my body relax when his smirk transformed his face back to the Kash I knew.

"Don't you just look perfect with a baby."

My head turned to look at Kash's grandma who had just sat down on my left. She was a short woman that, from my limited interaction with her, looked like she lived to feed her family and give hugs. She was absolutely adorable. My eyes automatically dropped to the sleeping baby, and I gave her a small smile as I laughed awkwardly. "Um . . ." How do you respond to that?

"That was a compliment, dear. You look very comfortable like that, like you were made to hold a baby."

"Oh, well thank you." That *so* didn't sound like a compliment. It felt like it should be followed up with Kash telling me I should be barefoot in the kitchen.

"So beautiful," she murmured as she touched my engagement ring and looked happily back up at me. "Do you plan to give me more great-grandchildren soon? I'll be here for only so long . . ." she trailed off and laughed heartily.

"I don't know about that, we haven't really talked about it. We're still young," I cut off quickly when I realized Ava was barely older than me and already had two kids. But for shit's sake I had barely turned twenty-two a couple months ago. I was still getting used to taking care of Trip, I didn't even want to think about having a baby.

"Of course you are, darling girl! You have all the time in the world. This is just an old woman greedy for more babies to spoil rotten. Though I'm sure with you and Logan being the only children in your families, both of your parents will be spoiling your children senseless."

My stomach dropped and I kept the smile plastered to my face. "Yeah, probably," I murmured.

A feeling dangerously close to what I'd experienced at the dress shop started unfurling in the pit of my stomach and slowly made its way up my chest to grip at my heart. My breaths were coming painfully, and I worked hard at staying in control of my outward emotions. The girls that had been braiding my hair earlier ran up to their great-grandma to ask when we were eating, and I'd never been more thankful for the distraction of little kids than I was in that instant.

When I was sure I had a handle on my emotions, I looked over at Kash again and immediately wished I hadn't. He was staring in my direction—once again at nothing—and the beer bottle in his hand was halfway to his lips, frozen in air. *What is with him today?* When I failed at trying to get his attention, I stood up from the couch, making sure not to jostle Shea.

"Excuse me," I mumbled to Kash's grandma, and made my way outside where tables were set up and most of the women were.

"Hi, future daughter-in-law." Marcy grinned at me and looked over at Ava. "I swear she is the best baby. Logan would never just sleep like this. He had to be in a car seat in order to fall asleep, and when he wasn't sleeping, he was screaming."

Ava launched into a play-by-play of Shea's usual days, and I turned to look at one of Kash's aunts, who touched my arm when I sat down.

"Marcy was telling us all of the wedding details! Are you so excited?"

Smiling widely, I readjusted Shea on my chest and nodded. "I really am, the next two and a half months need to hurry up. I'm ready."

"It sounds like it's going to be beautiful, we're all so happy for Logan." Leaning closer, she placed a hand on my knee and spoke softly. "She also told us about your parents, I'm so sorry to hear that."

This was not happening. Could I not get a break from this pain lately? I'd started healing before I moved here, and I felt like everything that had happened in the last few weeks had sent me spiraling back to the very beginning.

"Me too." I offered her a weaker smile and faced straight ahead.

"Do you plan to just walk down the aisle alone then?"

God. Breathe, Rachel. Keep breathing. The sickening pain threatened to choke me, and I struggled to maintain my unaffected facade. She wasn't being hateful, none of these people were, but it felt like they were cutting into me worse than Blake had done with physical blades.

"No, I uh—I have someone to walk me," I answered and cleared my throat.

"Oh good, that just about broke my heart when Marcy told us. You're a strong girl," she assured and patted my knee a few times.

"Thank you." I sat there silently as the table full of women continued their earlier conversations, and I soon excused myself for the second time in just a handful of minutes.

I held Shea's warm body in my arms and wandered around the backyard, pretending to be interested in the flower beds that lined the walls. But my thoughts were anywhere but on the exotic-looking flowers.

For the first time in close to a year, I felt trapped. As sweet as they were, I wanted to get away from the people here. As much as I wanted to marry Kash, I wanted to get away from all the wedding planning. As happy as I was being here, I wanted to get away from Florida.

I just wanted to run. I wanted to go back in time five years and enjoy the last few months with my parents all over again. I wouldn't have taken a second with them for granted. Hell, I wouldn't have let them go on that stupid trip in the first place. My throat burned, and I looked down at Shea when she lazily dragged her head so her other cheek was lying on me.

My parents hadn't been there for my high school graduation—and being in my catatonic state, I had felt like I wasn't present for it either. But everything happening now? Everything that was to come? They wouldn't be there, and I needed them.

I'd needed my mom there with me when I bought my dress. I needed my dad there to walk me down the aisle and give me away to Kash. And I needed them there for whenever we had kids. They were supposed to be there through all of it, and they couldn't. How was I supposed to get through everything without them?

Shea's little hand fisted around the collar of my shirt again and I swallowed the imaginary lump in my throat when realization set in. I wasn't sure I *could* get through everything without them.

Kash

"ARE YOU GOING TO TELL ME what was going on with you tonight?"

I glanced up from looking at her stomach just before she caught me staring and shrugged. "What do you mean?"

Setting down her purse and kicking off her shoes, she practically fell onto the couch. "I don't know, you've been really quiet for the last few hours. You didn't say anything to me on the drive home. I'd ask if I did something wrong, but you don't look pissed off anymore, you're just quiet. It's not like you."

"How many kids do you want, Rach?"

Her head jerked back as her eyes widened. "Um, I don't know."

"One, two, three . . . ?"

"Kash, I don't know. Why does it matter right now?"

Sitting down next to her, I pulled her into my arms and laid back. "I just want to know."

She stayed silent as she thought for a minute. "Uh, well I didn't really like being an only child. I mean, I always had Candice and Eli, but they weren't really my family and I wish now that I'd had someone else. Did you like being alone?" I shook my head negatively, and she nodded as her eyes got that faraway look. "I don't want a huge family or anything, I guess two."

If I would get to see Rachel holding infants like she had been this afternoon, I'd want to have a damn football team with her. My hands left her shoulders and slowly moved past her waist and my thumbs trailed over her flat stomach. I wanted the visual I'd had in my head all day so fucking bad.

Her mouth found mine and I whispered against her lips, "I want to have children with you."

"We will, someday."

"Now."

Rachel's body went rigid before she sat back to look down at me. "Slow down there, cowboy. Why don't we get married and enjoy a year first. What brought this on?"

My eyes automatically drifted back to her flat stomach the same time my hands did. "I was watching you with my little cousins all day, and I want that with you. I don't want to wait years. We're getting married in two and a half months, you wouldn't even be showing."

She burst out laughing and fell back. "Oh my God, Kash, no. Just . . . no. We're not having a baby right now, and we're definitely not getting pregnant before we get married! We can start thinking about it in a couple years."

"Why? What's the difference of now and in a year or two?"

"There's a huge difference! That's a lot of time of just us that I want. This is the most backward argument we've ever had. Shouldn't I be arguing your side and you arguing mine?"

"We're not arguing, we're discussing, Sour Patch."

"Okay, well discussion over," she huffed and crossed her arms over her chest. "No mini-mes running around."

Switching our positions from earlier, I curled my body over hers and pressed my lips to her throat. "I want a family with you, Rachel, and I don't want to wait for that. I had to watch you for hours playing with my little cousins and holding Ava's baby. All day all I've been able to think about, or see, is that image and wanting it to be ours. Wanting to see your stomach growing with our child. I want to start our family."

"Kash," she whispered and pulled my head up to press her lips to mine. "That was a really good effort, but no."

I growled and mumbled, "I'm going to hide your birth control."

Rachel sucked in a large amount of air, and I knew she was about to let me have it, but I'd just realized I knew where her birth control was.

She must have seen the recognition flash in my eyes, because hers widened and she gasped, "Oh no, sir!"

I jumped off the couch, but she grabbed me before I could land, and we both hit the ground with Rachel now caging me to the floor. Not that I couldn't get out, but I fucking loved the position we were in.

"Logan Kash Ryan . . . I swear to God if you hide my pills, I will go to my doctor and get one of those birth control things put in tomorrow. You know those ones last five years unless you get them taken out? Actually five years until kids sounds pretty good right about now."

My hands had been traveling up her waist, underneath her shirt; but when I realized what she was saying, I froze. "You wouldn't."

"I would and I will," she gritted out.

"Fine." I shrugged and ran my hands back down her flat stomach. Flashes of me running my hands over Rachel's stomach, round with our child, hit me hard. Just like they had been all day.

I'd thought about having kids . . . eventually. But now? It was all I could think about. Something about seeing Rachel holding Shea had made it all click today, and I wanted it so bad, it felt like it was all I'd be able to think about until I saw it through. And, Jesus Christ, I wanted to see it through.

"It's like you said"—I whispered, and my hands went to the button on her shorts—"they aren't one hundred percent effective anyway."

Her face fell. "You're using condoms again. Starting now."

"The fuck I am!"

"Kash." She sighed and sat up, but her body curved in on itself as I watched hidden exhaustion set over her features. "I don't want to even think about this right now. Okay? We can figure something out in a few years, but for now just . . . stop. Don't push the issue of having kids on me."

Whoa, what? "The issue of *having* kids? I thought you wanted kids."

"I don't know, Kash . . . I just—I can't talk about this right now."

"Rach—"

She pushed off me and had gone two feet before she turned and pointed a finger at me. "If you want kids so damn bad, figure out how to have them yourself!"

What the hell? When did she go from wanting kids eventually to not wanting to talk about it at all?

"Rachel," I called after her when she turned to leave again. "Come here and just talk to me."

She kept going. Slipping into her sandals, she grabbed her purse and headed toward the front door. I scrambled up and ran over to her, grabbing her arm just as she'd reached out for the doorknob.

"Are you kidding me? What the hell is going on? Why are you throwing shields at me, and how did that conversation just turn into you being upset and *leaving*?"

She kept her head down and refused to look at me. "I just want to go for a drive. Let me go."

If I let her go now, we would go back ten steps . . . and I wasn't willing to go back to how we'd been. Rachel keeping things

from me. Shielding me from her emotions. Pushing everyone—
including me—away. Hell no. Never again. "No. First off, you
don't leave when you're upset or if we're in the middle of a fight.
You talk to me. Second, I told you a long time ago we were done
with your shields, and we're not about to start up with them
again. So sit down and tell me what's going on with you all of a
sudden."

"Kash, just let me go clear my—"

She hadn't acted like this, or shielded me, for almost a year. To
be honest, it was freaking me the fuck out that she was starting it
again. Knowing she would keep this up until I dropped it or she
eventually left, I did the only thing I knew in order to get her to
listen. "I said sit the fuck down, Rachel!"

I hated yelling at her, but there was something about me
taking control of the situation, and being an asshole, that always
got Rachel to break down her walls and start talking. Not waiting for her to move, I grabbed her purse and dropped it on the
floor, bent so my shoulder was against her stomach, and stood
back up with her hanging over me.

"Why are you such an ass?" she grunted when I turned back
toward the living room. "All I want is to be alone right now!"

"Ah, my little Sour Patch. We're going to have to work on that
if you want to get married. Because after we are, you can't just
walk out on a fight."

"I didn't know we were fighting," she grumbled.

"We weren't until you started PMS-ing on me."

"I am *not* PMS-ing! Put me down!"

"Gladly." I let her slide down and pushed her so she was lying
down on the couch and crawled on top of her, caging her in.
"Talk."

Her blue eyes were on fire as they narrowed at me, and I watched as her jaw locked while she took deep breaths in through her nose. My girl was about to explode, and as much as I loved her when she was pissed off, I needed to know what had just happened.

"Drop the attitude, Sour Patch, and talk to me."

"I don't want to talk to you. I want a couple hours to myself, we can talk after."

"Too bad. You have me with you right now, and I'm not going anywhere. Why do you suddenly not want to have kids? I understand wanting to wait until after we are married, but you kept making it longer and longer until you tell me you don't know if you *want* kids. When did this change?"

"I don't know, okay? I. Don't. Know. You see me with little kids and your mind instantly goes to us having kids. You know where mine went? Exactly where it's been going the last couple months. The fact that I won't have my mom there with me when I go through pregnancies, and having babies, and taking care of toddlers, and dealing with teenagers with bad attitudes! I don't have her here to plan our wedding, she wasn't there when I bought my dress, she won't be there for *anything*, Kash, do you understand that?" Her temper flared out quickly and tears filled her eyes. "I've already been having a hard time with that, but today as I sat there and listened to Ava ask your aunts and mom dozens of questions, I realized I'm terrified of not having my mom there to call and ask questions when we have kids. What if I do it all wrong?"

"Babe," I crooned and moved my hands to brush my thumbs across her cheeks. "You're going to be a great mom whenever we have kids, you won't do it wrong, and you'll have my mom there if you have questions."

"I know, and I'll have Janet. But it won't be the same." Her eyes fluttered shut when a few tears dropped down her face and into her hair. "They were supposed to be here for everything."

"I'm so sorry, Rachel." Squeezing myself between her and the back of the couch, I turned her and pulled her against my chest. I hadn't known what to expect just then, but I had no idea she'd been struggling with not having her parents here for all of this, and felt like a jackass for not knowing. I *should* have known. "I'm sorry they aren't here, but you have a lot of people who love you and are here for you. They won't make up for your parents, I know that, and so do they. But they're here for you, and I'm always here for you."

She nodded against my chest and took a shuddering breath in.

"And you never leave when you're upset. Okay? We always talk things out."

" 'Kay."

Kissing the top of her head, I pulled her up until I could see her face. "I'll lay off the baby talk, and I'm sorry for pushing that on you. I got carried away with seeing you like that today. But from now on, will you talk to me about what's going on so we don't have to go through this again? I should have known this would be a hard time for you, and I'm sorry I didn't. Next time, though, please tell me. I can't help you if I don't know, and if we can avoid what just happened, I'd prefer that."

"I know, I'm sorry. I just let it all get to me and I didn't want you to think I wasn't excited about getting married, because I am. It's hard without them, but I *am* happy, I swear."

"I know you are, Rachel. I never questioned that."

She nodded and blinked slowly a few times before resting her head next to mine.

Rachel was so strong willed and always exuding her fiery attitude, which I loved, that I'd stopped looking for signs of anything being wrong. I swore to myself right then that I would never forget just how fragile she could be, and to never miss another sign from her. She was strong, but I needed to be stronger for us.

"Come on, sweetheart, let's go to bed. We can talk more about this tomorrow."

4

Rachel

"CANDICE, I'M SO SERIOUS, one of these days you're going to get pregnant and you're going to have no clue who the father is." I laughed sadly and flopped down onto the couch as a horrified gasp filled my ear.

"I am not about to have little Candices running around. You know I'm careful, and you don't have room to talk about being safe, Miss We-don't-use-condoms."

Oh Lord, I didn't even want to tell her about the pseudo-fight Kash and I had about condoms and birth control pills a couple weeks ago. "I'm only with Kash, though! You probably can't even count how many guys you're with right now." I could picture her face as she tried to remember everyone and shook my head. "I'll take your silence as confirmation that you can't."

"Whatever, I'm having fun."

"Obviously, that was never a—" I sucked in a large breath as something cold, wet, and fluffy covered my face. "Kash!" He barked out a laugh as I wiped the whipped cream away from my eyes and sent a look of death his way, making him laugh louder.

He smiled widely, and I hated him for that smile at that moment. "You look adorable."

"What the hell is wrong with you?"

He shook the can in the air, just in case I'd missed it being in his hand the first time. "Ice cream time."

"I'm on the phone!"

"Yeah, and it's time for you to get off."

"You—are you . . . ooo I want to punch you in the face right now." Candice was laughing loud enough for both of us to hear from where I'd dropped my phone on the couch, and when I reached for my phone, Kash took a step toward me with the can raised. "You wait!" Holding my hand up to stop him, I grabbed my phone and spoke slowly. "Candi, I have to go kill my fiancé now, I'll call you later."

"Have fun! Don't hurt him too much, love you!"

"He just whip creamed my face. No promises. Love you back." After tapping the END button, I stood slowly and never took my eyes off the weapon. "That wasn't nice."

"I'm sure you'll get over it. I made you a banana split."

"And you put the topping on my face! That isn't exactly something you should be proud of right now. It's sticky."

Grabbing my hand, he pulled me close and tried to fight a smile as his eyes roamed over my face. "Don't whine, Sour Patch. You really do look adorable, you're just missing something."

Before I could move away, he hooked his arm around my neck

and sprayed more whipped cream on top of my head, smashing it in as I maneuvered out of his arms. Wiping my hands across my face, I lunged at him, but he shot more out of the can, aimed directly at my face. At the last second I turned and took off, running toward the kitchen.

"You are such an asshole!" I screamed behind me as I ran, but I couldn't stop laughing even as my nose began burning from somehow snorting up some of the whipped cream.

I heard the clacking of Trip's nails on the hardwood behind me, but no Kash. Turning to look proved Kash wasn't there, but I heard the sound of heavy footsteps just as I turned back around. I screamed as Kash came barreling toward me from the opposite direction, and I tried to turn back to go the way I'd been coming from but ran into Trip seconds before Kash did, and we both went crashing down onto the hardwood floor.

Kash's arm came up with the can, but before he could spray more, I smacked the can away and tried to crawl away from him and closer to it. And yes, okay I'll admit I may have cheated by *accidentally* kicking him in the stomach as I crawled away. A half-laugh, half-shout of victory left me when I reached the can and turned it on Kash, but nothing came out.

"Are you shitting me?"

He laughed and ripped the can from my hand, and after a shake, more fluffiness was spraying out at my face.

"What the hell? That's not fair!"

"What can I say? The can hates you," he boasted proudly as the sounds of an empty can filled the otherwise quiet hall. "Don't pout. You look amazing."

I couldn't help it. I *was* pouting like a four-year-old and I couldn't stop even if I wanted to, which I totally didn't. "I'm *cov-*

ered. You just wasted nearly an entire can of whipped cream on my face, and it's in my hair!"

A look of shock covered his handsome face. "Oh God no, not the hair!" he smirked, and a small laugh left him when my pout increased. "Come here, beautiful." Kissing my lips softly through the whipped cream, he licked off what had transferred onto his face and kissed me again. "See? Beautiful and delicious. Really, you should be thanking me right now."

"*Hate* is a strong word and it's coming to mind when I look at you."

"Aw, I love you too, snookems."

"I will murder you."

"I know." He smiled and let his hands trail down my waist to my barely there sleep shorts. I moaned unattractively when his hand trailed over where I wanted him most. "What if I promised to help clean it off you?"

Yes. Please. "Much less likely to murder you."

He barked out a laugh that cut off quickly when his cell started blaring the tone he set for anyone at the police department. "Damn it."

Not happening. I need sexy time with my man while he cleans whip cream off me!

"Ryan," he answered and gave me an apologetic look a few silent moments later. "Yeah—yeah, I'm on my way."

"Gotta go?"

"Yeah." He grimaced and helped me stand up. "I'm sorry, Rach. I'll be back as soon as I can. Double homicide, looks like it's gang related."

"Don't be sorry, go do what you do best." He and Mase weren't even on call for over twenty-four more hours. I wanted to ask why they couldn't have called someone else, but I kept my mouth shut and smiled through my disappointment. He looked like he was beating himself up enough; he didn't need me making it worse.

"Thank you."

He took off for the bedroom, and I walked into the kitchen to wet a paper towel so I could wipe all the gross-ness off my face. By the time I was walking back into the hallway with a wet wash-cloth to clean anything else that had been sprayed, Kash was jogging back down the hall in a clean shirt while putting his gun in the holster, his badge hanging around his neck.

Grabbing my chin, he pulled me close and kissed me hard. "Be back soon, love you, Rach."

"Love you too."

After he was gone, I finished cleaning and called Candice back as I dumped the banana splits Kash had made.

"Did you hurt him?" she asked in way of greeting.

"Ha. No, he got called in."

"Bummer."

"Tell me about it, it was just about to get good too. He told me he was going to clean all the whipped cream off me, I was pictur-ing us in the shower . . . yeah, no. Didn't happen."

"That sucks. He should have told them to give him half an hour."

I laughed out loud and hung my head. "I'm just saying, whipped cream wars are not as fun as they portray them in books or movies. They're usually all sexy and whatnot. Ours? Not so much. I got whipped cream up my nose, I was running away from him and fell over Trip and hit the hardwood really hard. Like, I think my hip and elbow are going to bruise from it because Kash was on top of me when I went down. When I knocked the can out of his hand it somehow hurt me more than anything, my hand is throbbing. *Then* when I'm about to get one good hit in, nothing comes out of the can! I'm all sticky and gross, it was just one massive fail."

Candice was laughing so hard she was snorting, and I couldn't help but laugh with her. "I would have paid to see that!"

"I'm pretty sure I looked like the abominable snowman on crack. You didn't miss anything too thrilling."

"Uh-huh, sure sounds like it."

"I miss you, Candi. I can't wait to see you."

"I know!" I could hear her happy clap through the phone and smiled. "Just a couple weeks and then it's me and Rachie time!"

"You're such a nerd."

A few days after the big blowup Kash and I'd had after the family dinner, he'd surprised me with tickets to Texas for Candice's graduation, and then to California for the two weeks after. He could only get two weeks of vacation blocked off, so after we spent the remainder of the time with Candice's family, he was flying Candice back here for the month leading up to the wedding. I'd tackle-hugged him when he told me about everything. He was always doing whatever he could to make sure I was happy, and though I hated that I knew a big part was still because of guilt for what had happened last summer in Austin, I was so in love with him for the gift of time with my pseudo-family.

"I know, I— Oh, hey! Mike just got here, I gotta go."

"Have fun," I said in a singsong voice. "Be safe!"

"Always!"

I looked down at Trip licking my ankle after setting my phone on the counter. "Yeah, I bet I taste real good right now."

Grabbing one of Trip's treats, I headed toward the bathroom

to clean myself from the dessert war. After he was all settled with a toy and treat on the bathroom mat, I stripped out of my clothes and turned the water on as hot as it would go. I washed my hair and body twice to get any lingering stickiness off, and tried not to frown at how differently I'd seen this shower going.

Once I was done and dried off, I let Trip out before going around the house and locking up. From experience over the last few months, I doubted Kash would be home anytime soon. It was close to midnight, so there was no way I could wait up for him. Placing Trip on the bed, I crawled in after him before grabbing my phone.

> *Just so you know . . . cleaning up from a whipped cream war without you isn't nearly as fun. See you when you get home. Love you.*

I knew better than to wait for a response, he probably wouldn't get the text until they were done. But I couldn't help but sit there and stare until my screen went black, wishing for anything from him.

I was proud of him, and I knew he loved what he was doing. But nights when he was gone were really lonely. With a sigh, I turned off my lamp and plugged my phone in to charge before pulling an already snoring Trip close and closing my eyes.

MY EYES FLEW OPEN and my body stilled. I didn't know if I'd been dreaming or if Kash was home and I'd heard him, but my arms were covered in goose bumps and I held my breath as I waited for another sign of what had woken me. I started to think it was a dream when I didn't hear anything else, but my body locked up again when I noticed Trip standing at the foot of the bed growling low and as fiercely as a puppy could. Sunlight from the windows was filtering into the bedroom, and I quietly reached behind me for my phone. Kash always texted me when he was on his way home for this exact reason . . . he didn't want me to freak out if I was asleep.

My text from last night had gone unanswered.

"Trip," I whispered and sat up, my eyes widening when I saw the ridge of raised hair along his back. "Trip, come—"

A loud boom sounded from the front of the house, and Trip began barking. I froze for all of three seconds before grabbing him and shutting his mouth as I failed miserably at dialing 9-1-1. It shouldn't be that hard, three numbers and the CALL button, but it took me four tries before I got it. In that time I heard two men talking low in the front of the house as I turned in circles, trying to figure out where to go. Closet? Under the bed? Out the window?

"Tampa Bay, dispatch. Do you need fire—"

"Police! Please send police." I quickly and quietly spouted off our address as I tried to keep Trip in my arms. "Someone just broke into my house. This is Rachel Masters, my fiancé is Detective Logan Ryan, and he's out on call right now for a double homicide, and I don't—"

"Ma'am, ma'am, I need you to calm down and speak slowly. Someone broke into your house? Is he or she in there right now?"

"Yes, I hear at least two males." I inhaled sharply when I remembered the fake wall in our closet. Thank God for Kash being paranoid!

"Ma'am, are you okay? What just happened?"

"Nothing! Are you sending someone?" I hissed as I quietly ran to the large closet in the master bathroom.

"I dispatched officers as soon as you gave me the address, Miss Masters. Do you have somewhere you can hide?"

"Yes, I'm getting in there now." My entire body was trembling as I strained to listen for the men. I couldn't hear anything anymore, but that didn't mean much. "How far out are they?"

"About eight minutes. Are you in your safe place now?"

"Yes," I whispered and set Trip down next to me. *Please hurry, please God, hurry.*

"Can you still hear the men, Miss Masters?"

"No." All I could hear was my breathing, which sounded disturbingly loud, and the pounding of my heart. Thank God Trip was staying quiet as he huddled back into the corner.

"Okay, well I need you to stay where you are until officers get there, just in case."

I jumped back into the wall and slid down to a sitting position when a loud crash came from the bedroom, followed by more sounds of furniture being flipped over. My body was vibrating and it took everything in me to keep quiet and keep the phone to my ear. Tears were pricking the back of my eyes, and when Trip softly growled I threw my hand over his nose and mouth, praying he understood my silent plea.

"Miss Masters, are you still there?"

"Y-yes," my voice so breathy, it was barely audible.

"Is that you making the noise?"

I knew she couldn't see me but I couldn't do more than shake my head back and forth as the tears spilled over. I looked in front of me, and my heart skipped painful beats when I saw the edge of the fake wall had caught on one of my shirts. I quietly leaned forward and strained to hear absolutely everything as I reached for the corner of the material.

"Miss Masters? If you can, let me know you're still with me."

"I'm here, the—" The faux-wall was thrown back, and a scream tore through my chest as a large man's frame filled the closet, but I couldn't make out his face. It was dark in the closet, and with the light coming in from the bathroom behind him, it made a strange halo of light around him while darkening his features.

His hand slammed over my mouth while his other arm reached out for me. I kicked at him, and when both hands went for my foot, I screamed *help me* and *hurry* into the phone over and over as he dragged me out of the closet. I dug my nails into the short carpet helplessly as he pulled me into the bedroom and flipped me onto my back. Before I could attempt to kick at him when he let go, he dropped all of his weight onto me and started yelling.

"Bring it now!" he yelled and turned to look toward the center of the bedroom.

Another smaller man came into view, and I tried to scream, but the first man's hand covered my mouth again as the second handed him a small towel. He brought it toward my face and I tried furiously to turn my head to the side, but it was useless. The cloth was pressed over my nose and mouth, and before I could comprehend the odd smell, the room was blurring.

The last thing I heard before the darkness consumed me was a sincere, "I'm sorry."

MY EYES SLOWLY CRACKED OPEN to the foreign room, and it took my mind a few minutes to process that I shouldn't be here—that wherever *here* was, wasn't good. I jolted upright and immediately wished I hadn't as the room tilted to the side and my stomach rolled. Falling toward the side of the mattress in preparation for whatever was about to come up, something caught my shoulders, and I hung there limply as a deep voice spoke softly.

"Whoa, easy, easy, easy. You're okay. Let's sit you back up and I'll get you some water."

My body hunched over as I dry-heaved against his arms, and he never once moved as my empty stomach tried desperately to get rid of anything. When I quieted, he started pushing me back into a sitting position, and I flew back and away from his arms. The room tilted again, but passing out wasn't an option, I needed to get out of there. He reached for me when I swayed back, but I used my legs to launch my body in the opposite direction, and off the mattress.

I took off for the door, but my feet hadn't touched the ground twice before he had his arms wrapped securely around me, holding me to him as I swung and kicked, and screamed for someone to help me.

"Calm down, I won't hurt you." He grunted when one of my flailing limbs connected. "Please calm down."

"Let go of me! Help me! Someone help!"

"I won't hurt you, but I need you to calm down," he gritted, and when I kept trying to get away, he continued to stand there holding me to him.

The nausea and dizziness came back quickly, and soon my arms and legs felt like dead weight. I wanted to keep fighting against him, *needed* to keep fighting against him—but I was losing strength fast. Images of Blake on top of me were flashing through my mind and fear clawed at me. I needed to stay awake, and I needed to get out of here.

"Help . . . me," I pleaded to the door and scratched against my captor's arms. For the first time, I agreed with Candice that

I should have let my nails grow long. My legs gave out and the captor easily held my weight as he backed us up to the bed and I struggled to get his arms away from me. This couldn't happen. Not again.

"You ne—" A deep growl worked up his chest when I dropped my head and bit down on his hand as hard as I could. He took a few deep breaths in and out as I futilely attempted to claw my way out of his arms before he spoke again. "I'm not going to hurt you, stop hurting me."

Tears fell freely down my cheeks the minute he sat down, and he pushed himself back until he was sitting up against the wall, with me still in his arms. I tried calling out for help again—even though I somehow knew that if anyone was on the opposite side of that door, they weren't going to help me—but nothing came out.

There was no fight left in me. There was nothing but the purest form of terror. I'd faced Blake, but I'd been prepared for some of his crazy and I'd known him most my life. I didn't know the man keeping my body still against his, I didn't know where I was, I didn't know what I was up against . . . and I didn't know if I would ever see Kash again.

That thought broke me and my body sagged under the stranger's firm hold as tears alternated hitting his arms and falling onto my bare legs.

"Please," I forced out and tried once more to remove his arms. They didn't move, and he didn't respond for countless minutes as the dizziness and weariness won out.

My eyes shut against their own will, and like back home, the last thing I heard was his voice. "I'm sorry."

5

Kash

"YOU GOOD?" I asked Mason as we headed back toward the elevators.

He shrugged and punched at the buttons on the wall. "There's only so much you can do to get them to go in a different direction. He wanted to follow his brother."

The call from last night ended up being a drive-by involving a newer gang that we'd come across recently, and one of the two victims had been L'il Tay, a thirteen-year-old who Mason had been trying to get off the streets over the last few months. And though Mason was acting like this was just another case, I knew this was harder for him than the rest.

Knowing there was nothing I could say, I clapped his shoulder and let him be alone with his thoughts. Grabbing my phone, I smiled when I was finally able to open Rachel's text from last night.

> SOUR PATCH:
> Just so you know . . . cleaning up from a whipped cream war without you isn't nearly as fun. See you when you get home. Love you.

> We just finished up, be home soon babe. Love you too.

The doors to the elevator opened and we stepped in. As they were closing, someone started yelling my name from down the hall, and Mason caught the door just in time.

"Ryan! Gates!" Sergeant Ramirez ran toward us, and as soon as he was in the elevator he started pounding on the CLOSE DOORS button.

I suppressed a groan. All I wanted to do was get home to Rachel and Trip.

"We already have three units at the scene, and I'll be following you there."

Ramirez was a K-9 unit, why were they wanting his dog, Crush, there . . . and what scene? "Wha—"

"I know you're anxious to get there, but you know we're doing everything we can for this." The elevator was already moving, but Ramirez kept stabbing at the ground-level button. "How are you holding up? You look really calm, are you in shock? Maybe you should let Gates drive."

That seemed to snap Mason out of his thoughts. His hand jerked away from his mouth and his eyes widened. "Why would I need to drive?"

"And why would I be in shock?" My heart started racing as Ramirez started hitting the OPEN DOORS button.

Ramirez shot us a strained, sympathetic look before ushering us out to the underground parking lot. "You weren't informed?"

"Of what?" I was supposed to be the one in shock. So it had something to do with me. Everyone close to me starting flipping through my mind until a sinking feeling hit my chest and stomach. *Oh God . . . Rachel.* "What happened?"

"I'm sorry, I thought someone already told you, you were supposed to be informed already," he mumbled to himself as he kept walking toward the lot. "Look, I'm sorry I'm the one that has to tell you this." He stopped walking abruptly and turned to look at me. His expression was one I had seen so many times, and had even had to use myself. It felt like time slowed as I waited for him to tell me one of fifty scenarios that were speeding through my mind. "A call came in to dispatch about an hour ago. It was your fiancée, Ryan. The only thing that came from her end of the call was her saying her name, someone had broken in—"

I didn't wait to hear the rest. I took off running for my truck and had just gotten to the driver's door when Mason slammed me into the side and ripped the keys from my hand. After barking at me to get in the passenger seat, he fired up the engine and peeled out of the lot.

"This isn't happening. This isn't happening, Mase, tell me this isn't fucking happening!"

"Kash—"

"Damn it!" I roared and punched at the dashboard. "I don't even know if she's okay, Mason! What was Ramirez saying, did he say if she's okay? Is she— Oh God. Rach, baby, please be alive," I whispered and slumped into my seat, raking my hands over my face.

I heard Mason on the phone calling into dispatch and asking questions about what had happened, but I couldn't focus on his exact words or the muffled response coming from the dispatcher. I just kept praying over and over again that she was okay. I could deal with our place being broken into. I could replace all that. But I couldn't replace Rachel.

Mason nudged my arm and I snapped my head to the left to look at him. "Sorry, you weren't responding. They don't know if she's alive, but there's no blood. So just focus on that, Kash."

"W-what? No . . . What do you mean?"

He took a deep breath and gripped the steering wheel. "From what units at the scene—uh, your place—are saying, whoever broke in . . . they uh, they took Rachel."

Mason was saying something else, but I couldn't hear anything past the blood rushing through my ears. When we got to the house, the front door was hanging like it had been kicked in, but the rest of the front looked completely normal. Save for the dozens of officers and detectives that were walking in and out of it. Remembering the faux-wall in the closet, I prayed like hell that Rachel was using it and took off for the large closet in the bathroom.

When I flipped on the light in the closet, dread filled me when I saw the drag marks on the carpet. I called one of the officers that had been taking pictures of the bedroom to get a few pictures of the carpet before I walked in, and all hope left me when all I found behind that wall was our puppy. I grabbed him and pulled him into my chest as I fell back against the wall, and the tears that had been threatening started spilling over.

"Kash, you need to see this," Mason said softly from the doorway to the closet. I looked over at him, rolled to my knees, and stood. "Give me Trip. Go into the bedroom and look at the wall. We'll find her, okay? I swear to you we'll find her."

I handed him the golden retriever and rushed into the bedroom, which looked like a hurricane had hit it. My eyes widened when they finally landed on the wall opposite our bed. A roar filled the room, and before I could realize it came from me, two officers were holding me back and trying to get me to sit down on the bed.

On the wall in red spray paint were the words *DID YOU THINK WE WOULD FORGET?* Underneath was a symbol. One both Mason and I'd had tattooed on our left forearms during our last undercover narcotics assignment with Juarez's gang.

"How?" Mason was asking a detective who was in the room with us. And that was a damn good question. Juarez had put a hit on Mase and me before we could take down his gang, but it had died when the guys hired were thrown in prison for another murder. And I knew for a fact Juarez and his boys were all in prison. "Recruiting people from the inside who got out? Or just using people he trusts? Set up questioning with each of them separately."

I looked up when Detective Byson's cell rang. His mouth snapped shut from answering Mason, and he answered the call. "Byson." His eyes shot over to me and a grim look crossed his face as he listened. "Mmhm . . . Yeah. Set up something with Juarez and his attorney immediately. I'm on my way." He turned to face me and slid his phone back in the holder on his belt. "Rachel is alive."

"Thank God," I breathed and tried to stand, but the officers were still holding me there.

"A call was placed about fifteen minutes ago, demanding that every charge against Juarez's gang be dropped. Before the dispatcher could ask anything, the caller said they would call back in two days and expect progress on the charges being dropped, and would continue to call every two days until every member of the gang was released. If there isn't progress, there will be consequences, and if they aren't released within the month . . . she dies."

"Kash, Kash, Kash, calm down. Come on, man. Calm down. I know."

Mason gripped my shoulders and I tried to focus on him. The other two officers were now struggling to keep me down as I thrashed against them. Where I was going to go when I got away from them, I didn't know, I just needed to go. They had my girl. I needed to find out who *they* were, and I needed to get her back.

"I know this is hard. But we'll find her. I swear." Mason looked just as panicked as I felt, and it was then I noticed the wetness in his eyes he was trying to keep back.

When I finally stopped struggling, the officers let me go at Mason's request, but he kept me seated on the bed. "I need to get her back, Mason. I have to."

"We will."

"I'll do anything."

A determined look settled over his face and he whispered low enough that only I could hear him. "Anything to bring the fuckers down, right?"

I slammed my fist against his and swore, "Always."

I WALKED INTO MASON'S APARTMENT that evening with a bag slung over one shoulder and Trip in my arms. Our bedroom was still being considered a crime scene, and I was asked to stay out of it for the night as they processed more and continued to take fingerprints. Not that I thought I would be able to stay there even after they were done anyway, without Rachel . . . I didn't know how I would handle being there.

After dropping the bag in the room I'd occupied for years when Mason and I'd shared an apartment, I fell heavily onto the bed and kept Trip secured tightly to my chest as I stared at nothing.

A fear unlike anything I'd ever known had coursed through my body the moment I'd realized Rachel was at a murderer's home last fall, and that I'd let her walk away with him. When the call between us had been dropped after I'd heard her scream, I hadn't even let myself believe I wouldn't find her and bring her back alive.

But the fear I'd experienced that early morning could never be compared to the fear that had been crippling me all day. At least when she was with Blake, I'd had an underlying knowledge of what Blake was capable of. Now, though, I didn't know who had her, what they were doing to her, and what they could do. I just knew what they'd threatened to do.

For close to ten hours, a handful of detectives had questioned every member of Juarez's gang, the two men hired to kill Mason and me last year, and family members as well. No one was talking, and the only living extended family of Juarez and his boys that we could track down had either turned their backs on the members of the gang, or were afraid of them. I hadn't been allowed in for any of the interviews, since I was too close to the case—again—so I'd spent hours seeing if anyone on the street had heard anything, and looking for Rachel's cell phone, which we'd later found ten miles away from the house in a trash can at a gas station. A gas station whose indoor and outdoor cameras just happened to be down.

There'd been nothing to go off of from the anonymous call placed regarding their demands and threats for Rachel's safety, and although they said they'd call back every two days, I'd hoped like hell they would've called back again. But there was nothing. We had leads that weren't talking, and didn't have a reason to talk, and nothing else.

And my girl was gone.

Pain seared my chest and I prayed to God that he would keep her safe. He could do whatever he wanted with me . . . as long as she came back alive.

There was a shuffling near the other side of the room, and I looked over to see Mason standing in the doorway.

"How are you holding up?"

I sucked hard on my lip ring when my chin started shaking, and looked back to the wall. *How the hell does he think I'm holding up? Rachel's gone and probably being tortured, and I can't do anything!*

"We'll find her, Kash."

Unable to speak yet without breaking down, I nodded my head hard, once. *We have to find her, and we have to do it tomorrow.* I didn't care if they'd given her a month to live or not. They also said there would be consequences if there wasn't progress in two days, and I wasn't willing to let her find out what those consequences were. Seeing how the possibility of giving the takers what they wanted was slim, finding her was the only other option.

"I love her too, I'll do anything to get her back."

"Do you mean that?" I choked out when he turned to leave.

He turned back and gave me an odd look. "Of course I do."

"They aren't going to release Juarez."

"I know," he said with a sigh.

"Chief told me tonight before I left that I was off this case."

"Know that too. What are you getting at, Kash?"

I swallowed past the tightness in my throat and shook my head quickly. "We had to do a lot of things in the years that we were in undercover narcotics that I wish I could erase from my memory. But you and I agreed before we ever started, we would do anything to take the fuckers down."

"Kash . . ."

"And I'll do anything—*anything,* Mase—to bring these fuckers down too."

He stared at me for a few tense moments before responding. "I know what we agreed on, and we'll do what we always do. But don't do something stupid. There are a lot of people looking for her. We'll find her."

Fear was quickly turning to rage and determination. "Yeah, we will."

6

Rachel

WHEN I WOKE AGAIN, there was no dizziness, no need to empty the contents—or lack thereof—of my stomach, no headache, and no sense of how much time had passed. But there was fear, and very vivid memories of being taken.

Kash. My chest ached and tears burned my eyes. *He has to know by now that I'm gone. What is he thinking? What is he doing to find me?* And I had no doubt that he was trying to find me. I just didn't know if he would.

Finally opening my eyes to the dark room when a sob tore free from my throat, I covered my face with my hands and curled into a ball on my side before I heard a shuffling noise, and my entire body stilled.

There was someone else in the room with me.

Was it him? The man who had dragged me out of the closet and kept me from escaping the last time I'd woken on this mattress?

I brought my hands down from my face and waited the few torturous seconds while my eyes adjusted to the dark. Even having had my eyes closed for so long, it was still nearly impossible to see anything past my mattress, it was that pitch-black in the room. A large shape came into focus before I was able to make out legs stretched out along the floor and crossed at the ankles, large arms crossed over an equally large chest, and the whites of a set of eyes fixed directly on me.

"Are you awake now?" his low voice rumbled through the room, and for some reason I shrank away from it. "Do you feel up to eating?" When I continued to stay silent, he rose from the floor with a grunt and I watched his shadowed body stretch before turning toward the wall he'd been up against. "Don't go back to sleep. I'll be right back."

A bright light filled the room for the short time it took him to slip out the door, and I immediately bolted off the mattress and headed in the direction of the door. The room went pitch-black again and I felt along the wall for a handle. Beeps sounded—like electronic buttons were being pressed—before a series of short, staccato beeps, and then the sound of his heavy footfalls as he walked away from the door.

I finally found the handle and tried futilely to open the door, even though I knew, deep down, those beeps had been a code to lock the door from the outside. The tears were now falling freely as I alternated slapping my hands against the wall and screaming for help, and trying to open the door. I'd continued my useless attempt to get someone to help me even after I'd fallen to the ground, and after what seemed like half an hour later, the beeps came back and I shot to my feet in preparation.

As soon as the door cracked open, I pushed through it only to be caught by a pair of large arms and walked back into my room as I screamed for anyone to save me.

"Get off me! Someone help!"

He shut the door behind him with a foot and continued walking us both until my feet touched the mattress and he started pushing me down.

Oh God, no! "No, stop! Help me, please!" My body hit the mattress, and he kept his arms on my shoulders as he knelt to the ground beside me and I struggled against him.

"I need you to stay here, and stop fighting against me. If you get out of this room, I promise you there is no one who is going to help you. I can only keep you safe if you stay in here, do you understand me?"

My head was shaking back and forth as I sobbed and fought against him. I'd dealt with Blake and his psychotic claims; I wasn't about to believe this man.

"Stay here so I can bring you your food."

His body wasn't coming closer, but I continued to push against him and struggled to get out from under his strong hold. Without warning, his hands were gone and he was stalking back over to the door. I shot upright, and my mind screamed to make another attempt at getting away from here, but I knew he would bring me right back in. Besides, he only had the door open long enough to bend down and grab something on the other side of the wall before it was shut and he was making his way back to me.

He set something down on the bed next to me and walked quickly away again. "Close your eyes," he said in warning.

I kept them open.

The light flipped on and I blinked rapidly against it, refusing to cover my eyes for fear of what he would do if I stopped paying attention. When my eyes had finally adjusted, I looked to my left and saw a plate full of chips and a gourmet-looking turkey sandwich. The guy came back to me briefly to set a bottle of water down next to the plate, before retreating to the place and exact position he'd been in when I'd woken up. We stayed just like that for hours.

Him, sitting on the floor in front of the door, watching me.

Me, sitting on the bed with my knees up to my chin, staring directly past his head to the handle of the metal door.

The food untouched.

"GET UP, LET'S GO," the man ordered the next time I woke up.

Afraid of where he was about to make me go, I stayed on the mattress, staring at my knees, which I had pulled up to my chest.

"You haven't left this room since I brought you in. I know you need to use a bathroom, so either we go now, or you can wait until tonight."

I didn't even know how far away *tonight* was. I'd just woken up, but I'd been sleeping almost the entire time I'd been here. I desperately wanted to take him up on his offer, but a part of me didn't want to acknowledge that I needed him for a task as simple as going to the bathroom.

Wait. "Go." He's about to take me out of the room! My body began pumping adrenaline at a fast pace as I thought about what this could mean. Forcing my face to not give anything away, I kept my eyes off him as I stood and met him near the door.

"Don't try anything, and don't leave my side." When I didn't respond, he grabbed my elbow. "Understood?"

I looked up at him, making deliberate eye contact for the first time since I'd woken up here.

With a curt nod, he opened up the door, keeping his hand on my arm the entire time. Looking to the side, I saw a long hallway in one direction, and a much shorter one in the other with a door where it ended.

I didn't know if that was a closet, or a door to the outside, but when the man began walking me in the other direction, all I wanted to do was go to it.

We passed multiple rooms on each side and a kitchen before he stopped in front of a shut door. Opening it slowly, he flipped on a light inside and started to look around. His hand still hadn't left my arm, but he was facing me. I knew I wouldn't get another chance like this, so before he could look back at me, I quickly lifted my leg before shoving it into his groin as hard as I could. He bent and his hand loosened, but it was all I needed.

Wrenching my arm from his hand, I turned and started sprinting down the hall in the direction we'd come. Not long after, I heard heavy and quick footsteps behind me, but I didn't look back. Another few rooms had gone by when one of the doors ahead opened, and a guy stepped out. He wasn't facing me, but with the sound of our approach, he'd stopped walking and started to turn.

A muscled arm wrapped around my waist, yanking me back and into the kitchen. My scream was cut short when a hand slammed down over my mouth, and I opened my eyes to see my captor directly in front of me, his eyes dark and a finger in front of his own mouth, telling me to stay silent.

My back was against the wall, the man caging me in so I couldn't move. Every heavy breath from him had his large body brushing against mine.

"Oh, little girl," a sinister voice rang out in the hall behind me, and every hair on my body rose. "Have you finally come out to play with the rest of us?"

A low growl built up in my captor's chest, and my body started shaking uncontrollably.

"I won't bite . . . hard."

My captor pressed his body closer to mine, and after slowly moving his hand away from my mouth, moved close to whisper in my ear. I cringed back but couldn't go far. "Don't say anything."

"Where'd you go, you little bitch?" the voice said again, but this time the sinister tone was laced with hatred.

When my captor pulled back, his face was murderous. Tears sprang to my eyes, but I somehow knew that I needed to listen to him. Suddenly his head turned to the side, and I froze . . . not wanting to see the man that voice belonged to.

"Damn, bro, already claiming her?"

"Leave," my captor growled. "Now."

"No need to get touchy. I'll wait for my go at her."

"I said get. The fuck. Out."

"I'm going . . . I'm going. You better keep an eye on your bitch. Because next time she's alone, Marco might be the one to find her . . . and you *know* how bad Marco wants her."

"No one touches her." His body was vibrating, and I looked up at his face to see the barely concealed rage.

"For now," the voice said in a mocking tone. "Possessive doesn't suit you. You might want to be careful with that, you know how we all like a challenge." With a deep laugh, I heard footsteps retreating from us. "I'll be seeing you soon, sweetheart."

A few seconds passed before my captor looked back at me. His face was dark when he whispered, "Do not run from me again, understood?" Not waiting for me to respond, he pushed off me, grabbed my arm, and started walking out of the kitchen.

I shrank into him when he suddenly stopped, and we came face-to-face with three men.

"Look what we have here," one of them said.

"Told you I'd be seeing you soon, sweetheart," another said, and I would have recognized that disturbing voice anywhere.

"We need her." The third spoke directly to my captor, his eyes never once looking at me.

The man holding my arm pulled me behind him. A move the first two didn't miss. "You've gotten by fine without her, Marco. I'm sure you'll figure something out."

Moving me to his other side, and closer to the wall, he began walking again. Not four steps later, pain spread over my scalp, and a cry burst from my chest as I was yanked back by my hair. My captor's arm moved around my waist as he put himself between Marco and me, and his other arm was straight in front of him with a gun pointed at Marco's head.

"Someone's moody." Marco never flinched. But a smile slowly crossed his face as he let my hair fall from his fingers. "You have beautiful hair. What a shame."

"No. One. Touches her," my captor said low, his words full of warning.

"Just fuck her and get that pent-up anger out of your system already," he said to my captor, his smile never fading. Marco stepped back to the other two guys, his hands raising up in mock-surrender. "Until next time."

My captor quickly pushed me back, the hand not holding the gun never leaving me until we were in the room I'd originally woken in. Scrambling away from him, I darted toward the mattress and pressed myself to the wall. Our eyes never left each other until I broke down crying. My adrenaline had faded, and the fear of seeing the other men consumed me as I shrank down until I was sitting with my knees pressed to my chest.

I wanted to know what Marco had meant by "What a shame." I wanted to know what my captor planned on doing with me. I wanted to know why it felt like he'd just saved me, when he'd been the one to take me from my house. And I wanted to know why, for those few minutes, I had felt safe next to him.

7

Kash

"WELL WHAT ARE THEY DOING to try and find her? How are they going to get her back? Will those men in prison say anything? Will they give any type of hints? How could you wait two days to tell us about something like this, Logan? How could you keep this from us?!"

"Marcy, stop." My dad cupped Mom's shoulders and leaned in to whisper in her ear.

I rested my head in my hand and propped my elbow up on the granite counter as they spoke softly back and forth to each other. Well, Dad spoke softly. Mom was borderline hysterical and getting louder by the minute.

"She's been through enough! That poor girl has been through enough!"

"Marcy, sweetheart, why don't you go lie back down and—"

"No! No, we need to go find her, we need to call the news station, and we need to get people looking for her!"

"There are a lot of people doing everything they can . . ." Their voices slowly faded as Dad pulled her out of the kitchen and I just sat there, staring.

Not really seeing anything. Not really thinking anything. And sure as shit not feeling a damn thing. I was numb. I didn't even remember driving to Mom and Dad's, actually, I didn't even know if I'd driven or walked. I just remembered seeing Dad's face as he opened the door for me near five this morning, and finally telling him and Mom everything that had happened. I'd spent so long doing jobs where I couldn't tell them anything, that a part of me had been subconsciously rebelling against telling them; whereas the other part had finally realized that I *was* keeping it from them, and I couldn't continue to.

Chief was forcing me to take the week off. I'd spent all day and night yesterday going over everything I remembered from Mason's and my time with Juarez, and coming up empty. I hadn't slept, I couldn't remember if I'd eaten or not, and I felt like I was going insane with trying to make connections to other gangs that I knew weren't there. If I didn't get Rachel back soon, I was going to lose my goddamn mind.

Dad breathed heavily through his nose as he sat down on the barstool next to me. For a long time we both just sat there without saying anything. Eventually he got up, made coffee, and sat back down after placing a mug in front of me as well.

"She's not mad at you, you know. Your mom, that is. She's just scared."

"I know."

"Are, uh . . . shit, Logan. I don't even know what to say. I want to ask if you're going to be okay, but I wouldn't want someone asking me that." He set down his coffee mug and lifted both his hands in the air before letting them flop down onto the counter. "I just can't believe this is happening. This doesn't seem real; this is something you see in movies, and on TV shows. It's something you read about in the newspapers, but you never think about it happening to your family."

"This is my reality. This happens all the time in my job, but it wasn't supposed to happen to her. I caused this, Dad—"

"No, Logan, don't start going down that—"

I dropped my arm and looked up at him, noticing for the first time the redness and fear in his eyes. "But I did! My job, what I've done . . . that is why she's gone."

"I'm not going to let you put blame on yourself for this. I had to watch you blame yourself for what happened to her back in Texas when you did everything you could to prevent it. You can't keep doing this to yourself, Logan. It's not your fault; none of it is your fault. Blaming yourself is only going to make it harder, it's only going to cause you to go down a path that is dangerous for you."

I snorted. I was pretty sure I'd already been up and down that path a few times.

He rested a hand on my shoulder and waited until I was looking at him again. "I'm serious. This is going to be a difficult time for all of us, but especially for you. We'll be here for you every step of the way. We're all hurting, we're all scared for her, but no one other than the people who took her are to blame. All right?"

My eyes squeezed shut as my head fell back into my hand, and

I took a deep breath in and out without responding. I didn't know what to say, I didn't agree with him.

"I saw what happened to you before, and I see what's happening to you now. I know you're hurting, son. I know"—he choked out and his hand tightened—"and I can't imagine what this is like for you, but we can't lose you too."

The air in my lungs left in a heavy rush, and when I blinked my eyes back open, I watched as tears dropped onto the counter. I hated that he was talking about her like she wouldn't be back.

Rachel would be back.

I needed her back.

LOOKING AROUND THE OFFICE a few hours later, I wondered where the other detectives were as I quietly made my way toward my desk. If anyone aware of the situation were to see me, I knew they would make me leave. But I needed to look up records on Juarez and his boys that would be inaccessible from anywhere else, so I was willing to risk the suspension that would be coming for me if Chief found out. Turning the corner, I stopped midstep when I saw Mason hunched in on himself at his desk, his entire frame shaking and tense.

"Mase?"

His hands dropped from his face to hang between his knees, and he lifted his head like it was the hardest thing he'd ever had to do. When he turned to look at me, my day of going in circles with my parents quickly fell from my mind. Fear gripped my chest, my legs felt like they would give out on me at any moment, and I felt hot and cold all at the same time.

"Kash, you know you can't be here right now," he choked out.

"What—what happened? Why are you crying?" I knew that whatever had him looking like he wanted to die had to do with Rachel, I knew it to my core. I'd never once, in the years I'd known Mason, seen him cry.

Heavy tears fell down his cheeks, and I watched as his face crumpled before he burst into strained sobs.

I stumbled back until I hit a wall and fell down it as I waited for him to say words that I didn't want to hear . . . *couldn't* hear. It felt like my heart was being torn from my chest as I watched Mason struggle to speak. As the minutes passed, my dread began turning into a sorrow unlike anything I'd ever felt before, but no tears came. I was in shock and having trouble breathing. This couldn't be happening, she couldn't be gone.

"We'll find her, Kash, I swear," Mason choked out, and my head snapped back up to find him looking at me. "I swear to God we'll find her before they can do anything else to her."

"She's alive?" I whispered, and hope surged through me before his words sank in. "What happened?"

"You're not supposed to know anything, you're supposed to stay completely separated from the case."

"I don't give a—"

"But if the roles were reversed, I would hate you for not telling me." With one hand he wiped the wetness away from his eyes as the other reached over to his desk to grab something, before standing and walking slowly to me. Dropping to his knees, he handed over a folder and I hesitantly grabbed for it.

Flipping the top open, I pulled out the blown-up photograph and swallowed back bile before the tears started to fall down my face. An anguished cry burst from my lips and my hands gripped my hair after I dropped the folder and paper to the ground.

Mason put a hand on my shoulder, and spoke softly. "They called, they didn't even ask if there was progress . . . they already knew there wasn't any. They have to be in contact with Juarez or one of the guys, so the department is checking every call and visitor they've had. You could—" He paused, and the hand that was gripping my shoulder began shaking. "You could hear her screaming in the background, Kash, and they said they'd call back in another two days. This picture was sent an hour later. They had our techs working on it, trying to track it through the server, but these guys know what they're doing. It just kept coming to a dead end."

Another tortured cry left me, and I brought my knees to my chest as my head shook back and forth. "God, Rachel, I'm so sorry—I'm so damn sorry. We have to find her, Mase."

The picture was burned into my mind, so much that even after I closed my eyes, it was still all I could see. Three of Rachel's severed fingers. One still had the engagement ring that I'd put on it a few months before. The bright purple color she always wore on her nails a dead giveaway that they were, indeed, her fingers.

"We will, I swear we will. Byson is questioning Juarez again—"

I didn't wait for him to say anything else. I pushed him back and scrambled to my feet, already running toward the interview rooms.

Mason barked out my name, but I kept going. I passed the first two open rooms, and just as I was approaching the third door, it opened and Byson stepped out, looking down at his notepad.

Hearing my approach, his head snapped up, and his eyes widened. "Ryan! What the hell—"

Shoving past him, I kicked the closing door back open before slamming it shut and locking it, and came face-to-face with Juarez for the first time in almost a year.

"What a pleasant surprise," he sneered as I approached him.

"Where is she?" Slamming my hands down on the table, I leaned over it as I yelled, "Tell me!"

"You expect me to know what you're talking about?"

I would have thrown the table if it weren't bolted down to the floor. Rounding it, I went over to where Juarez was sitting and kicked his chair back into the wall.

"Don't fuck with me, Juarez!" Stalking over to him, I gripped the arms of the chair he was cuffed to and leaned in so my face was directly in front of his. "Tell me where my goddamn fiancée is!"

His only answer was a sardonic smile.

"Tell me or I swear to God I will make your death slow and painful," I growled.

"You mean like Rachel's?" Juarez whispered.

I punched him, and grabbed the collar of his gray prison shirt to bring him closer to me. "I will end you, you son of a bitch! Where the fuck is she?" I was so far gone—my mind only on finding Rachel and making every one of the sick bastards involved in her kidnapping pay for what they'd done to her—that I didn't even register what the yelling outside the room was about until I was being dragged away from Juarez.

"Kash, calm down," Mason grunted as I struggled to get away from him and Byson as they pulled me back.

"Tell me where she is!"

Another mocking smile crossed Juarez's face, and my frustrated roar filled the room.

"I will make you pay for everything that has happened to her!"

"Enough!" Mason yelled as they threw me out of the room.

I turned to go back in, but Mason slammed me against the wall and restrained me by pinning my arms behind my back.

"Kash, don't make me put cuffs on you," he said low. "You have got to calm down. I know you're upset, man, I *know*. But you're ruining your career, and making it worse for Rachel by doing this."

"He knows where she is," I gritted out, the adrenaline quickly leaving my body. "He fucking knows, Mase. He said her name!"

"Ryan! Gates!"

I turned, and my body sagged against the wall when I saw Chief standing there.

"My office. Now."

Mason swore under his breath as he pulled me from the wall and kept my arms behind my back as he walked us toward Chief's office. Byson was already waiting for us in there, and when Chief sat down at his desk, I knew I was about to lose my job.

WALKING SLOWLY, like I was expecting a bomb to go off if I made any noise, I stepped into the bedroom that just ten days ago had been destroyed. That just ten days ago had had a message about *why* they'd taken Rachel on one of the walls. That just ten days ago was considered a crime scene and had been full of officers. That just ten days ago Rachel had been taken from.

I hadn't been in here since that day, but since then Maddie, and Mason, and my mom had come in to clean the disaster that had been left over, and paint the wall. The TV was gone—I hadn't seen a need to replace it, since I hadn't wanted to come back here—and so were the mirror and lamps; but other than that, there weren't any signs that anything had ever happened.

Except one.

Rachel was still fucking gone.

The department hadn't gotten any closer to finding her, and even though Chief had been considerate enough to give me only unpaid time off for the rest of the week . . . I was still doing things every day that were sure to get me fired at the very least. I just made sure that everything was away from the department, and that no one other than Mason knew what I was up to.

Although he had strict orders not to, Mason had kept me updated on everything about the case, and I would always be thankful to him for that. But I wasn't sure how much more I could take.

It'd been ten days and already I felt like I was dying from what I had seen and heard. I didn't know how Rachel was still pushing through the torture we'd seen her go through. I didn't know how she was even still alive. And when I got her back—because I *was* getting her back—I didn't know what would be left of her fiery spirit I'd fallen in love with.

Putting Trip down on the floor, I watched him take off for the bathroom and followed him into the master closet. He went right to the fake wall and began crying, and for some stupid reason, something dangerously close to hope actually sprang up in me. I tentatively reached out toward the wall, a harsh huff escaping my chest when my fingers were just inches away, and I paused.

I'm fucking crazy. She's not going to be in there.

Shaking my head, I reached out to grab it, and yanked it back.

Trip ran in, and my hand fisted around the thin material as the worst type of disappointment washed away any form of hope I may have had.

I'd known she wouldn't be in there. I'd known, but I'd still let myself believe that by some miracle, she would.

"She's not here, bud, come on."

Letting the wall fall back into place, I walked into the bedroom and stared at the bed for a handful of minutes before finally sitting on the edge. Bending over, I rested my elbows on my knees, and my head in my hands—and groaned out the last week and a half's frustrations, devastations, and heartaches.

Exhaustion finally took over my body, and without even taking off my shoes, shirt, or jeans . . . I lay back on the bed and automatically rolled over to face Rachel's side. My heavy eyelids blinked as I looked at the empty space beside me . . . nothing about that was right.

Most nights I couldn't even sleep, the only times I did were when my body literally couldn't go from the stress and exhaustion anymore. I hated sleeping without her, and I hated sleeping knowing I could be using that time to try to find her. But what I hated most was waking up without her. Not only was it a cold reminder of what she was going through, but it also just felt wrong.

I wish I could hold you.

I wish I could tell you how much I love you.

I wish I could hear your laugh.

I just wish I knew that I would see you again.

You can't leave me now, Rachel. We're about to get married. We're going to have a family someday. We're going to get old and fat together.

Wherever you are, Rachel, whoever has you, and whatever is being done to you. Know that God can't stop me from finding you, and bringing you back to me.

I will hold you again, and I'll never let you go.

Gripping her side of the comforter in my fingers, I breathed out her name and surrendered to the exhaustion.

8

Rachel

I SPUN MY ENGAGEMENT RING AROUND on my finger just to give me something to do, since I'd just finished picking off the nail polish that had lasted this long. My eyes darted to the right of the door handle long enough to confirm he was still awake and watching me, before going back to the handle.

I didn't know how long I'd been there, I'd tried figuring it out, and tried keeping track of certain things . . . but still wasn't sure. The same man who had originally taken me out of the closet, and the home I'd shared with Kash, was always in my room save for an hour or so every day, and he'd finally given up trying to get me to talk to him. I believed him now that he wouldn't hurt me, but that didn't mean I trusted him as a person or wanted to talk with him.

Every day he took me out of my room twice: twice for the restroom, and one of those times to also shower. The first time after my attempted escape, I'd silently refused to shower, since he stayed in the bathroom with me, but the next day I couldn't resist washing what I was estimating was three days' worth of grime off me. He'd stayed in the bathroom, but he'd kept his back to me the entire time. Every day he brought me three meals unless I was sleeping through one of them, and after the first four meals had gone untouched, I'd begun tearing through them whenever he brought them.

I figured I'd slept through the entire first day, and past breakfast the next day, since the first two meals he'd brought me were generally for lunches or dinners. And since I slept as often as possible to pass the time, and sometimes that meant missing meals, I only had my showers to track the days that were passing. By the time I'd taken what I thought was my fourth shower, I realized I couldn't remember if it was really the fourth or fifth. And while I was about 90 percent positive that was three showers ago, it could have been four. Still going on the theory I'd missed two full days of showers, I was guesstimating I'd been gone for eleven days. Or nine . . . or I could just be going crazy and it had really only been five. But who knows.

I hadn't spoken a single word since the first time he'd brought me food and I'd tried to escape, which I think was day two. And somewhere on day *x, y,* or *z,* I got tired of referring to him as *him* or *he* and decided to name him Taylor, solely based on the fact that he looked like Taylor Lautner's twin.

Regardless of what I'd named my kidnapper—or how many days I'd been here—there was still nothing about a rescue, I didn't know why they had taken me, and I didn't know what they were going to do with me.

I'd seen a few other men on my walks to and from the bathroom, but no one had said much, other than speaking Spanish to Taylor, which I didn't happen to know much of. And not one of them had done, or said, anything to me since that first time out of the room. The men seemed to ignore me for the most part, but that could've had something to do with Taylor's reaction to Marco, or the fact that he now had his gun out every time we walked up and down the hall.

None of this was making sense, and as the days continued to pass, my fear had steadily grown into something deeper. Something I didn't have a name for. And in that fear was confusion, longing, and sorrow.

With a few grunts, Taylor stood from his faithful spot on the concrete floor up against the door, and stretched for a moment. Why he never brought a chair in here was beyond me, but I also couldn't fathom why he was babysitting me for countless hours on end, every day. He'd already taken me for the first bathroom break before he brought me breakfast, so I was guessing now was lunchtime.

When he walked up to me and grabbed my empty plate from breakfast and checked my half-full water bottle, I knew I was right. I didn't try to get away from him as I had so many times in the first few days. I just stopped twisting my ring and watched his every move . . . waiting for what I knew would come next.

"Don't go to sleep."

He was gone longer than he normally was when he went to get my food. How long did it end up being? I'm not sure . . . it felt like hours, but could have been only one. I knew there was someone else that had to be cooking in the house or building that I was in, because the longest Taylor was ever gone was probably half an hour. And I knew in that time he took his showers, ate, and would come back with meals that could have taken hours to cook.

Even though I never spoke to him, having him in the room with me had become something I was used to. And when he was gone, it felt . . . wrong. Not that I craved being near him, but to be honest, I was terrified when he wasn't around. I don't know why that was; *he* should still terrify me. *He'd* dragged me out of a closet, *he'd* knocked me out with chloroform, and *he'd* kept me locked up in a room that was barely large enough for me to fully stretch out in.

I guess in a way he did still terrify me, because the unknown scared me more than anything. I'd grown up with Blake, so I'd trusted him until he started changing—and he was easy to like, everyone had loved Blake. Taylor, despite the obvious first day, hadn't done anything to me. In a way, he'd been protecting and taking care of me, and I'll never forget those first two, pained *I'm sorry*s. But I also knew how fast someone could snap and turn into a different person entirely.

Shaking my head quickly to clear my mind of my confusion, I got off the mattress and paced around the small room for another immeasurable amount of time until I heard the echo of heavy footfalls, and the beeps of the lock for the door. I scrambled back to the mattress and had just brought my knees up to my chest, wrapped my arms around my legs, and rested my cheek on my knees when the door opened and Taylor walked in. He usually walked right over and placed my plate down next to me, but this time he didn't. When I heard the rustling sound of plastic bags, I rolled my head so my chin was on my knees now, and my eyes widened when I saw him standing there, weighed down with a local grocery store's bags, and bags and drinks from . . . *oh my God, Taco Bell!*

"I got you some stuff," he said gruffly and set the food and drinks down at his feet before walking over to stand directly in front of me.

I watched as he opened the first bag and began pulling out deodorant, a toothbrush and toothpaste, a hairbrush and ponytail holders, girly shampoo, conditioner, a razor, and soap—since whatever I'd been using was definitely meant for men. The next bag opened and he pulled out large packs of men's undershirts and boxer-briefs. I raised an eyebrow at first when he sat them down next to me, but I didn't say anything.

"There's no way in hell I was going to be able to pick out a bra for you, and women have too many different kinds of underwear. This was easiest, but they might be too big on you."

I couldn't even complain. My throat was closing up, my eyes were burning, and it was taking everything in me not to reach out and run my hands over it all. I hadn't brushed my teeth since the night before I was taken, and I hadn't put deodorant on or brushed my hair since the same time. Even though I was able to take showers every day, I had to put my old underwear, sleep shirt, and little shorts on once I was done; and it felt like I was never getting clean. If I could have clean clothes, even men's clothes, I didn't care.

The last bag opened, and a shaky smile crossed my face for the first time since I'd had the unfortunate pleasure of meeting Taylor, as he pulled out different colored nail polishes.

"I don't know if you like these colors, but I watched you pick off what you had on your nails. So . . . here."

A package of pens followed, and the smile fell as confusion set in; but then he brought out a journal, and my stomach dropped.

"I had to watch you for a long time, I don't know what you wrote about, but I know you used to write every day. Anyway, that's it," he said and took a step away from the mattress.

I picked up the journal and ran my hand over the front of it as tears fell down my cheeks. I knew sometime later I would be creeped out and put Taylor in the same zone Blake had been in, since Blake had people following me, and somehow had gotten cameras into our apartment. But right now, all I could think about was that I was going to be able to write to my parents again. It'd been over four and a half years since my parents died, and for four years I'd been writing in journals to them every day. Not being able to talk to them had been about as hard as not being with Kash.

My mouth opened, but it took four tries before any noise came out, since I'd gone so long without using my voice. "Why?"

Taylor froze and straightened from where he'd been bending down to grab the food—his eyes were massive when I looked up at him. "Why did I buy you all that?"

Shaking my head, I wiped away tears with my free hand and cleared my throat in preparation of speaking again. "Why did you take me?"

"You will never understand how sorry I am," he stated.

"If you're sorry, then why?"

"I didn't have a choice."

I could see the torment in his dark eyes, and I didn't understand it. My voice was still rough and low as I forced out, "But why am I here? What was the reason for taking me?"

He ran his hands through his hair and seemed to scramble for the right words to say. After a few moments of floundering, he exhaled roughly and shrugged. "I can't tell you. Just know that I didn't want to be a part of this and I'm sorry."

The depth of his apology had my mind traveling down a path I hadn't once considered since being taken, and I gasped loudly before I could cover my mouth. "Is he okay? Kash, is he okay? You didn't hurt him, did you?"

"We aren't touching him. He's . . . safe." The confusion on my face must have prompted him to continue. "I doubt he's fine because you're gone, but as long as you're here, he's safe. We aren't going to physically do anything to him."

"And—and me?"

He'd started to bend down to the food again, but his dark eyes flashed back to mine at my question. "I'll never hurt you."

I hadn't spoken in well over a week, but now that I was talking to Taylor, it was like I couldn't stop. Even though my throat screamed in protest from lack of use, I straightened out my legs and sat the journal down next to me as I leaned forward on the mattress. "If you don't want to be a part of this, why are you? Why would you do something like this?"

Taylor continued to grab the food and one of the drinks before walking over to me.

"Do you need money? Do I know you? Do you know Kash? Are you involved in drugs, or a gang, or something?"

"I'm not going to tell you anything, so stop asking questions."

I wanted answers. But when he sat down in front of the door and popped a straw in his own drink, I knew he was done answering; but I was thankful for the little he had told me. Minutes passed before he prompted me to eat, and I finally looked through the bags full of enough food to feed Kash and Mase. I'd spent enough time crying over being taken from them, but something about staring at all that food had tears welling up again; and I suddenly had the ridiculous cravings for pancakes, my fiancé, and that big bear of a guy.

"I can't eat all this," I whispered, and looked helplessly up at Taylor.

"Whatever you don't eat is mine, I haven't eaten yet."

Taking two burritos out of one of the bags, I set the bags down in front of the mattress and curled back up against the wall with my soda and food.

Taylor watched me eat in silence, and it wasn't until I was done and minutes had passed without me grabbing for the bags, that he leaned forward and snatched them up and inhaled the rest of the food. We didn't speak again for hours, but I wasted my time painting my nails and toenails, and writing in my journal.

Only this time I wasn't just writing to my parents, I was writing to Kash too. He wasn't gone, but I was. And despite the honesty in Taylor's words about not hurting me, that didn't mean one of the others wouldn't. So the question was the same as it had been in those first unnumbered days, I didn't know when I would see him again . . . or if I would.

Sometime after I'd stopped writing, he stood and grabbed all the trash from lunch earlier, and headed to the door to get what had to be dinner.

"Don't go to sleep."

I spoke quickly when he grabbed the handle of the door, and like he did earlier, his eyes looked shocked when he turned to look at me. "Why do you only leave me alone when I'm awake? Shouldn't you leave when I'm asleep? It just doesn't make sense that you're here all the time, and when you do leave, you tell me not to go to sleep. Aren't you worried I'm going to try to escape again?"

Those dark eyes of his filled with something that had fear sliding through my body, and there was no need for him to say the words out loud. The warning of what would happen if I did escape was clear. "I don't leave this room when you're sleeping because you're vulnerable. If I leave you when you're awake, then you can scream if something happens, and I'll hear you."

"If something happens?" I swallowed hard and blinked rapidly as I tried to understand this new look on Taylor. "Like what?"

He chewed on his bottom lip for a second before answering. "Let's just say, if someone other than me walks through that door, scream immediately. Don't wait for something to happen. It's not a matter of *if* something will happen to you, it's just a matter of how long they'll wait until they start trying to get in here." At my audible inhale, he nodded once and repeated, "Don't go to sleep."

I didn't.

Not long after, he was back with two plates of spaghetti, and for the second time since I'd been there, he ate with me. Taylor was always watching me, I guess probably because it gave him something to do in this room, so I was used to his eyes on me. But the way his eyes kept drifting over to me while we ate was freaking me out. When we were finished, he picked up the plates and stood, waiting for me to follow.

"Grab the bags for your shower."

I took the bags that held everything I would need, including new clothes, and followed behind him as he opened the door. I held onto the back of his shirt when he prompted me to, and stuck closer to him than I normally did as we walked down the halls to the kitchen, and then the bathroom; and I cringed even more into him when we would pass the other men who were in the building with us. After his warning earlier, I would have rather not left my room again, but it didn't have a bathroom.

Once I was done relieving myself, I didn't even stop to think about Taylor being in the same room. I never did anymore. I stripped out of my clothes and folded them into a pile on the floor before stepping into the large shower with my new shampoo, conditioner, razor, and soap. It felt so good to shave that I wanted to stand in the shower and continue letting the water pour over me once I was done. But something about knowing there were clean clothes to put on, and a toothbrush to use, had me shutting the water off and hurrying to grab the towel to dry myself.

My eyes shot over toward the counter, and lying on top was one of the shirts, boxer-briefs, the deodorant, both brushes, and toothpaste. I sent a glare to Taylor's back, and he must have felt the tension fill the bathroom because he shifted his weight and looked down.

"I didn't look toward the shower. I was just making it easier for when you got out, you never opened the packs of clothes and they still had stickers on them."

Oh, well . . . "Thanks."

I put the deodorant on before slipping into the clothes that swallowed me whole. Someone needed to give Taylor a lesson in buying women's clothes. At least the boxer-briefs had the elastic band, but I still needed to roll them a few times so it wouldn't feel like they were about to fall down. The hem of the shirt touched midthigh and covered the briefs, but I had to stop looking at myself in the mirror because it just reminded me of when I wore Kash's clothes to bed.

A deep ache filled my chest and I forced tears back as I reached for the hairbrush and spent minutes getting all the tangles out from however long I'd been here. After searching the bags and finding the hair rubber bands, I braided my hair low and off to the side, and finally, *finally,* grabbed the toothbrush and tooth-paste.

I had thoroughly brushed my teeth three times and was reach-ing for the paste for the fourth time when Taylor's hand caught my wrist to stop me. His expression was somewhat amused, but there was a hint of the apologetic look I'd seen this afternoon.

"It will still be here tomorrow. Three is enough."

The hand that was holding the toothbrush fell dejectedly to the counter, but I knew he was right. I went about rinsing off the brush and my mouth before turning to look at him.

"What do I do with the soap and everything in the shower?"

"Leave it in there."

"But, won't someone take it? Or touch it, or something?"

He shook his head and put the rest of the new clothes in one bag before grabbing my old clothes and shoving them in another and tying it off. "This is my bathroom. If you're not in it, they don't have a reason to come in here."

"Oh. Wait, this is your bathroom? So there are others? This *is* a house?"

"Somewhat."

I waited for him to expand on his response, but when he didn't, I followed him out of the bathroom and through a door to a bedroom filled with various workout machines and a bed that made my body yearn for it. I followed him inside and watched as he put the towel and bag with my old clothes down a chute, and when he saw me standing behind him, he gestured toward the rest of the room.

"This is my room."

"Why don't you sleep in here?" *Better yet, why can't I sleep in here? The mattress I'm on is thin and old as dirt. And at least in here there's carpet instead of a concrete slab for him to sit on.*

He looked at me but never responded. His dark eyes moved quickly back and forth as they searched my face. Ever since he'd come back with dinner, he'd been looking at me like he was making sure I was still there, or still okay. I didn't understand it, and just as I was about to ask about the change in the last half hour, he breathed out deeply and turned to go back to my room.

When I was back on my mattress, he turned off the light and I waited for the minutes to pass by until I could make out his form on the floor in front of the door.

"You never answered my question."

"Which one?" he asked, his tone teasing.

I rolled my eyes though I doubted he could see the action in the dark. "When I brought up your room. You know you don't have to stay in here with me; I really won't try to leave again. You should be able to sleep in your own bed."

After a minute he finally answered. His tone was dark again, and the way his eyes had looked earlier flashed through my mind. "I do need to stay in here with you. It's not you I don't trust; it's them. At least I can lock you in here well enough that it would be extremely difficult for them to get to you when I'm gone."

A chill shot down my spine at the thought of someone else coming in here; and confusion set in as I realized that, once again, I was thankful for Taylor. I didn't want to feel thankful to him for anything, and I didn't like that I felt indebted to him for what he'd done for me. Because despite his protection, he was still the one who had taken me from my house and was keeping me from getting out of here. I needed to remember that.

Instead of trying to continue the conversation, I pulled my knees up to my chest and shut my eyes. But even as I waited for sleep to come, I couldn't help but acknowledge that for now, at least, I was safe—and as long as Taylor was in this room, nothing bad would happen to me.

Taylor

MY HEAD HIT THE WALL BEHIND ME when I heard her breathing even out. Scrubbing my hands over my face, I bit back a groan and tried to get the images from earlier out of my mind.

I could see her, so I knew she was okay. But, Jesus Christ, the way Marco had used Photoshop to make those images always looked so fucking real. Going so far as to take pictures of her hands when we'd had her knocked out and making it seem like we'd severed her fingers. Taking the recordings of her screams from when we'd taken her and those first couple days she was awake here, and playing them out masterfully so it sounded like she was being tortured when they called into the police department. And I didn't even want to think about how they got all that hair that looked the exact shade of hers for the package they were sending tomorrow. Jaime had taken some of her personal things before we began trashing the room, and along with the hair matted in unknown blood, the earrings that had been on her nightstand were also spotted with blood and would be in the same box. If another two days went by without any progress, the detectives were getting the video.

In the twelve days since I'd brought her here, I'd spent practically every moment watching her like a hawk. I could pick her out in a crowd of thousands of people, if I were an artist, I could sketch her features from memory. Even so, I was having an impossible time making myself understand that whoever that girl was in the video, wasn't the girl in front of me now. Again, where had they found the video? I didn't know, and I didn't want to. It was fucking sick.

She's safe, I kept repeating to myself. But for how long? If she tried to escape again and one of them got ahold of her, I didn't know if they would listen to Romero's orders about not touching her.

Well . . . what I'd told them Romero's orders were. "Take the girl and do whatever it takes to make the department release us," he'd said to me. By that time, harming her was out of the question. It wasn't just because she was female; it was because it was *her.* I couldn't stand the thought of any of my brothers laying a finger on her, let alone torturing her.

When Romero gave an order, he only gave it to the person who was supposed to carry it out. With him in prison, none of us had an option other than trusting each other that we had relayed them correctly. Besides, if you changed an order, or didn't follow through . . . Romero would have you put out. There'd never been a thought to go against him like this . . . until she came into my life.

We wouldn't hurt her fiancé—that hadn't been a lie—even though he and his partner were the reason all this was happening in the first place. But Romero was sure this would work, and the brothers would do anything to get the core of our family back together. So until the department gave in to the demands, they were going to continue to get very authentic-looking pictures, videos, phone calls, and packages that suggested the girl asleep on that mattress was going through hell on earth.

Not that I would say anything to Marco or Jaime, but I knew eventually they were going to test the hair and blood and find out neither belonged to her. Just like eventually one of the brothers was going to slip up somehow and the detectives would realize everything had been faked. I'm sure I wasn't the only one who realized that, but I'm positive everyone was banking on the fact that Romero and the main brothers would be released before then.

Despite who and what I was, I felt bad for her fiancé. We may not be causing him physical harm, but that didn't mean he wasn't being tortured far worse than she could imagine. I couldn't even imagine what he was going through as he looked for her and got the "evidence of torture" the guys had been sending.

If I'd lost someone like her, I'd fucking lose my mind. And he didn't just lose her—she'd been taken from him.

If people were torturing my girl, I'd hunt them down and kill them. And I had no doubt that was exactly what he planned to do.

She rolled over on the mattress, and even through the dark of the room, I could make out her bare legs curled up to her stomach. Images of how she looked when she got out of the shower tonight hit me hard, and I welcomed each and every one of them.

I wasn't a fucking idiot. I knew she was going to drown in the shirts I'd gotten her. But I'd spent four months watching her every move as we waited for the right time to put our plan into action. Seeing her walk around in nothing but an overly large shirt had become one of my favorite things. So when given the opportunity of choosing what she wore, it had been simple . . . and worth the torture it would put me through.

I held my breath when I heard a harsh huff come from her. Every night she did this, and every night I felt like even more of an asshole.

"Stop . . . please," she pled. Her voice was barely above a whisper, and after repeating those two words a few more times, she was silent.

I wanted to take whatever nightmares she was having away, but I had no doubt I was the source of them. Who wouldn't have nightmares of being kidnapped? Especially after being kidnapped and kept in a tiny fucking room with the man who had taken you. Raking my hands over my face again, I wanted to die in that moment. Just like I had every night I'd heard her beg *someone* to stop. I didn't want to be a part of kidnapping her. I didn't want to be in this life.

But I didn't have a fucking choice.

Like I said, when given direct orders from the head of your crew, the rest of the brothers don't question them. They carry them out. When you're the one who let the only blood relative of the head of your crew get murdered, you're the one that's chosen to carry out the bad orders. Every. Time.

I'd had a nightmare of a childhood. My mom skipped out when I was young, my pop had been in prison most my life, and the uncle who raised me had always been strung out. When I turned fourteen, he'd celebrated my birthday by bringing in one of his gang's whore's daughters so I could become a man. He'd rewarded me with bags of smack he wanted me to sell at school for him.

My best friend, Dre Juarez, had been my only way to escape my uncle at the time. His brother headed up a neighborhood gang, and they'd always provided a sense of loyalty for me. But I hadn't wanted to be in a gang . . . even back then. I'd seen what it had done to my old man, and I'd had to live through the shit with my uncle. No matter how normal Romero Juarez's house seemed, I wanted a different kind of normal.

That all went to shit when I turned sixteen. Uncle was demanding I join, or get out, and I didn't have anywhere to go but to Dre's brother. Dre was already fully in, had been for years, and the rest of the brothers were ready to welcome me. That weekend my uncle was arrested, and it was all over the streets that his boys blamed me.

One night they came looking for me, and in looking for me, ended up murdering Dre instead. It'd been a drive-by that I hadn't even been present for; I'd been hooking up with some chick from school. But after that, I hadn't had a choice, Romero made me join as a payment for getting Dre killed. The other half of the payment was retribution on the men involved in the drive-by.

Those were the first three men I killed. But they hadn't been the last in the eight years since I'd gotten in. Most of the brothers could do as they pleased, as long as they followed the rules. Me? If I didn't do what Romero asked, Romero swore he would make me join Dre six feet under. I hated this life, and I hated who I'd become. But I swore to myself that one day I would get out and start over far away from this shithole. Now, more than ever, I was craving that life because of the girl not ten feet away from me. I *would* get out . . . someday. Until then, this fucked-up family was all I had.

About four years ago, the core of our family—the "originals"—

started cooking up and dealing meth out of a house in the ghetto. Part of initiation into the gang was spending a year there; after that, you were introduced to the rest of the family. From there you could choose to come and help keep the family running, or stay in the meth house. Or, as Romero liked to put it: "work or play." Close to a year and a half ago, Romero started up saying two of the new brothers were cops. He was so sure they were and was waiting for things to play out. But that waiting had cost him, and the rest of the cores, their freedom. Every member in the meth house was in prison now, including all of the originals.

Once the two cops started showing back up around Florida after a few months of lying low, Romero had Jaime and I begin the long journey of making them . . . disappear . . . in a way that couldn't come back on the family. It would have been a perfect time for me to try and get out. But Jaime and Marco had taken over the family and were stricter than the originals had been. A week before we were supposed to do the hit, one of the pigs got a girl, and everything changed. Jaime was sent to watch the cops, and I was to track the girl's every move.

Over the next four months, that's exactly what I'd done.

Unfortunately, I hadn't just tracked her every move. I'd fucking fallen for her. A girl who, at the time, I'd never spoken to. And now . . . a girl who would always hate me.

9

Kash

Jumping out of my truck, I put my hood up and kept my head low. I was well known in this part of town, as was Mason, starting back before we'd been made while we were with Juarez's crew. People knew us for the gangs we had been in, and now people knew us because we were in the gang unit.

For the most part, the residents around here were cool with us. They knew our background, and knew that we tried to help them when shit went bad around here. Which was pretty much all the time. But that didn't mean they didn't start alerting the entire damn neighborhood that cops were nearby when they saw us either.

Looking around to make sure activity looked normal, I waited until I spotted the lookouts. When I was sure they were going about business as usual, not noticing me, and people weren't running into their houses, I took off through an alley behind me. Turning on Second Street, I walked and rounded the corner at Maple before slowing down. Just before I hit Third Street, I ducked my head even lower and looked to the left as I brought my right hand up the back of my head and over. Just as I hit my forehead, I paused and tapped twice with my index finger before dropping my arm and continuing my slow walk.

Not more than four steps later, another pair of feet came up next to me.

"What up?"

I snuck a quick glance and tried not to smile to myself. Shawn. Little, gangly Shawn. Exactly the kid I'd been hoping for. I fucking hated that they were sending him out to confirm their deals, but at least he would scare easy.

"Nice night, yeah? Lots of stars out." His voice shook as he looked back and forth.

I knew this game, and I knew it well. "If nights are what you're into."

Shawn tried to look in my hood at my response, and I dipped my head lower. "Yo, man. I think you're on the wrong street if you're looking for something else. The walkers are on Seventh."

"Street's right. I'm just not looking for stars, understood?"

"All we got are the stars out here, ya feel? I think you best find your way home." He started to turn around, so I hurried to make my request.

"No price tonight. I don't want stars. I want to see the Sun."

"Sun's not out, ya know?"

"I'm sure the Sun will make an exception." Turning my head toward him, I quieted my voice so it wouldn't carry over the street. "You say my name out loud, or you make me, I put Sunny and his boys away for this operation they got going on. And since you're out here setting up drug deals, then that means you'd go down too. If you cooperate, then I don't say a fucking word. Got me, Shawn?" His body started to tense so I spoke quickly. "You alert a lookout, and you're all in prison, I'm not playing around. I want. To see. The Sun."

Shawn worked at relaxing his body and turned to face me as he pulled his phone out. I lifted my head enough that he could see my face, but not so much that anyone watching us would be able to. His eyes widened momentarily, but he did a good job at remaining calm and searching through his contact list.

"I help you," he said so soft I almost didn't hear him. "I got your word I don't go down for trying to sell to a jackbooted thug?"

I snorted. "As long as all of you cooperate. I came alone. Sunny's boys can check me for wires inside. Now make the call."

"Whatcha coming 'round here for anyway, Kash?" he asked as he lifted the phone to his ear and looked around the street.

"Don't say my name out here. Just get me in to see him."

Nodding, he waited until someone answered. "No stars, he wants to see the Sun. That's what I said, but he said the Sun will make an exception"—he lowered his voice—"and I really think the Sun *should,* ya feel? Yeah. Yeah."

"Tell them," I prompted him, and Shawn looked at me like I was insane. "Tell them, but don't say my name."

"It's K-money. Understood? Came alone, prepared to leave without words to others, but he wants to see the Sun." He jerked his head in the direction of the house, and we began walking toward it. "Yeah, we comin'."

As soon as we hit the steps to the house, I unzipped my hoodie and stopped when we reached the door. It opened, Shawn and I stepped in, and as soon as the door shut behind us, I raised my hands in the air and instantly had three of Sunny's men around me.

"All that's on me is the duty weapon in the holster on my right hip."

Taking my hoodie off, lifting my shirt, patting me down, and disarming me. All were routine when coming onto their territory the way I was, and all were what I'd been prepared for. I waited quietly as they went through all their *necessary* steps of making sure I wasn't wearing a wire, before they reluctantly handed my gun back to me and stepped away.

After I'd reholstered, I kept my hoodie off, partly because it was hot as shit outside and in the house, and also because I knew it would help keep Sunny's boys calm if they could see my weapon.

"Shawn said no stars?" one of Sunny's boys, RJ, asked.

"No stars."

"Not wearing a wire, and don't want stars, why you here?"

"What, I can't come around just to check up on you? See how your night is going?" I sneered and looked away. "I need to talk to Sunny. That's all you need to know for now."

Just then the door to the back of the house opened and Sunny walked out. Sunny wasn't a big guy by any means, he was shorter than me by a good five inches, and didn't have as much bulk on him. But this motherfucker was terrifying. It wasn't the tattoos, because, well, honestly, I'm sure I had more than he did. It wasn't the scar that ran down the left side of his face from his temple to his jaw that he'd received in a deal gone wrong years back. And it wasn't his near-black eyes, which made him look dark and demonic and completely contradicted his name. It was all of it mixed in with this alpha-male, badass leader vibe he had that made men terrified to fuck with him.

Too bad I kinda thought I was a badass too. So instead of cowering when he walked into the room, I straightened and raised an eyebrow at him. We both eyed each other before cracking smiles and reaching out to shake hands and pull each other in.

"Hoping this is a good visit, Detective. K-money, huh? That was a good one, Shawn, quick. I'm impressed." Sunny took a step back and crossed his arms. "Why do I have the unfortunate pleasure of having you hide out on my street, Kash?"

I smirked and matched his stance. "As I told Shawn, I won't say a word about you, your men, your operation, or being here as long as you all cooperate. I just need to speak with you, I need a few favors."

"And why would I do anything for you? I know your history, as far as I know, you're back in the game of bringing crews down."

"You and I both know I didn't bring *crews* down. I stopped dealers. If that's what you're afraid of, like I said, I'm not here for that. I'll leave here acting like I don't know what's happening in this house and with your crew."

He laughed and brought his arms out before crossing them again. "I don't know what you're talking about."

"Stars, Sunny, really?"

Nodding his head to one of his men, they all began laughing as the guy walked over with a plate full of cookies in the shape of stars.

I glanced up at the man holding the plate before turning to level my glare at Sunny. "If I were you, I wouldn't be playing me right now. You do me this favor, then I'll turn a blind eye to your operation. But don't make me out to be a fool, Sunny, you know who I am, you know what I've done, and you know what I'll do to you and all your men."

"Then talk."

"Alone."

He studied me for a few minutes, the tension in the room continuing to grow as everyone waited for him to make a decision. Finally, with a nod, he turned toward the door he'd originally walked out of and called over his shoulder, "Let's go."

I followed him through the door, down a hall, and through two more rooms before he finally shut a door behind me and shot me a dark look. "The fuck is wrong with you, Kash? You trying to come in here and screw all this up for me? You don't just walk into *my* house . . . into *my* operation . . . into *my* assignment. Jesus Christ, you could ruin *everything* by being here." He gritted his teeth and ran his hands over his head.

"Are you done?" I asked and went to sit in one of the chairs. "I don't have time for your dramatic fits, Sunny. I really do need your help. I wouldn't have come here if it wasn't crucial, you know that, man."

Sunny had been in undercover narcotics for closing in on fourteen years. He was the one that had originally gotten Mase and me in with right crowds so we were able to easily slide in with our first crew. I knew he was right, I knew he had every reason to be pissed at me for showing up here. If I'd still been undercover, me showing up on his street while in another crew could have just been grounds for a fight, but as a known detective, it was suspicious on Sunny.

He huffed loudly and took the chair next to me. "It better be. Talk to me."

"Before we get into what I need, please tell me Shawn isn't on stars."

"Kash . . ." he said in warning.

"Look, Sunny, I was glad he was the one to come at me tonight. But the kid is, what, fifteen? Bad enough you have him as the one going out to set up the deals, but even you can't sit back and watch him waste his life on meth."

Sunny rested an elbow on the arm of his chair and massaged his bald head as he answered me. "I'm not, and he's not. I don't want him setting things up either, he's a good kid . . . but he was determined to get in a crew. I'm sure you've seen that. Has been since he was a little runt. So I took him under my wing so I could keep an eye on him, but I haven't let him touch the product. He wanted more responsibility, and it would have looked weird making older members do grunt work when we have him. I have to do what I have to do. I know you understand that."

I frowned because I did. Sunny and I shared a look that said everything. Neither of us liked the situation, but what could you do other than blow your cover? And Sunny's was a lifelong cover, not something you could easily jump in and out of in a year and a half or so like Mason and I had.

"Enough about how I'm running my crew, tell me why you're here."

I got comfortable in my chair and folded my arms over my stomach. "Did you catch wind about Mase and me getting sent to Texas, and why?" When he nodded, I continued. "I met a girl there, and it's a fucking *long* story, but short of it is . . . I'm in love with her. I'll be in love with her until the day I die. She moved back here with me, knows all about my past undercover work, and knows about the job that went wrong that ended up sending us to Texas."

"She got a drug problem?"

"No, Sunny, fuck."

I rolled my eyes and kept my outward emotions turned off as I told him the rest. In the last few days, everything had changed. I'd done all I could to find her without the department's knowledge. It'd been difficult, between going to work and doing my own investigations without letting anyone else catch wind. But it was about to get a hell of a lot easier. Starting today, Rachel and I would have been on vacation in Texas for Candice's graduation, and then California to visit with her family for two weeks. When Chief asked if I wanted to still take the time off, or if I'd needed the work as a distraction, I'd chosen the time off. No one would be expecting anything from me, and I would be free to look for her more than I had been. He'd nodded and told me he understood it was a difficult time, that if I needed anything, to let him know.

I didn't need a goddamn thing other than my fiancée back.

I'd gone to see living relatives that Juarez and the other boys had, and I'd spent days on the streets, talking to people. But I knew I was missing things, and that's why I was coming to see Sunny now. He had a massive operation in Tampa Bay, the only reason it was still running was because he was a cop, and we weren't about to shut him down because he was working at taking down suppliers that went much larger than Tampa Bay . . . that went much larger than Florida. So he knew pretty much everything there was to know, and if he *didn't* know it, he knew who to talk to in order to find out.

"She doesn't have a drug problem, but she was abducted two

weeks ago right out of our bedroom. Mason and I were working a double homicide when it happened. Department has leads, but nowhere to go with them, and they haven't gotten any closer to finding her than they were on that first day."

"Shit, Kash. You serious?"

I stared at him, unblinking, not responding.

"Man, I had no idea. I can't remember the last time I watched the news, and I haven't checked in with the department in months. Are you—I mean, damn. Are you okay? I would be losing my shit."

"Already have, and, no, I'm not okay. My future wife's gone. And I just watched a video of her being tortured . . . a couple days ago, we received her hair covered in blood." Bile rose in my throat, but I swallowed it back down. I was supposed to stay off the case, but her hair had been in a box made out to me. Mason and two other detectives had had to actually cuff me when I'd opened it in order to restrain me. "I'm not fucking okay. But I'm going to find her, and I'll do whatever it takes. I think you understand how serious I am if I'm sitting here asking you for favors. I'm willing to do whatever."

Sunny studied me before leaning in and saying softly, "A man that looks like you has nothing left to lose. Your eyes are dead, Kash, but you still have a job, you still have a family, you could still lose everyth—"

"No, if I've lost her, I've already lost it all."

He sucked in air between his teeth and shook his head hard once. "Okay, how far gone are you willing to go?"

"Back to how I was undercover."

"All right, then tell me what you need help with."

I explained the spray-painted message left in the bedroom, the

phone calls made to the department, the torture they'd been putting her through, and what they'd sent us. I told him about the
demands the kidnappers had been making, and how well they'd
been covering their tracks.

"I've gone to visit the family of some of the guys, but most of
them have no contact, they're scared of them. I know most of the
guys had some women, some had baby mommas, and some had
regular whores, but I can't find any of them. I was hoping you
knew something we were missing, or you'd be able to help me
find some people who could persuade some of the crew to talk."

Sunny drummed his fingers on the arms of the chair and
dropped his head back as he thought for a bit. "I'll have to get
in touch with some people to find out more. For the most part, I
left that gang alone because the two of you were headed in when
they started getting bad, there was no reason for me to really pay
attention, you know?"

"Yeah. I'd been afraid of that."

"But I do know there's a walker over on Seventh Street. RJ
was hitting it for a while, and she was here getting her hits, they
just called it even. What I'm getting at though, is she was a talker.
So I know she was the main bitch of one of Juarez's boys. She'd
be buck-ass naked in my living room, just got done with RJ and
getting ready to go walk. All the while she'd be talking about
her man being in prison and how she was walking so she could
support herself and their kids. Can't remember the guy's name
though."

"You know hers?"

"Yeah, um . . . damn it . . . uh, Serena?"

"Ah, Deon's woman."

Sunny snapped and pointed at me. "Yes!"

I should have known when Sunny said she was a talker. "Deon would kill her if he knew she was working corners on Seventh Street. But that won't help me much right now."

"No, but don't forget she and Deon got three kids. Before RJ finally got tired of putting up with her, she made him take her to the prison every Sunday to go see Deon. I'd bet she still goes to see him, and RJ knows where she lives. I would say she's worth a visit, if you understand what I mean. She's not someone who can keep her mouth shut."

"All right, I get it."

He stood and leaned close to me. "I'm sorry about your girl, man. I really am. I'll help you with what I can, I'll make some calls and I'll see what other people know about Juarez. But don't show up at my house anymore like this, people are going to start thinking something's up, understood?"

"Completely, I appreciate it."

We exchanged numbers before he opened the door and yelled for RJ to join us. After finding out where Serena lived, and a few more displays of authority for his territory by Sunny for the members of his crew, I left the same way I'd come. Quiet, and hidden by the shadows.

10

Rachel

MY EYES FLEW OPEN and I heard the sound of heavy breathing fill the small room. Trying to keep my breathing even so I wouldn't give myself away, I barely turned my head from where it had been smashed in my arms to look over toward the door. Terrified of what I might see, and who might be there, I almost cried out in relief when I could make out Taylor's form doing push-ups.

I stayed quiet as I watched him silently work out and wondered if he did this every night while I was sleeping. He had to be doing something, because his massive frame never seemed to change over the course of my time here in this room, and a part of me felt bad that he was resorting to this rather than using the equipment in his room.

"Go back to sleep," he said roughly, never once stopping from the crunches he was now doing.

Instead of following his command, I let my earlier curiosity bubble out. "Do you do this every night?"

"Yep."

"Why don't you use the equipment in your room?" I bit my lip as I waited for his response, remembering how this conversation had gone over last time.

"I already told you."

"But I could stay in there with you, and then when you're done, we could come back here." Did I sound as desperate as I felt to sleep on that bed?

He stopped suddenly and turned to look at me in the dark. "Are you trying to make something happen? Do you want to put yourself in more danger than you are already in? Unless we have to, we aren't leaving this room," he snapped, and I flinched.

"No," I whispered and felt my cheeks burn at the tone in his voice.

"Shit"—he sighed and crawled toward the mattress—"I'm sorry. I shouldn't have talked to you like that, but I don't understand why you keep pushing the issue. I know you know the danger is real. I can see the fear in your eyes every damn day, so I don't get why you keep bringing it up."

"I feel bad that you're making yourself so uncomfortable to make sure I'm safe. And I know that's stupid, I shouldn't feel bad because of what you did. But then when I think that, I can't figure out for the life of me why, if you would steal me from my home and my life, would you suffer so much to make sure I'm safe?"

Taylor just stared at me, and when I thought he wouldn't

answer, I turned my head back into my crossed arms and shut my eyes.

"Because you didn't do anything to warrant this, and you deserve to have someone protecting you in this fucked-up situation."

My head snapped back up and I turned to look at him, my mouth open to ask him—again—what I was doing here, and why I was here; but I knew those were questions he wouldn't, or couldn't, answer.

"Just go back to sleep," he pleaded, cutting me off and crawling back to his spot on the floor before starting up his crunches again.

What kidnapper says something like that? What kidnapper *protects* his captive for that matter? Everything that had happened so far was flashing through my mind, and none of it made sense. His presence alone was terrifying, but I wasn't sure if that made me feel safer from the others, or if I still feared him. The way he'd been so quick to apologize when he'd yelled at me just added to the confusion and mystery that *was* Taylor.

I didn't understand him, and at the time, I didn't know if I ever would. But as I had been so many times in the week since he'd shown up with new clothes and other things for me, I was thankful for him.

PAIN THREATENED TO CRIPPLE ME as I impulsively struggled against the handcuffs. I screamed against the gag when Blake moved the blade from my left arm, and slowly ran the scalpel down the inside of my right. Tears were streaming down my cheeks as I watched him begin to methodically move the blade over my stomach, a smile on his deceptively handsome face the entire time.

"Not my Rachel," he whispered. "You don't deserve her beauty."

I continued screaming, my body wanting nothing more than to escape the intrusion. But Blake's weight on my hips, and the sickle curving around my throat, prevented any movements other than my arms, which were chained to the iron headboard.

Blood trickled steadily from my arms onto my shoulders and in my hair. I tried begging him to stop, but all that came out was wordless screams. My vision was darkening as I watched the deep red liquid pooling on my stomach. I needed to stay awake; I refused to let myself believe I would die like this. Kash would find me, I just had to keep repeating that to myself.

"Not my Rachel," he repeated again.

His arm moved up, and I gave up on my futile attempt at shrinking back into the bed as he moved the scalpel from my hairline to my jaw, the blade staying close to my face, but never coming in contact.

"You could have been mine. You were always meant to be mine. Why couldn't you be her?"

Another muffled scream tore through me when the blade pressed into my chest.

"Wake up! Stop—fuck! Wake up!"

"Stop, please! Get off me!" I screamed, and thrashed wildly. Another curse came from him when I connected with his face again.

"Wake up!"

My eyes flew open and blinked quickly against the blinding light in the room to find Taylor directly above me. He'd grabbed at my arms to pin my wrists down above my head, the other was pressing down on my hips to keep me from bucking against him.

"Get off me," I pleaded hoarsely. Taylor's form blurred as tears gathered in my eyes, and eventually fell.

When I could see him again, I noticed his dark eyes fixed on my chest, a look of horror on his face. Slowly, his eyes went up to where my arms were being held down. They widened marginally, and bounced back and forth a few times before coming down to rest on my face.

"Please let me go."

His face morphed into an expression I didn't understand as he released me and sat back on the ground. I quickly pulled at the large shirt I was wearing to cover my chest. The V-neck collar wasn't deep and usually hid the scarred MINE; but I knew with it being stretched down, he'd seen it just then.

"I'm sorry," he said, his voice gruff. "You were screaming this time, and I—I just . . . I don't know. I'm sorry."

"This time? W-what do you mean *this* time?"

"I hear you beg me to stop. Every. Night. The same words you screamed when I took you and kept you from escaping. I won't hurt you," he assured me. "I know you don't believe me, but all I want to do is keep you safe."

My body stilled for long moments, and I subconsciously rested my hands over the scars on my chest and stomach. I just stared at him for long moments, watching as indecision played over his features. It wasn't hard to understand why being kidnapped had brought back continuous nightmares of Blake. I just hadn't known I talked in my sleep. Kash had never said anything. But, then again, he was all about avoiding anything that had to do with Blake.

Taylor stood and walked over to the light switch on the wall, and my body began shaking. I needed the light right now. I needed to be able to see everything. And I needed to stay awake.

It took me three tries before I managed to blurt out, "Will you tell me something about you?"

Turning, he eyed me warily before walking back toward the mattress, and sitting in front of it. "If that's really what you want to do to make you fall back to sleep. You know I won't answer if I can't, so don't push those questions."

I swallowed roughly and nodded my head. Taylor had only talked to me like this twice so far; but both times I'd started asking the wrong questions immediately, and he'd shut down. Right now I just needed my mind to get off Blake and what had happened almost a year ago, so I would do anything if it meant Taylor kept talking.

"How old are you?"

"Twenty-four."

"How long have you lived in here?"

When he answered, his voice sounded worn out. "Eight years."

"Don't you have a girlfriend? Or a wife . . . kids . . . anything?" When he didn't respond, I asked hesitantly, "Is that a bad question?"

"No to all of the above," he finally said. "No one should have to deal with my demons."

"What demons?" I asked quickly, and cringed as I waited for him to shut down our conversation.

"They're just something I've brought on myself throughout the years."

I studied his face as I replayed his tortured words over and over again. "I don't believe that," I said later. "I don't know why . . . and part of me can't believe I'm about to say this . . . but I know you're not a bad person."

He scoffed, and when he spoke again, the tortured strain was gone from his voice. "If I'm not a bad person, then why are you here? Better yet, tell me why you've been having nightmares of me every night."

My mouth opened, but nothing came out.

"Exactly. Don't ever let yourself believe that I'm not as bad as your nightmares are portraying me. I assure you, I'm worse."

I watched Taylor stand again and quickly walk over to shut off the lights. Darkness engulfed us, and all I could hear was him settling down in his spot against the door.

"I don't have nightmares about you," I said softly. The phantom pain of Blake's blades was making it hard to breathe. Each labored breath seemed shallower than the last.

"What?"

"The man who haunts my dreams was evil. You . . . you're not a bad person."

The sound of Taylor moving back toward the mattress filled the small room. "What do you mean? Who do you dream about?"

"Just . . . not you."

"Those scars," he said after a few moments of silence. "Where did you get them?" When I didn't respond, he spoke again . . . his voice strained. "I'd seen your arms, but I . . . I thought it was something different."

"You thought I'd done this to myself," I guessed, and took his silence as acknowledgment.

"Who did that to you?"

I sat there for a long time without answering his question. Taylor didn't have a right to know about my life, and yet, some part of me wanted to tell him. "A man that I'd grown up with and had trusted. Something changed in him though, he became

obsessed . . . he was evil. And, to put it simply, he wasn't accept-
ing of the fact that I refused to be his."

"Is he who you dream about?" he asked. The darkness in his
tone caused me to shrink away from him.

"Nightmares," I corrected him. "I have nightmares about
him. I *dream* about Kash and my life before you entered it."

It felt like all the air was sucked from the room at my attempt
to hurt Taylor. It was ridiculous, but an apology was at the tip of
my tongue. I hated that I felt bad for hurting him . . . but I knew
my earlier assessment was correct. Taylor may have done bad
things, but he was not a bad person.

With a heavy sigh, Taylor moved back across the room. He
didn't say anything, and neither did I, but I felt his eyes on me
until I eventually fell asleep.

"WHAT COLOR DO YOU THINK I SHOULD USE?"

One of Taylor's eyebrows shot straight up, and with his dark
eyes, strong features, and large arms crossed over his chest, I suddenly felt stupid for asking him. But I was bored, I needed someone to talk to, and he was the only candidate. Candice would've
helped me pick out a color, so this beast was about to help me
pick out one now.

"Well?" I prompted and gestured toward the six nail polishes
sitting on the bed.

"You're serious?" Despite his deadpan expression and tone, I
didn't give up.

"Uh, yeah." It'd been over a week since the night Taylor had
woken me up from my Blake nightmare, and in that time, something had changed between us. I don't know if it was telling him
the smallest bit about Blake, or if it had to do with Taylor men-

tioning his personal demons. Whatever the reason, we talked more every day. While it made the days go by faster, I was also struggling to remember why I'd ever been afraid of him. That alone should worry me and shoot up red flags; but I could see the torture he struggled with internally, and I knew this whole situation was the last thing he wanted for either of us.

He huffed and uncrossed his legs before switching which one was on top. "Isn't it enough that I buy you those, and braved buying you tampons last week?"

My cheeks flooded with heat, but I squared my shoulders and stared him down. "Well if I was home, you wouldn't have had to worry about that! It's not my fault you weren't prepared for having a woman locked up for this long."

His face dropped and turned an odd shade of white for his normally tan skin. "I'm sorry—"

"I know you are, and I know you don't even have to do what you've been doing. So thank you, but could you just humor me, and help me pick out a color? Please?"

"Sure," he said softly, and didn't bother standing as he crawled over to the mattress. His brow drew together as he studied the different colors, and picked them up individually, before picking up two at a time and setting one aside.

I laughed softly and raised my hands in surrender when he glared at me.

"This one." He dropped the electric blue polish in my lap and sat back but stayed close to the mattress. "You're trying to turn me into a girl," he grumbled and ran his hands through his shaggy hair.

"Um, not? You just have to put up with me because you signed up for the job of taking care of me. Lucky you."

He grunted and watched as I started with my toes first, and then made my way to my fingernails.

"You having fun watching me?"

"I wouldn't say fun is the right word, but it's something to do. And your concentration face is cute."

Rolling my eyes, I let the *cute* slide, even though I would have normally punched Mason's or Kash's arm if they had called anything I did *cute*. Not now, though. I'd take the *cute* title and wear it proudly if it meant being near them.

Funny how things like that change when you're in these kinds of situations. Kash usually drove me crazy. He was so stubborn, and such a smart-ass, but I missed those annoying traits so much. I missed the way our personalities clashed and resulted in us fighting; I would give anything to fight with Kash again. The thought of having children with him used to terrify me, and now I was afraid I'd never get to have that opportunity. And I hated the nickname Sour Patch so damn much, but I would never complain about it again if it meant hearing Kash's voice.

Tears pricked my eyes, and I blinked quickly to keep them back. Taking a deep breath in to tamper down the emotions bubbling up, I concentrated on finishing the last nail and screwed the top on before looking up at Taylor. "Do you know my name?"

"I do."

"Why don't you ever use it?"

He bit down on the inside of his cheek and looked away from me as he thought about what to say. "I stole you away, I didn't meet you. When you meet someone, if they want you to know their name, they give it to you. It's like a privilege, and you didn't give me that privilege."

"I named you," I admitted softly.

He jerked his head back to look at me again, and his brow scrunched together. "What?"

"Uh, well, I named you. I was always thinking of you as *him* or *he,* and I eventually got tired of it."

When I didn't offer anything more, he leaned forward and put a hand out, palm up. "Well . . . ? What's the name you gave me?"

"Taylor." In my head, it'd been easy to think of him as Taylor, but now that it was out there, a blush was creeping up my neck and over my cheeks.

He barked out a loud laugh and leaned back. "Oh God, not you too? That's not the first time I've gotten that."

I'd been stunned by his laugh, but then joined in with him at his admission. "Well! You look just like him!"

"Thanks . . . I guess?"

"It's a compliment, trust me."

His dark eyes met and held mine, and I looked away momentarily to break the connection. When I looked back at him, I cleared my throat and offered a small smile. "Um, my name's Rachel."

"I know," he whispered roughly.

"And yours?"

He seemed to think for a few seconds before flashing me a sad smile. "You can call me Taylor."

My first reaction was disappointment before I realized the danger for him in this situation. He was a criminal, and I could already give a very detailed description to an FBI sketch artist. Knowing his real name would just add to his likelihood of being caught when this was all over. If it was ever over.

Biting back the disappointment, I smiled and offered him a hand. He took it carefully, making sure not to touch my nails. "I

would say it's nice, but that probably isn't the right word. It's . . .
very interesting to meet you, Taylor."

"I'm glad you decided to 'meet' me, Rachel."

"Me too." And honestly, I was. If this were under normal circumstances, I knew Taylor and I would be friends. He was a mix
of Candice's brother, Eli, and Mase. But as it was, I didn't know
how to feel about him.

All I knew was that every day I was more positive than the last
that he wasn't only my way to safety, but he was also the key to
my freedom. And I was going to cling to that safety net, because
my life and freedom depended on it.

11

Kash

TAKING OUT MY LIP RING, I ran my hand through my hair one more time and grabbed the file off the passenger seat of my truck before jumping out and smoothing down my tie as I walked toward the closed-off building. I went through the process of checking in and going through the metal detectors before I walked through the halls to the meeting room. I watched as families, lovers, and friends met up with inmates and talked at tables, and waited until I saw both Deon and Luke escorted in.

Their faces pulled together in confusion when they didn't see Serena and Nadia sitting at a table waiting for them, but per my request, Deon and Luke were seated at a table in the corner. The guards stood there waiting until I walked in, and with a practiced smile and flash of my badge, excused them.

"Thank you, gentlemen, I appreciate your help today."

When I looked down at Deon and Luke, I was met with twin glares, but neither said a word until I sat down.

"You fucking pig. We're in here because of you."

"Where's your partner? Or did you two break up?"

I smirked and steadily tapped the hard edge of the file against the table. "Aw, good to see you two too."

"Wipe the smile off your face, you piece of shit."

"Deon, I'd like to remind you that I'm not the one shackled to a table right now."

"I'm surprised you're even able to smile," Luke said, and attempted to cross his arms through the cuffs. "What was it I heard recently? Your wife was kidnapped?" He clucked his tongue and shook his head slowly. "Tragic. Just tragic. Isn't it, Deon?"

"Absolutely. I figured you'd be more torn up about something like that. She must not be a very good lay."

At any other time, I couldn't imagine not lunging over the table and beating the shit out of them. But I knew this meeting was crucial, and if I let them see any emotion, if I hinted at the grief that was tearing at me, this would all be for nothing. So I kept my smile in place and continued tapping the file on the table.

I'd tried hardening myself to what was happening, and as far as everyone knew, I was too far gone to be helped. Not being able to handle the guilt and heartache, I'd stopped looking at the evidence coming in of Rachel's torture. Now all I wanted to know every two days was if she was still alive. Anything more than that, and this facade I'd worked so hard at creating would crack. I'd lose it, and if I let myself give in to the pain and grief . . . I *would* be gone.

"Any luck on that case, Kash-man? Or maybe she's dead?

Maybe that's what's happening? Did you ever find the *bastards* who took her?"

"Enough of the bullshit"—I cut Luke off and set the file down—"you and I all know who took her. What I find funny is that the two of you—well, and I'm guessing the rest of the crew—still think she's gone. She escaped, we got her back a couple days ago."

Both men went silent, but their faces gave nothing away.

"I'd love to tell you the department's plans, but that would just give you time to warn the men that took her. So I'll keep that information to myself. Funny that they haven't told you she slipped through their fingers yet. They must just be too scared because they don't have a backup plan to get any of you out of prison yet. Oh well."

Silence continued to greet me, so I opened the file and pulled out the large photographs, keeping them facing me.

"You know what else I find funny? That Serena and Nadia finally got over their hate for each other. Good to see they became friends and are living together." I put down the photograph of the girls' house on the table, facing up. "Even better, they are helping each other raise the kids." I slapped down the picture of Serena, Nadia, and all seven kids playing out front on the table. "Jesus Christ, can you imagine having to go from not working, to supporting seven kids combined?"

Deon's and Luke's eyes were wide, and their breathing had deepened, but still they weren't saying anything.

"Oh, but don't worry about that either. Because Nadia and Serena were getting along so well, they got a job together." I laid down three pictures of the girls in next to nothing, standing on a corner, and leaning into car windows.

Deon's hands fisted on top of the tables, and the chains tightened when he tried to pull them into his lap to hide them.

"But, as we all know, your whores had meth habits. And from what their new supplier is telling me, they're spending a lot on it. When they're not fucking other guys to get it, that is. So, of course, *this* has been happening quite a bit." I smacked down a picture of both girls unconscious on the couch of their home, with glass pipes on the table. "Which obviously means *this* happened." I laid down a series of pictures of child protective services taking the children from the home, and both Nadia and Serena being arrested. I clicked my tongue and huffed a laugh. "Ah, man, good times."

"I'll kill you," Luke growled.

"What is it you want?" Deon asked.

"Oh, no, no. I'm not done. So before the children were taken so they could have a chance at a normal life, and before your women were arrested so we could take some more of the filth off the streets, and before my girl escaped . . . yours talked. And they talked a lot. Even if Rachel hadn't escaped, your girls gave up the rest." I grabbed the second-to-last picture and my expression darkened when I looked back up at the guys sitting across the table from me. "But not without a little persuasion first." Setting down the picture, I waited for the reaction I knew was coming.

Both men tried to lunge over the table, but being shackled to the ground and table didn't let them get far. I turned and held up a hand to the guards who had begun making their way over to us, and with reluctant nods, they backed off. I'd gotten the pictures of the women and the kids, while sitting in my car, across the street from wherever they were at the time. The ones of them doing drugs and sexual favors to get more drugs: Sunny and his crew had helped out with those. How he got RJ to get back with Serena for that time, I didn't know, and didn't give a shit. That last one, though; Mason and I had paid the girls a visit for that.

They remembered us and knew we were the reason their men were in prison. We'd cuffed them to chairs and had shown them some of the pictures I was showing Deon and Luke now, in order to get them to stop screaming that they would tell the boys that we'd threatened them. When asked where they were keeping Rachel, both immediately shut up.

The picture Deon and Luke were looking at was of two of my guns pointed at their heads as they cried and kept rambling about "the house," how "she's at the house." Neither of the girls had been hurt that night, we'd gone there to scare them, and that's exactly what we'd done. But when Mason and I broke into the house where we'd lived with Juarez and his crew two days later . . . we'd come up empty. By that time, we'd already anonymously called child protective services and given copies of some of the pictures as evidence, and the women had already been arrested.

And because of our last visit to them, visiting them in jail wasn't exactly an option right now.

I focused back on Luke and Deon. Both had their eyes narrowed into slits and glued to me, both were breathing so hard their nostrils were flaring, and both had gone back to not speaking.

"So you see"—I said darkly and leaned close—"you played this game with me, took what's mine, and tried to ruin my life. I can't be positive, but I'm pretty sure I just won. And now I've started my own game . . . now I've taken what's yours. Only difference between your game and mine is, you'll never get yours back."

Luke growled, and I smiled.

I began gathering all the pictures together and put them in the file. Just as I started to stand from the bench, I waved the last picture in the air, facing away from them. "Oh, I must have missed this one. Did you want to see the picture where their new suppliers are fucking them while someone else shoots meth in their arms for them? No? No, didn't think so. Have a good life in prison, gentlemen."

Deceiving people was natural . . . it had been my job for so long that lying to protect myself, or those I loved, was as easy as breathing. I'd promised Rachel that there would be no more lies, forgiving or not. When it came to her, there hadn't been, and there wouldn't be when she came back. But all bets were off until I found her. I would deceive anyone, lie about everything, and do anything to get her back.

The wicked grin I'd been forcing myself to wear to continue taunting them fell as soon as I turned and began walking from the room. I thanked the guards gruffly as they let me out of the secured doors.

As soon as I was in my truck, I called Mason and told him I was on my way to his apartment.

Once I was there, I went over the meeting with him before we destroyed all the pictures I'd taken and received from Sunny. Just as we were planning out what he was going to say when he went in to meet with Deon and Luke tomorrow, my phone rang. Glancing down at it, I stared at the name for long seconds before I finally hit the green CALL button and brought the phone to my ear.

"Hey."

Sniffling met me on the other end for a bit before her shaky voice choked out, "She's going to be okay, right? You are going to find her, aren't you, Kash?"

My eyes hit Mason's, and I put the call on speakerphone before responding. "Yeah, Candice, we're gonna find her. We're looking for her right now, I swear to you we're doing everything we can."

"I've, uh, I've been thinking. Maybe I should still come to Florida, help you look for her. Eli, Mom, and Dad want to come too."

"No." Mason and I both responded at the same time.

"Candi, babe, that's not the best idea."

"Mase? But, but maybe we could help, you know?"

"Candice we're doing everything we can to find her, we have a lot of really good people looking for her," he said. "And being here might end up just being too hard for you guys because you'll be faced with it every day. It's constantly on the news, in the newspaper . . . it's everywhere here."

"But it can't hurt to have more people looking," she argued.

"Candice," I said softly, "we're not searching for her body. If we were, we would need more people. Right now, they're hiding with her, so we're looking for them. It's different, and I agree with Mason, it would probably be harder for you all to be here."

Her quiet sniffling turned into sobs and she cried out, "I just feel like I can't do anything, and I've never been there for her when she needed me!"

Candice called me every day and we had this exact same conversation. I got calls from her parents just as often. Eli was the only one who called solely to get the details of everything that was happening before he hung up on me. To be honest, I think he blamed me for all of this too. At least I wasn't the only one.

I looked up at Mason helplessly as Candice continued crying, and he grabbed the phone from my hand, took it off speaker-phone, and walked away, talking quietly to her.

As much as I hated to say it, I couldn't handle talking to them right now. I knew they were devastated, I knew they felt lost and helpless, but I was trying not to feel anything at all . . . and I had to stay focused on finding her. If I went back to making sure that they were all constantly taken care of throughout this, then I would go back to feeling like I couldn't make it another day . . . another hour . . . another minute without her. The second I let myself feel all of the pain I knew was waiting just below this ro-botic mask I was wearing, I'd crumble, and I couldn't afford to crumble right now.

I already had to see my parents, and they were doing worse than Candice and her family was. Because not only were they mourning Rachel's loss every day, but they also had to see what I was turning into as a result of all this.

I waited on the couch until Mason came back into the room and handed me the phone.

"What'd she say?"

"They're not going to come right now, and I made her put her dad on the phone. I advised him that even if—when . . . I'm sorry—when we find her, it wouldn't be a good idea for them to come immediately, or possibly anytime soon. I told him that although they'd want to see her, she might not be ready to see anyone, and we'd have to be careful with her. I think he under-stood. I'm not sure if Candice and her mom will though."

"Yeah. Thanks, Mason, I appreciate it."

"No need for thanks, you know I'm here for you. And I know you don't want to, but both our parents are waiting for us at my parents' house. So let's take my truck. We can go pick up Trip, and on the way there we'll talk about what I'm going to say to Luke and Deon tomorrow."

I ground my jaw, and Mason began pushing me toward the door.

"You can't do anything more today, Kash. You're waiting on word from Sunny, I'm gonna talk to the guys tomorrow, and you have been working nonstop since you saw Sunny over two weeks ago. You need to relax for a night. Just relax, maybe get some sleep, recharge, and go back to it tomorrow."

"It's not like this is just some job that I'm devoting my life to. I'm trying to find Rachel!"

He locked his door and shook his head slowly as he turned to look back at me. "I know, Kash. But with the way you're going, if you find her, I don't know what kind of guy she'll be coming back to. I've never seen you like this, not even undercover. You're changing, you can't lose yourself in the process."

"I'm doing what's necessary. I wouldn't expect anything less from you."

12

Taylor

"Did you get food for everyone?"

I stopped walking and held back a curse before turning to face Dominic and Marco. "You were all eating when I left, why would I bring you food?"

"Why would you bring *her* food?" Marco asked, his tone challenging.

"She needs to eat too."

"No, what she needs to do, is get that fucking jackbooted thug boyfriend of hers to release our brothers. We need her to get some more evidence put together. Bring her to the lab later."

Shaking my head, I took a step back and turned to head down the hall. "No."

"You're crossing a line, *brother*." Dominic spat the last word out, and I turned to face them again.

"This whole fucking thing is crossing a line. Besides, I'm following orders from Romero. Take the girl, but don't harm her. Yours is to get the brothers out by using her. From what I've seen, them thinking she's the girl in all your videos and recordings *is* using her. You just haven't succeeded in getting them free. I'm doing my job, you're the ones who are failing at yours."

"If we don't get them out, then we all fail. There's been no response from anyone in the police department in weeks. We're watching them, everyone including the boyfriend stopped looking for her a week ago!"

My eyebrows rose at Marco's words, and he sneered a laugh.

"Exactly. We need more from her. Bring her to the fucking lab."

Turning again, I called over my shoulder, "If they've stopped looking for her, that's your problem, not mine. You don't get to touch her."

"Is this really coming from Romero? Or maybe it's someone else. Yeah, we're supposed to use her to get the brothers out, but how the hell are we supposed to use her when you don't leave her unprotected?"

Freezing, I schooled my features before turning back to him. Dropping my head low, I slowly looked up at him from under my eyelashes, a sadistic smile pulling at my lips. "You want to go question Romero's orders . . . be my fucking guest. I'll start counting down the days until he has you killed."

I had him, and he knew it. No one questioned Romero. Not unless they had a death wish. Just the same, if Romero ever found out I'd changed his orders so I could protect her . . . I would end up with Dre, six feet under.

When Marco's face acknowledged defeat after our conversation, I turned and blew out the breath I'd been holding.

"Cruz! Cruz! If you know what's good for you, you'll bring her. Our brothers need her!"

With my free hand, I threw up a middle finger and continued walking away. I wasn't worried that the department had stopped looking for her. A sick, twisted part of me was excited. My first thought had been, *If they stopped looking for her, was it possible that Rachel would one day stop waiting for them to find her?*

As I walked toward the room, I kept trying to force those thoughts away. *I stole her. She isn't mine to keep,* I continued to chant to myself, but that fucked-up side of me couldn't stop smiling. She'd changed since she'd been here. She was comfortable with me . . . that was clear. I knew it was too much to hope that she might ever feel something for me. But was it wasted time imagining that day would come?

Rachel

THE SOFT BEEPS SOUNDED from the opposite side of the door, and in walked Taylor with a mischievous smile on his face. Snapping my journal shut, I set it down beside me. One of my eyebrows rose when I tried to sit up to see what he'd brought for dinner, and he turned the food away from me.

Sitting back against the wall, I eyed him and hated that I could hear the pout in my voice when I said, "You were gone a long time."

His full lips tilted up at the corners and he dipped his head. "I went out."

Must be nice. "Where'd you go?" *And when the hell did I turn into the clingy woman?*

"Close your eyes."

"What? No! Why?"

Taylor's expression went blank, and he prompted me to close mine again.

I shot him a glare before closing my eyes but stayed still as stone and strained to hear every movement he made. Other than a couple heavy footsteps and the telltale sounds of food containers being opened, there was nothing suspicious. But, oh God, the food smelled amazing.

I heard Taylor lower himself to the ground before he said anything again. "Open your eyes, Rachel."

He didn't have to tell me twice. My eyes flew open, and I gasped and lunged toward one of the boxes. Not even caring that the expensive-looking chicken pasta dish was sitting in front of me. There was freaking cheesecake, and I'd been deprived of sweets for far too long.

The massive slice had been mere inches from my mouth—and yes, I was about to eat it without utensils—when it was snatched from my hands, and I looked up to see Taylor holding it away.

"That would be dessert, you can wait."

Not only did Taylor suck at picking out clothes for women, but he also didn't understand the need to have sugar. And I happened to be one of those women addicted to it.

"If you value your balls and your life, you will hand that back over right now."

His dark eyes widened and a smile lit up his rugged face. "And I say you'll wait for it."

Without warning, I lunged for him, being careful not to land in the actual food sitting in between us. Taylor flew back until he was lying on the ground, and he stretched his arms way above his head to keep the container away from me. But I'd landed on him, which meant I had the advantage here. And that cheesecake was mine.

I started crawling over him, but he just laughed and brought one of his arms down to restrain me. "Since when are you impatient?"

"Since you brought cheesecake, damn it!" If he didn't release me soon, I was about to go full baby-mode and start making grabby hands toward the dessert; maybe I'd even cry. "Please!"

His rich laugh filled the room, and he barely grunted when I punched him in the side. I managed to wiggle my way a few more inches up his body and didn't even notice his laughing had stopped; because at the same time, the arm around me stopped restraining me, and just simply held me.

Which meant I could make another grab for it.

I dug my knees into the concrete floor and pushed myself closer, and nearly cried in victory when my hand grabbed the cheesecake right out of the container and brought it to my mouth. I took a huge bite out of it and moaned before rolling off Taylor. Not caring to go back to my mattress, I stayed there, on my back, and finished my cheesecake.

It was so fucking delicious I wanted to cry.

Turning my head to the side, I smiled at Taylor, but the smile slid from my face when I noticed him watching me intently with those dark eyes.

"What?"

His eyes seemed to focus, and he shook his head and turned it to look at the ceiling. "Nothing, just didn't know a simple piece of cheesecake would turn you into a crazed fiend looking for their next fix."

"Hmm, next time, Ben and Jerry's. It's like water for me."

"Ice cream"—he huffed a laugh and sat up—"got it. Now come back here and eat real food, or are you not hungry anymore?"

"Does it matter? I got what I wanted," I said with a smile.

"Yeah, I noticed that," he said so softly that if I hadn't been passing him to get back to the mattress, I wouldn't have heard him.

I sat across from him, and like he always did, he waited for me to start eating before digging in himself. Other than a few jokes from him when he began eating his own slice of cheesecake, we'd eaten in silence. He'd had a faraway look all through the pasta, and even when we were both done and talking about nothing again, he kept averting his eyes from me. I was dying to ask what he was thinking, but I'd learned from Kash that if someone wanted you to know something, they'd tell you.

So I bit down on my tongue and let him continue to act like there wasn't a weird charge between us that just thirty minutes before hadn't been there.

When we got back that night from my evening trip to the bathroom and to take a shower, I'd crawled onto the mattress and grabbed for my journal.

"Can you keep the light on for a while? I want to finish writing."

Taylor's hand dropped from the light switch on the wall and

he sat down in front of the door. "What is it you're always writing?"

"Uh—"

"Do you write songs or poetry? Or do you just write?"

I knew he was trying to get rid of the awkward vibe we'd had between us the last couple hours, but this wasn't something I was willing to share with him. "It's kind of personal," I said softly and glanced up to see if I'd offended him.

"I'm sorry, I didn't think about that, I'll let you get back to writing."

"I . . . I just don't usually talk about it."

"You don't have to explain, it's—"

Suddenly the lights went out, and we both went silent. I heard Taylor stand up and the door open, but for the first time, no light filtered in from the hall. "Rachel, do not move. If anyone other than me walks in here, scream, you hear me?" he whispered.

"Yeah." I put my journal back down and crawled to the back of the mattress. I was shaking, but it wasn't in fear. Some part of me was imagining Kash and Mason cutting the power and coming to rescue me. It was ridiculous, and *so* silver screen . . . but I couldn't help it. It had been twenty-two days since Taylor had brought me the journal, which meant I had been gone for over a month. After that amount of time, I was allowed to have silly fantasies of being rescued.

"Rachel, it's me."

I frowned when Taylor's voice filled the room.

"There's a really bad storm and the power is out, at least on this street."

"Oh," I said dejectedly.

"Come on, we're gonna go to my room."

My head snapped up, and I could make out the shape of his body in the doorway but nothing else. "What? Why?"

"Because this room needs power to lock, mine doesn't. So come on, let's go."

I stood and walked the few steps over to where he was, and with my hand stretched out in front of me, waited until it bumped into him. He laughed and grabbed my wrist before towing me out of the room. We stopped in the kitchen and at a hall closet on our way there, picking up water, candles, and matches. And by the time we got to his room, I was practically sprinting into it and urging him to lock the doors. Something about being in those halls and not being able to see the other guys had chilled me to the bone, to the point that even after I was sitting on Taylor's bed with my knees pulled up to my chest, I was still shaking.

Taylor went around the room, lighting enough candles so we could see, before using a flashlight app on his phone to check under the bed, in the closet, and the bathroom. I didn't need to ask what he was doing; I knew he was checking to see if the others were in here with us.

When he was satisfied with his search, he stood next to the bed with arms crossed over his chest and stared down at me. "Did you get your journal?"

Even though I knew I hadn't grabbed anything when we'd left the room, I still patted his bed beside me, looking for it. "No."

"Can you sleep?" When I nodded my head, he took a step back and spoke softly, "Then I'll see you tomorrow."

ROLLING OVER TO MY OTHER SIDE, I let my eyes adjust and watched Taylor at one of the weight machines in his room. Unlike the times he worked out in my room, he had his shirt off and was only in a pair of running shoes and mesh workout shorts. He did each rep with ease, but sweat was running down his body, and I wondered how much of a difference this was for him now after spending so long without it.

Minutes passed before his voice caused me to jolt back. "I know you're awake, Rachel."

"Uh—"

"Do you need anything, or are you just bored?"

"I can't sleep." And I wished I had stayed facing the other way. Getting caught staring at him while he worked out was still beyond embarrassing. But he spent days on end staring at me, it was only natural for me to do the same when he finally did something.

He let the bar go all the way to the top before releasing it and turning his body so he could look at me better. "I'll go shower."

"Wait, what?"

"That's too loud, I'm keeping you awake."

"You're not, you don't need to stop . . . I just can't sleep."

"I'll be back soon," he said when he stood, but he paused when he turned toward the bathroom. "Anything happens, Rachel, you scream. Understand?"

There wasn't a point in arguing with him about working out; he was always trying to make me as comfortable as possible. If he thought he was keeping me up, then there was no changing his mind. "Yeah."

"Don't go to sleep."

"I know, Taylor."

He turned back and shot me a smile, but it quickly faltered. "It feels so wrong to leave you in here."

It felt wrong to be left alone, but I didn't want to voice that. "I'm fine, go shower."

"Scream," he whispered.

The water turned on a minute later and I got out of the bed and walked around his large room as I waited for him to come back out. I wished I could spend time walking around here with the lights on, so I could see if there was anything personal laid out. I wanted to know what kind of guy Taylor really was, other than a confusingly protective and sweet kidnapper.

I picked up one of his free weights and about died under the heaviness of it. I had spent over a month sitting on a mattress, not moving. Although he kept me well fed and I'd had no form of exercise, I still felt like I was thinner than when I'd been brought here. And not that I'd had much muscle before, but I was positive there was nothing there anymore.

Just as I was putting the weight back in the designated slot, the door to the hallway rattled, and I turned to watch the handle twist back and forth as someone continued to put pressure against the door. Another couple attempts to open the door, and my body finally unfroze and I hurried into the bathroom, thankful that Taylor had left the door unlocked.

"Rachel," Taylor said softly. Just as I was about to explain why I'd rushed in, I heard his voice again—and this time the husky tone of it had every inch of my body covered in goose bumps. "Fuck, Rachel."

My eyes widened and I turned to face the mirror. It was starting to get steamy in the bathroom, but not enough that I couldn't see the reflection of Taylor through the glass door of the shower. What I saw had my jaw dropping, and my next inhale becoming audible.

Taylor's left arm was out in front of him, his hand keeping him leaning toward the wall. His arm closest to the glass door was moving back and forth in a controlled motion. I tried to turn around, but my eyes flashed down and I couldn't seem to take them off his hand going up and down his long length.

There's no way I'm seeing this, this isn't happening. He's not doing this, and he's definitely not doing this while thinking about me! Look away, Rachel, for the love of God look away.

"God—yes."

I stared, transfixed, as his hand gradually moved faster and faster. Something inside me heated, something in me wanted to watch him finish. My fingers twitched watching him, and it was his next "Rachel" that had me snapping out of it and realizing what I was doing, what I was feeling, what I was thinking, and what I was craving . . . from him.

I felt sick. My eyes burned as tears pricked them, and I turned and rushed into the bedroom, not even remembering about the others trying to get in until I was already in his bed and covering my shaking body with the comforter. I wasn't okay with what I'd just seen, I wasn't okay with my reaction to watching him, and I wasn't okay with the images that were still racing through my head at what I wanted him to come in here and do to me.

Biting down on my fist in an attempt to quiet my ragged breathing, I tried not to burst into tears. I'd just gotten my body to stop shaking when I heard the water turn off and the glass door open. I kept the comforter up, covering most of my face, and a couple minutes later when Taylor walked into the room, I didn't move.

"Rachel . . . ? Goddamn it, you weren't supposed to go to

sleep!" he whispered harshly, and I heard him walking quickly around the room as he checked the door, under the bed, and the closet.

I should have tried to answer him to tell him no one else was in there. I should have told him that someone had been trying to get in the room while he was in the shower. I should have assured him that I hadn't fallen asleep so he wouldn't have to worry himself more the next time he had to leave me. But I couldn't. All I could do was lie there and want for things to be different.

Up until about ten minutes before, I'd never thought of anything romantic or sexual with Taylor—and I knew the only reason I was now was because of what I had seen. I wanted those thoughts gone. I wanted to go back in time and decide to stay in the room when the others had tried to get in, and just be prepared to scream if they had succeeded.

And most of all, I wanted my Kash. I wanted to be wrapped in his arms in our bed. I wanted to go back to the night of the whipped cream war, and beg him to stay home with me so none of this would have happened. I wanted a way to tell him I was okay. I wanted to know that I was going to see him again. And I wanted to know if he was trying to find me.

A couple of drawers opened and shut before I heard the familiar sound of Taylor making himself comfortable on the ground, in front of one of the doors. For the first time in a long time, I wondered why he would go through this day in, day out. I'd believed him that he wanted to keep me safe from the others. But who would go through this just for that reason after kidnapping the person?

Taylor made me feel safe, that hadn't changed, but now I

couldn't help but wonder if he was waiting for something from me. I still didn't know why they'd taken me, and it still didn't make sense that Taylor would be the main one doing the kidnapping, when all he ever did was take care of me. Was I there for him? Was it some weird form of stealing women to be wives, and was Taylor waiting for me to forget about Kash and fall in love with him?

That wasn't about to happen. I quietly brought my hand up and twisted my engagement ring around my finger. I didn't know what the date was, but I knew our wedding date was coming up soon, and I wondered what Kash had told everyone.

Has he told them anything at all, or is he hoping he'll find me before then? Has he told them it's postponed until I'm back? Has he told them the wedding is canceled? And if so, what was his reason?

I knew he at least had to know I'd been taken. The dispatchers at the department would have told him if Taylor and the other guy there hadn't done enough damage in the bedroom for him to figure it out.

So is he telling people that I've been kidnapped and he doesn't know when they'll get me back, or if they'll get me back? Or is he telling them that I was kidnapped long enough ago, and that without any word, they're assuming I'm dead?

My chest ached knowing that Kash may indeed think I was dead. I couldn't help but wonder how long he would have searched for me before giving up. How long he would grieve before eventually trying to move on with his life. And how long would I be here before I came to terms with the fact that I would never get out again?

Taylor's breathing evened out, and I vowed to someday get out of this place, and get back to Kash.

I BARELY HAD TIME to sit up in the bed and see what was happening before Taylor was throwing himself in front of me and reaching into the nightstand with his free hand—his other hand was holding a gun pointing at two men who were standing just outside the doorway that led to Taylor's bathroom.

"Don't move," he said in warning and pulled the second gun up so he had one aimed at each man.

"Just give us the girl, bro," the one on our right said. Both had their arms up, but one of his started slowly inching down to his waist.

"Keep reaching for your gun, Jaime, and I'll put two bullets in your chest."

Jaime's hand went back up, and both men took a step away from each other, like they were about to round both sides of the bed. Taylor was already practically sitting on my feet as he kept his guns trained on them, but my body was shaking, and I felt like he was better protection than the headboard I was sitting up against. I forced my legs to move and slowly scooted myself down the few feet on the bed until I was pressed up against his back, and gripping his shirt.

The muscles in Taylor's back were tense and vibrating as I let my forehead fall to the point right between his shoulder blades, and prayed that if anything happened, it didn't happen to him.

"You can't keep her locked up with you anymore. They're taking too long at releasing everyone, something's gotta give. You know they stopped responding to our calls and e-mails, we need to take action; and they want her."

"You touch her, you die. Get the fuck out," Taylor growled.

"You're really going to turn against us over a piece of ass?

What do you think Romero will say when he finds out? You'll be out, and you know—"

"I don't fucking care, get the fuck out!"

I heard shuffling, and then a short scream burst from my throat when both guns went off. My ears were ringing, and although I knew they came from Taylor's guns, I still let out a shaky breath of relief when I heard his deep voice again.

"Next time, they're aimed at you. Get out, don't come in here again, and don't come near her."

"Fuck you, you're out. You got it? You're out, and she *will* be used to get them back—we're going!" one of them yelled, and I figured Taylor had aimed his guns at them again.

We sat quietly for a few minutes until Taylor finally broke the silence. His voice was dark and soft. "Are you okay?"

I just nodded my head into his back and tried to force my hands to loosen their hold on his shirt—they tightened instead.

"I need you to let go, Rachel, I need to go lock the doors again if they didn't bust them, and put something in front of them so they can't get back in."

"Yeah, okay—yeah . . . I'm trying," I cried out, half-frustrated that I was feeling like a child unable to make her body do what she wanted it to do, half-terrified and wondering when I'd started crying.

Taylor leaned forward to set the guns down before reaching behind him to grab for my hands. His large fingers wrapped around my shaking fists and gently began massaging them, down to my wrists and back again until they loosened their death grip on his shirt and finally let go.

We sat there for a handful of minutes—with my forehead still pressed to his back, and his hands holding on to my wrists from over his shoulders—not moving, and not saying anything until he twisted around and set my hands on the bed before releasing them.

His eyes searched my face, and his mouth opened like he was going to say something before he shut it and shook his head. "I'll be back," he said and got off the bed and headed into the bathroom.

When he was done locking the door and moving his workout equipment in front of the doors leading to the bathroom and hall, he grabbed the guns off the bed and put them on top of one of the nightstands. I was staring at one of the two holes above the bathroom doorframe where Taylor had shot, when his hand grabbed my chin and turned my head to face him.

"You okay?"

I nodded and swallowed through the tightening in my throat. When I opened my mouth to reassure his worried-looking eyes, nothing came out and tears clouded my vision again.

The hand holding my chin released me and grabbed around the back of my neck, bringing me into his chest so he could wrap his other arm around me. "I won't let them get to you, Rachel. I swear I won't."

He held me as I cried, and when I could speak again, the questions came out all at once. "W-what is going on? Why am I here? Who were they talking about? Don't give me your bullshit about not being able to answer! Who *are* you?"

When he didn't respond for a few minutes, I thought he wouldn't say anything at all. But with a heavy exhale that hinted at the stress he was carrying, he tightened his grip and whispered into my neck, "I'm just a guy who got caught up in a bad situation a long time ago."

I pulled back and cradled his cheeks roughly as I pleaded, "Then get out of it! Get me out of here; you don't have to be this guy. You're not him. I don't know what you did, but I know what you've done for me. I've told you, you're not a bad person, Taylor."

"Trent." When I just sat there staring at him, he placed his large hands over mine and repeated, "Trent Cruz. That's my name."

I knew what this meant. I knew how big this was. He trusted me with that; and in giving me his name, he was letting me know again that I could trust him. As bizarre as that sounded. "You don't like Taylor?" I asked and earned a somewhat-relieved smile from him.

"If it's coming from you, then, yeah, I like Taylor." Pushing me away gently, he stood from the bed and waited until I was lying down. "Go back to sleep, Rachel. It's going to be practically impossible for them to get back in, but if they somehow do, I'll always protect you."

My body tensed up when he stepped away from me and was already shaking by the time he sat down next to one of the equipment benches in front of the bedroom door. I'd felt safest when Tay—Trent was in the room with me, but after waking up and realizing that two of the others had gotten in, and had guns with them, even having him in the room wasn't enough.

I squeezed my eyes shut and tried to steady my breathing, but minutes passed and I was coming close to breaking down again, worse than I had when it had all been over. Not waiting to think about what I was doing or what it meant, since I was the captive and he was the captor, I flew out of the bed and over to where he was sitting before throwing myself onto his lap and burying my head in his chest as sobs tormented my body.

"I'm sorry," he repeated over and over as he held me close and let me soak the front of his shirt with my tears. "I wish I could change everything, Rachel, I'm so damn sorry."

There was nothing for me to say, I didn't know why he'd taken me, and I knew I might never know. I also knew deep down that if he could take me away, he would do everything to make it happen. But he wasn't, and he wouldn't even attempt it. That told me everything—that whatever was happening was so much bigger than me being kept in this place.

When my sobs quieted, Trent gently pushed my shoulders back and spoke low, the warmth in his tone making my body shiver. "Go get back in bed, I'll be here to protect you."

I responded by throwing myself back at his chest and wrapping my arms around his neck. He didn't hesitate, he just moved his legs under us and stood up, with me still in his arms, and walked us over to the bed. Laying me down on the bed, he grabbed my hands and unclasped them before placing them on top of my stomach. My hands shot out when he straightened, but he was already removing his shirt soaked with my tears, and climbed over me to the other side of the bed.

As soon as he was on his side, facing me, I curled my body up against his and pressed my head into his shoulder. It was ridiculous, but like when I was little and I felt like the monsters couldn't get me if I was hiding under the covers, my body stopped shaking and relaxed into Trent when he pulled the comforter up over us.

I knew Jaime, the guy with him, and any of the others could still get in here; but with the comforter surrounding me, and Trent's arms holding me close, I finally felt like the monsters couldn't touch me.

Trent

KEEPING ONE ARM AROUND RACHEL, I brought my other hand up and ran it down my face, exhaling heavily into it when I reached my mouth. I couldn't believe I'd fallen asleep and allowed them to get into the room before I'd woken back up. They hadn't made a fucking sound; I'm still not even sure what woke me. They could have easily grabbed her, taken her, and I wouldn't have known. It would have been my fault.

I couldn't stop thinking that my reaction to Marco and Dominic tonight had been what led Jaime and Carson to break in.

My fault. All of it.

But, Jesus Christ. Rachel was asleep in my arms. The warmth of her breath on my bare chest should be insignificant, but right now it seemed like the most vital connection to this world. Her long hair tangled in the hand holding her close to me, and the heat of her body against mine was something I'd craved for months; and I felt like I was riding a high more extreme than any drug could ever give me.

The way she'd thrown herself into my arms tonight was playing in my mind on repeat; and even now with her pressed against me, I could still feel the way her head had felt buried into my neck, the way it had felt when she'd thrown her arms around me after I'd tried to push her back.

I'd known she'd been changing, but something had happened since the power had gone out tonight. The feisty Rachel I'd come to know over the last few weeks was gone. She was terrified, like she always should have been . . . but instead of retreating from me like I would expect her to, she was clinging to me. I didn't understand it, but I wasn't about to question it. Because nothing about my feelings had changed, even though everything about *her* had.

I'd already completely fallen in love with a girl who could never be mine. Only now, she was making it impossible for me to grasp ever letting her go.

13

Kash

MY HEAVY EYELIDS SLOWLY BLINKED OPEN when the warm body in my arms stirred, and I automatically tightened them around her waist. I buried my face in her hair and a lazy smile crossed my face.

"Morning, Sour Patch."

She mumbled something unintelligible and I laughed as I moved her hair away to kiss her neck. "Where are you?" she asked suddenly as my hand made its way down her torso and stopped just at the edge of her underwear.

"Uh . . ." I forced out another laugh in an attempt to wash away the eerie feeling that hung in the air after her panicked question. "Should I be taking that as an insult, or—"

"Why aren't you coming to find me, Kash!"

"What the hell?" I pushed away from Rachel at the same time her voice filled the entire room. But it wasn't coming from the girl lying next to me. It was as if it were playing through speakers in the wall. Her screams and cries were all I could hear, all I could focus on. "Rachel!" I yelled and went to turn her body toward me, but the body was no longer there.

"Please! Somebody help me! Please!"

I struggled to get off the bed as a mass of Rachel's bloody hair clung to my hands. My legs got caught in the sheets and I fell out of the bed, landing on my back. I crawled away on my hands and knees, the sheets still twisted around my legs; and gave up when her screams got to an ear-piercing level. On my knees, I pressed my forehead into the floor and put my hands to my ears. My own anguished cry joined hers as I listened to her screaming for help over and over again.

"No! Stop! Help me . . . please!"

The noise stopped suddenly and I opened my eyes to stare at the carpet as I slowly removed my hands from my ears. I put my hands to the floor to push my body up and froze when my fingers grazed something. Cries started back up in the room, and my body filled with dread at what I might find next to me. Looking to the left, all the blood drained from my head and my stomach churned. Rachel's severed fingers lay there directly below mine. Dry heaves rocked my body as the auditory assault steadily grew louder again and a new visual one began.

"Get off me! Help!"

Like a movie being played directly in front of me—even when I closed my eyes—my worst nightmares replayed over and over. Rachel being whipped, waterboarded, and beaten. Being raped by two men. Her struggling to get out of the chains binding her to a chair firmly anchored into the ground while blinding lights surrounded her and ear-piercing sounds and music filled the room and drowned out her screams.

I pounded my fists against the carpet and my voice boomed over everything else. "Rachel!"

I sat up quickly in bed and pulled in ragged breaths as my heart and mind raced. My hand hit the right side of the bed and touched nothing but cool sheets. Trip raised his head off his paws from where he'd been sleeping near my feet, and I fell back onto the pillows with a frustrated grunt as I gripped at my hair.

"Fuck!" I yelled toward the ceiling.

Almost every night I'd dreamed of waking up next to Rachel again. But those images that haunted my every waking thought hadn't been torturing me in my dreams as well . . . until now. I couldn't keep doing this, I couldn't keep wondering what had and hadn't been real anymore. I couldn't keep living every moment being terrified that I wouldn't see her again. The department had been testing things, like the hair and the blood. We knew the hair wasn't hers and the blood wasn't even human. Two of the videos of Rachel being tortured we'd already found were actual videos found on the Internet from years ago. But there were still countless other things that they hadn't been able to figure out if they'd been real or not. And it was driving me insane.

I slapped my hand down on the nightstand when my phone rang, and I glared at the bright display before fumbling to answer.

"Hello?"

"K-money," he said low, and then chuckled. "Rise and shine, cupcake, it's almost dawn."

I squeezed my eyes shut and tried to steady my breathing. "Don't call me if you're just gonna sit there and mess with me,

Sunny. Do you have something for me or don't you? Because the days that she's been gone have more than doubled since I saw you."

"My men have been giving me strange looks and I've been getting questioned because I've been going out on a limb for you, you got me? I'm putting my life on the line for you and your woman, so I deserve some respect from you."

My eyes shot back open and I growled, "Don't forget I know who you are."

"You know, I think I'll keep my information to myself. Have a nice day, *Detective*."

I growled and slammed my free fist onto the bed. "I will bring your entire operation to the ground, and your time undercover will be over, Sunny! Do not fuck with me on this one! We had a deal!"

He didn't say anything for a long while, and I lay there, my breathing rapid as I waited for something . . . anything.

Sitting up, I looked over at my gun sitting on the nightstand. My next words were dark and full of promise. "This is my future wife's life you're screwing with. If you don't tell me what you fucking know, your so-called *crew* will start turning up dead one at a goddamn time, and the only one who will have a clue will be you. Leaders come up dead all the time, Sunny, and if I'm using guns from your own house, no one will ever know once you're gone."

"Jesus, Kash." He didn't sound worried about my threat. He sounded disappointed. "Fuck, you're so far gone. Man, you need to pull back, you can't let this change you into this."

I was about to lose it. I was so close to breaking from all this, and as the days went by, I was getting desperate. Having Sunny tease me with information was sure to push me over the edge. "No. What I need is my girl back. I told you before, I'd do anything to get her back."

After a few silent moments, Sunny finally said, "He has a house."

My eyebrows slammed down and I blinked slowly. "Who has a house?"

"Juarez."

"Yeah, and I already checked it. It's still vacant from when we did the bust in it."

"Uh-uh." Sunny clicked his tongue three times. "He has another house. Ya feel?"

"House . . . do you have the address? But that still doesn't make sense. Who would take her, the department has interviewed everyone!"

"Kash, listen." He paused for a few moments before repeating, "Juarez has another *house*."

"He has another operation?"

"Not exactly. Where *you* were, was the other operation. This other place—"

"Home base," I guessed.

"Smart man."

"Holy shit, how did Mason and I not know? There was never any talk, no word about another house."

Sunny made some sort of affirmative noise. "From what my men could gather, no one knows about this place. One of them knows a guy, that knows a guy, that's fucking this chick, who belongs to Juarez. She's been to both places; she's the one that spilled about the other house. Said something about not knowing why she couldn't live at the main op while he was locked up, but that Juarez was locking it down so no one could get in or out. Locking down a house from prison . . . now if that doesn't sound like a man hiding something—or someone—I don't know what does."

I was already out of bed and grabbing at the nearest clothes I could find.

"So we brought the girl to our place, got her high, and waited for her to start talking. Looks like the reason no one knows about this place is because if they've been privileged to learn about it, they can live there. But if they've been told about it, they don't ever make it out of the crew to tell about it."

"Where is it, Sunny? Did she tell you where it is?"

"She did, but I'm going to tell you to cool your ass, because you're not going in right now."

I straightened from grabbing a shirt and pulled it over my head. "Why the hell not?"

"I told you, they're locked down, which means they're waiting for you or the department to show. And this isn't just some house, it's a warehouse turned into a fully functioning house and office for his business. Juarez's princess looked like the type that was well taken care of, and she wanted to live there. So it's not going to be as simple as busting down the door and running out with her. It's going to be big, they're going to be waiting for you, and it's going to probably be locked up good. You need to go do some surveillance, sit on it for a while, and make sure you know what you're doing first."

My head dropped back and I groaned. I hated it when Sunny was right.

"Hey, K-money."

"What?"

"I'm not taking offense to what you said, because I'd probably be in the same state you're in now. But I'm telling you . . . don't let this change you into that person. It's one thing when you're on assignment, it's another when it's just *you*. Ya feel?"

"I'm sorry, man. I just—fuck. I don't even know." I didn't know how I felt about the fact that I'd just threatened an entire crew, but I hated that I'd just threatened another officer . . . especially one putting his career and life on the line to help me.

"I'd go in with you if I could, but you know I can't. Don't go in it alone. And make sure no one at the department is watching you, because if they are, you know they'll stop you before you can take action."

"Got it."

Sunny rattled off an address and grunted in confirmation when I repeated it back to him. "Be safe, go get your bitch."

I huffed lamely and sucked hard on my lip ring. "Hey, uh, thanks, man. I really do appreciate everything you did for me on this. I'd send you an invite to the wedding whenever I get her back, but I know you wouldn't show."

He laughed, and suddenly the Street Sunny was gone, and the Cop Sunny was there. "Just love her man, take care of her. And maybe send me a picture of you two on the day so I can feel like I was there, yeah?"

"Yeah, man, I'll do that."

"Later."

I pressed the END button and sat on the bed as I pulled up the address on the map and memorized the location, as well as a handful of ways to get there. Pulling up my contacts, I hit Mason's name and waited.

"Mmm?" Mason groaned when he answered his phone.

"Get up, get over here . . . we need to go. I got info, Sunny just called me. I know where she is, man. Come on, let's go."

"Kash? The hell—do you know what time it is?"

I looked around me until I found the clock. Just as I started to apologize out of habit for calling him at three in the morning, I stopped and huffed. "Do you think I give a shit? She's been gone for thirty-four days now! Who cares what time it is? My fiancée was snatched and I think I know where she is, so we need to get her back, you asshole!"

He grunted a couple of times like he was sitting up, and yawned. "I know, sorry. I wasn't thinking. Kash, man, you know they're not going to let you go anywhere without watching you. Wait, did you say Sunny called you? When?"

"I haven't seen any units sitting on my house since the beginning of this. Do you know something I don't?"

"They aren't *sitting*. But there are a few in your district that are doing close patrol on you. They're afraid with what's happening, and your expertise in this, that you're gonna do something bad."

I laughed sadistically and got off the bed again to begin pacing. "Obviously they know me well."

"Okay, now that I'm somewhat awake, start over. You said Sunny called?"

"*Yes,* Mason. He called and I'm ninety-nine percent positive that the location he gave me is where she is."

"And why would you think that? Have you checked it yet?"

"No, we need to go check it!" I yelled. "Which is why I'm calling you to get your ass out of bed!"

"Tell me why you think she's there."

"Because apparently this is Juarez's other house. His *main* house. Like main operation, home base, whatever the fuck you want to call it, and his orders from prison are for it to be locked down. No one other than his men are to get in or out."

There were a few beats of silence before Mason asked, "When are we going in?"

"As soon as you get up."

"We need to sit on it for a few days, we can't just rush in."

"I know. We will."

"Patrol is going to notice if you don't come home after work, it'll raise flags. And we need to make appearances at the department so they don't go calling us to see where we are."

I thought for a second before responding. "Okay we'll do all that, and I'll ask my parents to come stay at the house so it looks like someone's here. We'll use your truck so mine stays out front. Now can we just start this already?"

"All right. Let's do it, you know I'm in. I'd never let you go into anything alone, and I'd never let you try to save Rach without me." He paused for a minute before quietly asking, "You don't sound good, Kash. Like, you sound like you're breaking. What's going on?"

"Within a year's time, I've walked in on a serial killer literally slicing Rachel's arms, stomach, and chest. Before Blake had gotten his hands on her again, I'd watched as he tortured her psychologically. I watched how it drove her crazy and haunted her. Now with this? I've seen pictures of physical torture done to her by different men. We don't know what is and isn't legit, but that's a moot point. Because once again, I can't do a damn thing to stop whatever *is* happening to her."

"Kash—"

"It is killing me to have her gone. It is killing me not to know what is happening to her. And though we *know* some of the evidence is false, it doesn't change what I've seen in those pictures, on those videos, and heard on those recordings. I have watched and listened to my future wife go through hell, and I feel like it is literally killing a part of me with every passing day. And now she's so fucking close, I'm shaking because it's like she's right there, *right* fucking there, and I'm about to lose it if I don't do something about it right now. Understand? I feel like I have every right to not sound okay right now."

"Okay, I understand. I just—I'm sorry. You've been so dead these last few weeks and now you sound like you're on the verge of going on a killing spree— Oh . . . wait, never mind."

"Yeah."

"All right, I'm getting ready. Get some things together for overnights out at this place, and for work. And get your 'oh-shit' bag ready for when we do the takedown."

"Call me when you're on your way."

I tossed my phone on the bed, let Trip outside, and hurried to get everything together.

Hold on, Rachel. I'm coming.

14

Rachel

THE STORM HADN'T LET UP AT ALL, and over the next two days, the power continued to go out. Only staying on for maybe fifteen minutes at a time, a few times a day. I was feeling desperate suddenly. I knew I needed to get out of there, but I had no idea what had come over me that morning that was terrifying me.

I'd spent hours after breakfast trying to convince Trent to get me out of there, but he wouldn't budge.

"I don't know how to explain it, but I know something bad is about to happen!" I hissed and grabbed onto his forearm before bringing his hand to my chest so he could feel my racing heart. "I won't turn you in, Trent, I swear, but we *need* to get out of this place."

"Rachel"—he pinned my shaking hands to the bed—"you're

just feeling anxious because the power has been off. You know we can't get out of here."

"No, I don't know that!"

"Look, I want to get you away from here, you have to at least know that. And you heard Jaime the other night, because of what I'm doing for you, I'm *out*, do you understand what that means?"

"No—"

"It means, when Romero gets word of this, or gets out, I'm dead. Trust me when I say I want to get out of here just as much as you do. But you're out of your goddamned mind if you think they don't have men stationed at the exits!"

I flinched away from his harsh tone, and immediately one of his large hands cupped around the back of my neck, forcing me to look at him again.

"Shit, I'm sorry. We just can't get out of here, okay?" When my eyes kept going down to my lap, he spoke gently. "Don't be scared of me. I'm sorry for snapping at you. You have to understand that I would do anything to get you away from here, and it's killing me that I can't."

I nodded and waited until my heart was going at a normal pace before asking more questions. "Who is Romero? Where is he getting out of? Is he in jail or something?"

"Rachel," Trent said in a clear warning, but I didn't stop.

"Why is he the one that decides if you're 'out'? Oh my God, are you in a gang, Trent? Are all of you in a gang?"

"Please stop asking questions," he begged and stood quickly from the bed. Dragging his hands agitatedly through his hair, he blew out a heavy breath and began pacing.

"You are!" *Oh my God, thank God.* "He's going to find me. He knows all the gangs in this area better than anyone. I know he's going to find me." I started chanting to myself, and for the first time in days, I had hope that Kash would come rescue me.

"Who is going to— Oh. No, Rachel, he . . . he's not."

It felt like my heart had dropped to my stomach as I forced out, "W-what . . . did you . . . you said you wouldn't hurt him!"

"And we haven't," he hissed and stalked back to the bed, bending over me enough that I fell back onto the pillows. "They stopped looking for you over a week ago. They *all* stopped looking for you."

Fat tears began rolling down my cheeks before I even realized I was crying. "No, he wouldn't. He can't. He has to be looking for me . . . right?"

"Rachel." He reached out for my cheek, but I smacked his arm back and turned away from him. "Please talk to me."

But there was nothing for me to say to Trent anymore. He'd just confirmed everything I'd feared the other night. Kash probably thought I was dead. And the department, Mason, and Kash had all given up hope of finding me. A hollow feeling had filled me, and I'd wondered if this was what it felt like to give up on life.

Even when I'd been terrified, and afraid that I wouldn't make it out of here alive, I'd always kept hope that Kash was coming to find me. And now that I knew he wasn't, I felt my body succumb to the knowledge that I was gone from Kash for good. I hadn't even felt that way when I'd been with Blake last year, or when Kash and I had broken up.

I was positive that being tortured by Blake was easier than dealing with that sense of loss.

Hours passed before Trent tried to get me out of his bed again. "Come on, we're going into the kitchen, and you're going to eat something."

I didn't respond.

"Rachel, let's go. You didn't eat lunch, and I'm not about to let you starve yourself. Get up."

When I didn't make any attempt at even moving, he lifted me out of the bed and walked me toward the door before setting me on my feet. He made sure I wasn't about to fall over, and when he stood directly in front of me, he sighed heavily and pulled my body close to his. I stumbled over my feet and smacked into his chest but didn't make a move to get away from it.

"He stopped looking for me. He thinks I'm dead," I whispered into his chest.

Trent's arms tightened around me. "I'm sorry."

"I have—I have to do something. I have to let him know I'm alive." A thought hit me, and the desperation I'd felt this morning came flooding back to me. I pushed away from Trent, and lunged for the workout equipment blocking the door.

"What are you doing? I'll get that."

"I have to get out of here! I have to find him, I have to let him know I'm alive!"

Trent's arms went around me, pulling my back against his chest. "If you try to get out of here, they will catch you. They won't let you out, don't you understand that?"

"I need to try! Kash needs to know!"

"Rachel, no!" Spinning me around, he wrapped one arm tightly around my waist, the other hand cupping the back of my neck so I would look at him. "I can't let you do that, you don't understand what these guys will do to you if they get their hands on you. I can only keep you safe if you're with me. What you saw that first time you tried to escape, and what you saw last night, is *nothing* compared to what they have planned for you."

"I don't care!" I nearly shrieked. "You can help me this time, I have to try to get back to him!"

Turning us, Trent pressed me against the wall and covered my mouth with his large hand. After a dark look, he dropped his head, and turned it slightly as he listened for anything coming from the hall. When minutes passed, and nothing happened, he removed his hand and leaned in to whisper softly in my ear, "You can't yell things like that. If one of them heard you, they're going to be waiting for us. There are men waiting upstairs, there's no way for both of us to get past them without them trying to take me down . . . and *take* you."

"I *need* Kash to know I'm alive," I said hoarsely. "I'll do anything, I'll risk it, I don't care." I hadn't tried to escape since those first couple days here . . . but at the time, I'd known Kash would try to find me. Knowing he'd given up had changed everything for me. "If he isn't coming for me, then I'll die trying to get back to him."

A brief, choking noise left Trent, and the arm still curled around me tightened. "I can't let you do that, I wouldn't be able to live with myself if I let something happen to you now. I— Fuck. If I . . . Rachel, if I try to get in contact with him, will you please make an effort to keep yourself alive while you're here?"

My head flew back, and my gaze rested on his pained expression.

"But know that even if I do get in touch with him without one of the others finding out, it might not end well for him. This place is full of armed men; he might not get in here, and get you out, alive. I can't be the person responsible for that. You would hate me."

"Trent, please! Please, anything, I'll do anything! Just let him know where I am and that I'm okay. I know they'll come for me."

His dark eyes took on more hurt as he nodded his head. "I'll try. I can't promise anything, there's no cell service down here, so I'd have to go up toward the top. Getting close to the outside right now with everyone against me might not be easy. They might already know if Romero wants me out, and if they think I'm trying to leave, they'll kill me in a heartbeat. It would leave you unprotected, and without him knowing. I just . . . I don't know. I can't put you in that position."

"It'll be okay." I tried desperately to reassure him, and just watched as the pain on his face turned to sorrow. "Everything will be okay, but we need to try!"

He watched me for a few seconds before nodding and releasing me. "I'll do it, if that's what you want."

Yes, that's what I want. I want my fiancé back. I want my life! I want to get out of here and never leave Kash's side again.

I launched myself back into Trent's arms and hugged his neck hard. "Thank you. I can't say that enough, thank you."

"Don't thank me yet, let's see if this works first." He pushed me back and turned to move the exercise machine away from the door leading to the hall. It then hit me what he was doing for me.

"When they come for me, I'll let them know what you've done for me. I'll do everything to make sure you don't go to jail for this, Trent."

He dropped his head, stopped pushing the heavy equipment, slowly straightened and faced me. "For what I've done, I deserve to go to jail at the very least. That's not what's hard about doing this for you, Rachel."

"Trent," I whispered and reached for him, but he moved my arm away.

"Let's go get something for us to eat, and then get back in here. All right?"

I nodded hesitantly and grabbed onto his shirt when he opened the door.

Trent hadn't felt comfortable leaving me in his room while he'd gone to get our food during the power outage, so I'd been going with him and sticking closer than usual as we did.

We stepped into the hall and quietly made our way to the kitchen. I watched as he quickly went through the pantry and pulled enough food down to last us for a while, I guess in case the power stayed off throughout tomorrow so we wouldn't have to come back out.

That same feeling I'd had all morning was back, and I knew we needed to hurry. Something wasn't right, and the hair on the back of my neck stood on end.

"Trent, we really need to go," I whispered and turned to look around us in the dark kitchen.

"Okay, come on. Hold on to me."

"Something bad is coming."

"I told you, Rach, it's the weather. It's hurricane season, but we're underground, we're okay if anything happens."

"No, I—" My scream was muffled by the hand that went around my mouth, and I immediately began thrashing against whoever was holding me.

I heard all the food drop to the ground and watched as Trent spun around to look at us.

"Carson, let her go."

"Fuck you, Trent. They've completely stopped trying to get everyone out. We need her to get them out."

"Carson, let. Her. Go."

The hand around my mouth tightened and my eyes widened when I saw what was in Trent's hand. "What are you going to do? Shoot at me in the dark when she's in my arms? We need her to get them out, and when we're done, you can have your whore back. What's left of her anyway."

"If you do anything to her, know that your death will be painful," Trent said, and the sincerity in those words chilled me.

"Jaime! Come get her!"

"Already here." Jaime's voice came from behind Trent, and I watched as Trent straightened and raised his hands in surrender, gun still in hand. "Go take her to the room, I'll be there as soon as I finish this."

Carson didn't wait for anything else; he turned and started walking me away from Trent. I bucked against him and bit down on his fingers, and when he began cursing, three gunshots went off in the hallway. I cried out, not from the loud echo in the hall, but because I knew Trent was dead. And it was my fault.

Before I could try to turn away from Carson and run back to Trent's body, another shot rang out, and Carson and I fell forward. Landing with my hands behind me hurt like a bitch; and with Carson's weight on me, I knew I was going to be bruised all over. But still I didn't move, and I didn't make a sound as I waited to see what Jaime was going to do.

Loud, running footsteps pounded down the hall and suddenly Carson's weight was off me, and another, much louder, shot went off aimed directly next to me. I couldn't force myself to look at Carson; I didn't want to see what he looked like after those.

"Rachel, get up, we need to get back to the room. Now. Let's go, come on."

I looked up at Trent and sat there in shock until I heard distant yells echoing down the hall. I jumped up and, when Trent took my hand, sprinted back with him to the room with the mattress on the floor.

"I'll be back," Trent whispered and I grabbed his arm.

"No, Trent, don't!"

"Trust me, I'll be back. If anyone else comes in here—"

"I know, I know, I have to scream." I sobbed and scrambled to the mattress when he rushed out the door.

Over a dozen shots went off and my hands clamped down over my mouth as I waited for what happened next. I now understood why all those stupid girls in horror movies couldn't shut up. Though I tried to hold back my sobs, I was still making a choking noise, and my breathing was rough and heavy. A minute that felt like hours after I'd heard the last shot dragged by before the door slammed open.

I screamed.

"Rachel, it's me!"

I'd never been so happy to hear Trent's voice, and I ran toward him to help take the heavy chairs from his hands.

"Move back," he ordered and went about putting both under the lever handle of the door until he was sure it would hold.

"My room locks, but they can shoot through it. They don't have the ammo to shoot through these walls. My magazine is almost empty, and the rest of it is in my room, but I'll do everything I can to keep you safe."

"I know you will," I cried and wrapped my arms around him, fitting myself to his body. "God, Trent, I thought Jaime killed you!"

His big arms tightened around my waist and he led us over to the mattress. When we were sitting, he pulled me onto his lap and held me there like a child. "I'm okay." His labored breathing was all that filled the room for a torturous amount of time before he admitted, "I killed three others in the kitchen."

That should terrify me, but right now, I was just so happy that he was okay. My hands gripped his shoulders, and I looked at his blurry face when his hand went under my chin.

"Are you okay? Are you hurt from falling? I'm sorry, I didn't have any other option, I had to shoot him."

"I hurt, but I'm okay. I've had worse. How did—how did you know it wouldn't go through to me? I was right in front of him."

"I have hollow point bullets, it was highly unlikely it would go through him to you. Where are you hurting?"

I sat up and looked him in the eye through the dark room. "How are you worried about me right now? Did any of them get you? Oh God, Trent, did they?" I started to get off his lap, but he quickly pulled me back down.

"No, they didn't. Tell me where you're hurt."

"I'm fine, it was just a lot of weight to fall on me when I couldn't stop the fall. I'll be fine—"

There was a loud banging coming from the metal door and I cringed into Trent's chest. I felt his right arm go up and stay there as he waited for something to happen. But the chairs held under the handle, for now.

"You're out, Trent! You're out, you hear me? You will pay for every one of our brothers! I'll fucking kill you, you son of a bitch!"

The screaming and pounding continued for countless minutes until it eventually slowed, and then stopped completely.

Trent and I sat there, gripping each other as we waited to see if it would start up again. When nothing happened for a long time, my eyes started drooping as the exhaustion set in. Trent gently removed me from his body and laid me down on the mattress before dropping to his side next to me, so his body was closest to the door, and pulled me into his chest.

"I'm sorry you had to kill them," I murmured before I fell asleep.

His breathing suddenly halted, and the hand around my waist curled tighter. "I'd do it again if it meant keeping you away from them."

I nodded into his chest and blew out a shaky breath. "I'm so glad you weren't hurt, Trent. Thank you for protecting me. I don't know how close you used to be with them . . . so just, thank you."

"Don't thank me, Rachel. Just know that I'll do whatever it takes for you."

My chances of escaping were rapidly weakening, and it was hard to keep hope that I had a chance of getting out of here. But if by some miracle the department found me, I knew I would do whatever it took to keep them from hurting Trent or blaming him for this.

Trent

I WAS IN SO MUCH FUCKING PAIN, and all I wanted to do was sleep . . . but I knew I had to push through that. If the guys tried, they could easily hit the door hard enough that the chairs would start coming loose, and eventually give out. A part of me knew I would wake up if that happened, but I also felt like I was on the verge of passing out, and I was terrified I wouldn't wake if that happened. Staying awake was the only option I had if I wanted to keep Rachel safe.

Unwrapping myself from her, I sat up on the small mattress and ran my right hand through my hair a few times. I thought about Carson and Jaime, Dominic, Eddie, and Miguel. Since I'd been with Romero Juarez and the rest of the brothers, I'd always been forced to end people's lives. And every time after, I'd gotten physically sick. I could still see every single one of their faces clearly in my mind, like they were right in front of me. I still hated myself for what I had done. Regardless of acting under the pressure of Romero's gun pointed at the back of my head, I was the one who had pulled the trigger and ended so many lives.

But with the five tonight, I felt absolutely nothing. I didn't know if it had to do with the fact that I'd hated every minute of my forced life with those men, the pain that seemed to get worse with each passing minute, or if it just had everything to do with *her*.

I knew now, without a doubt, I would do anything for the girl asleep behind me.

I stayed silent as I listened to Rachel's breathing. Making sure it was deep and even, I prayed to God she stayed asleep. Keeping low to the ground, I searched the dark room until I found a plastic bag. Trying to keep quiet, I grabbed the first shirt my hand touched and pulled it out. Once I got a small tear started in the material, I gritted my teeth and ripped the shirt open. The pain in my left arm exploded and I had to bite back a string of curses. Pulling in a ragged breath, I held it in as long as I could manage before attempting a silent rush out.

Once I was able to breathe somewhat normally again, I moved over a couple inches on the shirt, and repeated the same process until I had two thick, long strips of the cotton. I knew I wouldn't be able to make a tight enough tourniquet, but I had to try something. Tying them together on one end, and using my teeth and right hand, I wrapped the material around the entry wound and tied it off as tightly as I could above the bullet hole. I ground my jaw as the pain intensified, and sat still as I tried to calm my breathing, but it was so goddamn painful.

Moving so I could lie down on the mattress again, I stilled when a scraping noise accompanied my harsh breaths. Turning, I let my eyes slowly roam the dark floor until they fell on Rachel's journal.

She never had told me what she was always writing about, and after we'd been interrupted the other night, I hadn't asked again. If it were something trivial, she would have told me by now. But it had to be significant in her life, because all I could see was the way she had choked up when I'd given it to her.

Knowing that if she ever saw this journal again, I would already be gone from her life in one way or another, I felt around the floor until I found one of her pens. Sitting down on the mattress, I stared at the journal in my hands, trying to talk myself out of what I was about to do . . . but I needed to do this. I needed her to know.

Opening it up to the last page, I looked over my shoulder and took in Rachel's sleeping form one last time before bringing the pen down to the paper.

15

Kash

WE HAD BEEN SITTING OUTSIDE THE BUILDING for nearly thirty-six hours—other than the few hours when we'd made appearances at the police department yesterday and today—and I was getting anxious. I had a feeling something bad was going to happen if we didn't do something soon, and it was making me restless, and just pissing Mason off.

"I swear to God, if you don't stop moving I will shoot you."

"I'm telling you, Mase, something doesn't feel right."

He threw his hands up around him and whispered harshly, "It's probably this fucking storm we've been sitting in for two days! We're probably going to get struck by lightning or something."

I stopped my pacing and my expression went blank as I turned to look at him. "Really, Mason? Really?"

"Or maybe it's the fact that it's now dark again and the power is *still* out in this neighborhood, and it's creepy as shit."

Sitting down with a grunt, I crossed my arms and stared at the building in front of us. "When we rescue Rachel, I'm going to tell her about how scared you were of the dark neighborhood as we scoped out the place. I'm sure she'll get a kick out of it."

"Fuck you, Kash. We should just get back in the truck."

"We can't see anything from the truck. The building is too far from the street."

Mason grumbled but didn't argue anymore. He knew I was right.

The power had been out when we'd gotten here early yesterday morning, and other than a handful of minutes of flickering on and off yesterday and today, it'd mostly stayed off. It had been pouring rain up until this afternoon, and the lightning and thunder had been insane yesterday. But it was already down to barely sprinkling, and Mason was just being a bitch. I wasn't about to leave.

I knew Rachel was in that building. I could feel it. I could fucking taste it.

And I needed to pace some more before I took off running inside.

"Sit. Down," Mason growled.

"Just keep watching to see if anyone comes out of that door. I'm going to go check around the building to see if anyone is using the other doors."

"Kash . . ."

"Don't start with me, Mason. I need to move or I'm going to go crazy. I won't go in there without you, I don't have a death wish."

Grabbing two handguns and holstering them, I took off in the dark and tried to keep calm as I made a wide perimeter around the building. I strained to hear anything coming from inside, but there was nothing. And, unfortunately, with the power being out, I couldn't see the activity with lights or electronics I normally would watch out for.

The quiet and darkness continued to put doubt in my mind that anyone was there. That we would go in and it would be empty, just as the first house had been. But something was *telling* me Rachel was in there, and I couldn't ignore that. I also could not get past this fucking stupid bad feeling. It hadn't been there yesterday, it just randomly started this morning and had steadily gotten worse as the day had progressed.

As soon as I finished walking the perimeter, I turned and went around the other way, making a wider berth and weaving in and out of other buildings around. I looked for buildings that were abandoned, and when I finally found one, forced my way inside. It had the same setup as the one we were watching, a few doors of entry, but there was practically nothing inside.

I made my way past remains of a squatter camp and rodent nests, and walked straight to a random room standing in the middle of the massive space. As I got closer, I withdrew one of my guns and turned on the mounted-on flashlight. I kicked back the door that was barely hanging on its hinges and flashed the light down the steps. Taking a deep breath, I walked down and stopped when I hit another door. *Mason is going to kill me when he finds out I cleared a building alone.* Preparing for anything, and hoping for nothing, I grabbed the knob and shoved the door open.

"What the fuck?"

As soon as I was out of the building, I quickly made my way

back to where Mason was sitting and dropped down on the ground next to him.

"Where the hell have you been?"

"I found a building that's set up the same as this one. There was nothing upstairs except for these four walls pretty close to the main door. At first I thought it was a room, but it just held stairs that led to a basement. Down there, there are no doors to get in or out, except for the stairs. This basement was as empty as the upstairs, but these guys live here, and it's Juarez's main house. So I know they had to have done a lot of construction inside. But I'm betting they have the housing downstairs."

He looked over at me, and then back at the building. "Why?"

"Because the buildings around here are all abandoned or closed up because of the storm. So they're dark anyway, but all the houses on the other side of these buildings? There are flashlights, candles . . . you can hear people talking. There's nothing in there."

"Maybe there's nobody in there then," he said softly.

"No, she's in there, I'm just betting she's downstairs. But we need to do this tonight, Mason, like, now. I'm not shitting you, I have a really bad feeling."

He took in a deep breath, held it for a few seconds, and then released it in one hard rush. "Okay, get ready and let's go get her then."

After putting on our bulletproof vests, we quietly opened up our "oh-shit" bags and took out zip ties, magazines, boxes of ammo, glow sticks, and extra cuffs. After loading extra magazines with ammo, we started putting everything on us, and looked at each other.

"You ready?" he asked.

"You have no idea."

"Let's do this." He put his fist out, and just as I went to slam mine down on it, my cell phone began vibrating in my pocket. "Is yours ringing?"

I nodded. "Yours too?"

"Yes, shit." He grabbed his phone and I reached for mine. We both stepped away from each other and the building, and answered as quietly as we could.

"Ryan."

"Hey, Ryan, it's Detective Browning in Homicide."

My heart skipped painful beats as I waited for him to continue. *Not now, she couldn't be dead when we were so close.*

"We had a shooting outside an underage nightclub. One dead, three en route to the hospital in critical condition. From what the witnesses that were on scene are saying, gangs were involved, and it all started after people had been yelling about their territories. But everyone we've talked to so far doesn't know who the shooters were, doesn't know what gangs they're in, and doesn't know what the shootout was for exactly. You know, the usual. We need you to come over here, and help us sort through some things if you could."

No. No, I can't.

"Ryan? You still there?"

"Uh, yeah. Yeah, I'm here."

"Can you meet us in homicide, we have the witnesses over there."

I gritted my teeth and was suddenly spun around by Mason. "Tell him you'll be there." I shook my head and Mason gripped my shoulder roughly in his hand. "Tell him you'll be there."

Hanging my head, I choked out, "Yeah, on my way."

After hitting the END button, I looked up at Mason and tried to calm myself so I wouldn't react against him.

"This is our job, someone just died, and three are in critical. We have to go help them."

"But, Rachel—"

"Will still be there later. I know this is hard, Kash. After all this time, I know it's hard. But we need to do our job."

I flung my arm out and tried to keep my voice at a normal level. "Three in critical, one dead. That is going to be *hours* gone. At the very least we're going to be gone for five, probably nine or twelve. I can't be gone that long, I have a bad feeling about this, something is going to happen to her!"

"Maybe your bad feeling was about these people, did you think about that?"

"No, it's her. I know it's her."

"People are dying and one already died, we have to—"

"And Rachel might die tonight if we don't do this *now*."

Mason exhaled roughly and spun on his heel to walk away before walking back to me. "No matter what we decide right now, neither one is the right choice. If we stay here and go in and get Rachel, it's the right choice for us and for her. If we go and do our job, it's the right choice for our job, and for the families of the deceased and wounded. We made a commitment to serve and protect. We need to help the detectives find out what started this so they can find out who shot these people so the family of the deceased can find some sort of peace in all of this. Okay?"

I was shaking my head, I needed to get Rachel. We'd barely sat on the house long enough, but I knew we needed to go in there *now*.

"Why don't we call backup, have SWAT go in there?"

I looked at him like he was insane. "And then what, Mase? Both get kicked off the department for doing exactly what we were ordered *not* to do? For all we know, they wouldn't even send backup because they're going to think I'm just losing my fucking mind trying to find her. They'd tell us to stand down, or demand that we go to the department to have a meeting with Chief for all this. Do you not remember last year when you tried to take down Blake and save Rachel? How many times the chief from the Austin department told me to back off? The only reason he even listened to me was because I'd talked to Rach and her god-damn car was there. We have *nothing* right now other than in-stinct. Unless we have proof, we're fucking screwed."

Mase's hands raked roughly through his hair as he groaned. "Okay, okay. I got it. But we can't skip out on our job because of an instinct either. Kash, if we decide not to take this call, and she ends up not being in there, we'd end up in more trouble than if we called for backup right now. As soon as we're done, we'll come right back here, and we'll go in that building. I swear to you."

Looking at the building, I was completely torn. I knew I couldn't go in there alone, and I knew Mason was about to leave, with or without me. A part of me knew this was my job. I loved my job, I loved helping people, and while death was a very un-fortunate part of my job, we still had to deal with it. But at the moment, I just couldn't see past what was right in front of me.

"As soon as we get back?"

"I swear."

With one more look, I growled and turned toward Mason's truck.

16

Rachel

I WOKE UP with my face pressed into a hard chest, and for a moment, I smiled and curled myself into the warm body as much as possible. My smile quickly faded when I took a deep breath in and didn't catch a hint of cinnamon or Kash's cologne. What I smelled was a dirty mattress below us, and the body wash I'd been using my first week and a half here.

Trent.

Trying not to wake him, I slowly began uncurling my aching body to move away from him—but one of my knees was sand-wiched between his legs, and the movement had his arm tight-ening around me and a low grunt bubbling up from his chest. Giving up my efforts, I failed at keeping my focus off every part of my body that was hurting. Including my full bladder and empty stomach, the entire front side of my body felt like I'd been run over.

"Go back to sleep," his deep voice rumbled.

"I don't know if I can. I hurt all over, and now that I'm awake, it's all I can think about."

Trent began pushing me away from his body, and I hissed out a curse when his hand touched my shoulder. Withdrawing his hand, he grunted as he rolled away from me, and suddenly his dark eyes came into view above mine. Even without light, I could see the worry embedded in his features.

"Is it that bad?" he asked and moved so he was on his knees, his hands planted on either side of my body.

"I'm fine, just sore. Are you okay?"

"Just?" he asked, his tone clearly disbelieving. Before I could respond, he brought his hand up to my cheek and I tried to hold back a whimper when my face automatically tightened from the pain. "This is going to hurt, but let me make sure you didn't shatter any of the bones in your face. I can see the bruises even though it's dark."

His hand pressed down hard against my cheek, sweeping back and forth as he made his way to my nose and chin. To keep myself from crying out in pain I had clenched my jaw so hard that by the time he was finished I was sure it would break if I tried to unlock it.

"Did you fall on your right side, or did you just turn your head before you hit?" he asked and ran his thumb lightly just under the cheekbone as he waited for my response.

"I turned my head, I fell flat."

"Okay, try not to move," he mumbled and sat back on his knees so he could press his hands to the front of my shoulders, across my collarbone and back again, and down my arms. I brought my hands up to his wrists to stop him when I finally noticed his body.

"Are you okay? You're shaking."

"Fine," he said on a shallow breath.

"Trent—"

"I'm fine, please just let me make sure you're okay."

With a nod, I released his wrists and let my arms drop to my sides. I tortured my bottom lip as he felt along the bones that stuck out, and stopped breathing for long seconds when his hands hit my hip bones, and then worked their way down my legs to my knees and ankles. The image of him in the shower a couple nights before was dancing through my mind as his hands started making their journey back up.

When my chest began rising and falling quickly, he grimaced and whispered, "I'm sorry if this is hurting you. I'll be done soon."

That wasn't what was making my breathing ragged and, ultimately, causing me even more pain. It was the internal battle I was having with the sane Rachel, and the genuinely confused Rachel.

Sane Rachel was screaming Kash's name at the top of her lungs in order to keep him forefront in her mind. She was going over wedding details and imagining what their wedding would be like once she got out. She was picturing her future with Kash and the family they would have. The other Rachel was trying not to moan over the way Trent's large hands felt running over her body. She was replaying that night when he was in the shower, and imagining walking in there and taking over for him. She was fighting to break free from Sane Rachel so she could move Trent's hands over other parts of her body that were aching to be touched.

My body was so on fire I could hardly feel the pain anymore.

"I don't feel anything wrong, you're just bruised."

I huffed loudly when his hands suddenly disappeared from my body. My eyes shot open to see him kneeling over me; his labored breathing matched my own, and there was a look in his eyes that I'd seen plenty of times before. Only before, I hadn't comprehended what I was seeing. There was heat, and there was passion—and it was scaring the shit out of me.

"We can't stay in here, Rachel. We have no food, no water . . . there's no bathroom, and everything I have that can protect us is in my room."

"I know."

His eyes searched my face before he sat back and ran a hand through his thick hair. "Leaving this room could be a suicide mission. If we get out of here without anyone seeing us, it won't be long before they find out. We have to make it to my room, get what we can, and try to escape."

I knew he was right, but despite all my fantasies of getting out of that place, I had the sudden urge to never try to leave. I didn't want to know what faced us outside those walls. "I thought you said it would be impossible to escape."

"It still might be. There's more ammo and guns in my room, but we just have to hope what I still have in here is enough to get us there," he said grimly and pulled out his gun, released the magazine, and stared at it for a second before replacing it and setting his gun aside. "I only have four bullets left."

"You're thinking . . . that . . . we, uh . . ." I trailed off when I realized his breathing had suddenly spiked. Before I could bring it up, he spoke.

"We'll have to fight our way out, I have no doubt of that. They'll either wait us out in here, or they'll eventually get in. So, Rachel, if you still want to get out of here, then this is what we have to do. I know I gave you an alternate plan yesterday, but after last night, it's not an option anymore."

I wanted to get out of here, needed to get out of here. But the risk was proving to be too great; someone was going to get hurt. "I can't let you get hurt because of me."

"And I can't let you die because of me. If it weren't for me, you wouldn't be here, and you wouldn't be in this position."

"But, Trent—"

"I'll take whatever's coming for me gladly. I should have never stolen you, and I hope you'll find it in you to forgive me one day. Rachel, meeting you changed my life."

Tears were sliding down my cheeks, and when he brought a hand up to the uninjured side of my face to wipe them away, I held his hand to me and begged, "Please don't let anything happen to you."

"I'll do whatever it takes to get you out of here alive," he promised, and suddenly his lips were on mine.

Trent

A SURPRISED NOISE SOUNDED in the back of Rachel's throat, and I pulled back, breaking the kiss almost as soon as it'd started.

"We need to move," I said before she could protest what I'd just done. "And we need to move fast."

Her blue eyes found mine, and I hated that I hadn't gotten enough time to look at them like this. Even wet with tears, they were the most beautiful eyes I'd ever seen. "All right, I'm ready."

Using my good arm, I forced myself off the mattress and made my way to the door. Moving around the chairs, I put an ear against the metal and held my breath, listening for any sounds until my lungs protested the lack of oxygen. Stepping back, I removed one of the chairs and bit back a curse from the pain that kept shooting through my arm as I went back to the door to listen again. There wasn't any noise, but that didn't mean much. The door was solid metal, and they could be waiting.

"Come here, Rachel."

Turning around, I watched her struggle to stand and flinched when she gasped in pain.

"Are you sure you're okay to do this?"

"I'm fine."

She was lying, but this couldn't wait. "Stand behind me, and when I say run, run as hard as you can to my bedroom."

After having her remove the second chair, I stood back and counted to twenty before making sure she was hidden behind my body, and opening the door as quietly as possible. I took three steps forward with Rachel gripping the back of my shirt, my arms shaking so much I was barely able to keep my gun in the air as I prepared for anyone that might meet us in the hall.

When both sides of the hallway came up empty, I put my lips to her ear and whispered, "Walk until I say otherwise."

We made it to my room without seeing or hearing anything, and as soon as we were inside, I pushed the workout equipment back against the doors.

"If you have to go to the bathroom, go. If anyone gets through that door—"

"Scream, I know." She ran to the bathroom and I collapsed against the equipment, my breathing heavy and ragged.

Even with the makeshift tourniquet, new blood had made its way through the material, and was steadily dripping down my arm from the use of it just now. Using my shirt, I tried to rub off as much blood as possible before pushing myself up, and making my way to the closet.

After loading the magazine in my gun, I pulled out another handgun and made sure it had a full magazine before pulling out one of my assault rifles. The weight was something I was so used to, but at the moment, it felt like I was lifting a car just to get the strap around my neck.

"We need to get out of here. I have that same bad feeling I had yesterday."

I turned and nodded as I eyed Rachel warily, trying not to show any pain as I put the shoulder holster on and placed both handguns in there. If I had just listened to her the day before, we wouldn't be where we were now. She wouldn't be hurt, and I wouldn't be about to put us in a situation I thought we wouldn't make it out of alive.

"Ready, Rachel?"

"No . . . let's do it."

In any other situation, that would have made me smile. In any other life, I would give anything to have met her under normal circumstances and made her mine. As it was, I lowered my rifle and wrapped an arm around her body to pull her close.

She wrapped her hands around my neck, letting me hold her, and her voice was shaky when she said, "I don't know what you did before you came into my life, and I don't care. You may have done some bad things, but you're not a bad person. You're caring and brave, and I will never forget what you've done for me."

My chest tightened and I pulled back enough to look at her face. It took all my restraint not to crush my mouth to hers again right there.

"Get us out of here, Trent," she said, and the hands around my neck slid down my arms. Her grip wasn't tight, but it was enough.

I choked out a cry of pain and tried to turn from her, but one of her hands went up to my shoulder and stopped me. The other didn't leave my bandaged arm.

"Trent . . . what . . . what is this? Are you—are you bleeding? You said they didn't hurt you!"

"I'm fine, we need to go."

"No!" she cried, and the tears that had been threatening earlier began falling down her cheeks. "No, you can't be hurt, tell me what happened! Why would you lie to me?"

"It just grazed me, I'm fine."

"You're not fine!" she hissed and pulled her hand away from me to inspect it in the dark. "You wouldn't be bleeding through whatever this is on your arm if it just grazed—" She broke off, and a muffled cry came from where her clean hand was covering most of her face. "Trent . . ." she sobbed. "I'm so sorry."

"Don't say you're sorry. I told you, I'll do anything to keep you safe."

Before she could stop me, I bent and gritted my teeth through the pain as I shoved the workout machine away from the door. More blood flowed past the bandage, and Rachel's hand slipped down my arm when she grabbed at it.

"Trent, stop!"

"I'm all right, but we need to get out of here, we need to stay quiet. Okay?" When she didn't say anything, I grabbed her bloodied hand, and squeezed it once. "I'm going to be fine, Rachel, I swear to you."

She nodded, and I turned quickly away from her. I hated lying to her, everything about it was wrong. I knew if we could get out of here and find a hospital, I would live and have no problems from the gunshot wound. But while I knew I would go down fighting to make sure she escaped, I didn't believe for one second that the guys would let me live. If by some miracle we both got out, I would be arrested as soon as I got her to safety. Once I was in prison with Romero and the others, my life would be over. They would already know what I'd done to the rest of the crew; it would all just be a matter of how and when they killed me.

Opening the door, I held up my rifle, my arms so weak I could barely keep it out in front of me. "Stay behind me, Rachel," I whispered over my shoulder.

I stepped out with Rachel clutching my shirt, and began making my way toward the entrance of the underground building. We made it past the kitchen and the room I'd spent over a month in with Rachel, and had barely gone another dozen feet when the eerie feeling of being watched washed over me.

I stopped and listened for a few seconds before continuing forward—but the closer we got to the door that led upstairs, the worse the feeling got. It was too quiet, even with five of the guys dead. Something was wrong; they wouldn't have let us come out of both rooms without bombarding us. The guys weren't calculating enough to be stealthy and to wait for you to come to them. They were impatient and wanted nothing more than to get what they want. Granted, they would have waited for us to come out of the rooms, but they wouldn't have stayed hidden like this.

The entrance that led upstairs came into view in the dark hallway, but I immediately stopped advancing and drew Rachel back instead.

"Where are we going?"

"It's too quiet, it's not right. They have to be waiting outside that door." I turned to face her and waited, listening for any other noise. My quieted breaths and her hushed sniffling were all that filled the space around us before I spoke directly in her ear so my voice wouldn't travel down the hall. "There were thirteen of us here, that leaves seven after the five I took out, and myself."

"Is there another way out of here?" she whispered back, and I shook my head.

"Not out of the underground part. Once we're on the main floor there are three ways to get in, but they're worried about the door right behind me. Not the others. Stay here, Rachel."

I stepped back, and her panicked voice filled the hall. "What are you going to do?"

Grabbing behind her neck, I pulled her close again. "If they're all waiting outside that door to ambush us, I'm not willing to have you in the middle of that. Stay close to the door, but don't follow me out until I come back for you."

"Trent—"

"If someone ends up being down here with you, just scream. I'll be back for you."

She was quiet for so long, I thought she wouldn't answer. Just as I started to pull back, she nodded and whispered, "Okay."

A deep ache filled my chest, knowing this would most likely be the last time I saw this brave, and frustratingly stubborn girl. Grabbing the back of her neck, I captured her mouth with mine . . . but this time, I didn't pull away immediately. She met my kiss easily, and I almost groaned when my tongue met hers.

I could have stayed there with her forever. But I knew we didn't have much time. Reluctantly, I broke off the kiss, and pressed my forehead to hers as I whispered, "Rachel, I know you're not mine to take, and I know I'll never hold a part of your heart the way he does . . . but thank you for giving me a little taste of what loving you would be like."

A choked cry left her, and one of her hands, which had been resting against my chest, covered her mouth as she gathered herself. Her voice was so soft, I could barely hear her next question. "Why are you acting like this is good-bye?"

Because it is.

Taking a step back, I pulled the rifle up and kept my eyes on her face as long as possible as I said, "Stay."

"Freeze," a low voice ordered, and I felt the muzzle of a gun press up against the back of my head. My hands released the rifle so it was hanging in front of my torso, and I raised my hands in the air. Counting down the seconds before I could go for my guns waiting in the shoulder holster, I looked at Rachel's shock-frozen body and silently vowed to fight to keep her safe until I stopped breathing.

"No." Rachel's horrified whisper reached my ears at the same time I saw a large, tattooed arm wrap around her chest. "No!"

17

Kash

MASON AND I FINISHED ZIP-TYING numbers six and seven, and made sure they wouldn't be waking up for some time before we silently made our way back down the stairs. After thirteen hours at the department, Mason and I had rushed back to the building and wasted no time in coming in to find Rachel. The bad feeling I'd had the night before had only increased, and with each member of Juarez's gang we came upon, I knew I was getting closer and closer to my girl. Capturing the first seven members had been easier than expected. None had heard us approach them; they hadn't even been expecting us. It was almost like they weren't worried about anyone getting in the building . . . they were making sure someone didn't get out. I knew who that someone was, and I was about to get her back. Putting my ear up against the door at the bottom of the stairs, I counted to ten, and when no sounds could be heard from the other side, I nodded my head at Mase. He opened the door and we hurried through with our guns drawn.

Making our way to the large, metal door where numbers six and seven had been stationed, we repeated the same process and opened the door. There was an old mattress pushed to the back wall. Other than that, it was empty.

We retreated out of the room and walked down the hall, clearing rooms and a kitchen. I heard a low snap and looked over to Mason. He was pointing down at the floor, and for the briefest of seconds, he flipped on the light that was mounted onto his firearm.

There was blood all over the floor. Mason and I had made this a completely silent mission so far, and we hadn't shed blood of any of the guys we'd come across. The possibilities of whose blood that could be had me straining to keep calm. We moved out of the kitchen and continued down the hall, coming across more blood as we did. As soon as we found the second patch of stained concrete in the hall, we heard movement down the hall and froze.

Turning, I pointed down the hall, and we moved silently back toward the entrance. I slipped into the room with the mattress, and Mason motioned he was going closer to the door. Peeking out, I watched him enter the open doorway of one of the first rooms we'd come across. It was dark as hell underground, but not willing to let them even see a shadow, I withdrew back into the room and let the metal door shut enough without it latching.

Whoever was coming was staying as silent as we had, but the softest sound of shuffling went past the door, and I slowly opened the metal door enough to fit my body between it and the doorjamb. When the shuffling continued toward the entrance, I peeked around the corner and stopped breathing.

Rachel.

I could see her hair pulled back, and even in the dark, I'd know those bare legs anywhere. I'd spent countless hours in the dark worshipping and memorizing them, there was no way not to recognize them. The form of a large man was in front of her, and even though Mason and I had sworn to only knock the people out to keep them quiet, I knew if I got close to him, it would take an army to pull me off him.

Just as I started to slip into the hall, they stopped and he pulled her back a few steps. I moved just inside the doorjamb again, and waited for when they would pass me.

"Where are we going?" Rachel asked, sounding terrified. God, just hearing her voice was about to bring me to my knees. Over a month without her. Over a month of wondering if I would ever see her again. Over a month praying that I would hear that voice again. And now it was about to all be over.

"It's too quiet"—a deep voice responded—"it's not right. They have to be waiting outside that door."

His men were outside that door, though they weren't waiting. But I sure as shit was.

For a couple minutes, there was nothing. I held my breath as I waited for the signs of movement, and growled when I heard Rachel's panicked, "What are you going to do?"

If he touched her, I would kill him. If he hurt her, I would do it slowly.

Not willing to give him the chance to do anything, I turned in to the hall and put one foot silently in front of the other as

I got closer and closer to Rachel's back. I barely caught sight of Mason creeping up behind the man when everything in me locked up.

What. The. Fuck.

I stared in disbelief, and agonizing horror as I watched my fiancée kiss him. I waited for her to fight him, or tell him to stop. Neither happened, and I couldn't figure out if I was going to throw up, or kill him with my bare hands when they parted just a few seconds later.

Hushed whispers filled the hall, and I somehow found the strength to move toward Rachel when I caught sight of Mason creeping up behind the man again. Forcing myself to focus on Rachel instead of on the man I wanted to kill, I had to bite back a growl when I heard his deep command.

"Stay."

He took a step back and Mason's low voice filled the hall. "Freeze."

Rachel froze and whispered, "No."

I watched the man raise his hands and noted the rifle hanging from around his neck. But I knew if he reached for anything again, Mason wouldn't let him get far. Knowing she would expect it to be one of the other members, I prepared for her to fight back, and holstered my gun before wrapping an arm around Rachel's chest to pull her away with me.

"No!" she screamed and bucked against me, but I didn't let go.

The man brought his arms to his waist and I retreated faster. "Mase, gun!"

"I said freeze, you son of a bitch!"

Rachel stopped fighting me, and I heard a loud inhale coming from her at the same time the man said, "Let her go."

"Kash?" Rachel whispered.

My legs felt like they were going to give out when she said my name. "Yeah, Sour Patch," I managed to say. "It's me."

"Kash!" she yelled, and turned to wrap her arms tightly around my neck.

Dying. It felt like I was dying for a different reason than I had over the last month. She'd just been kissing someone else. Pushing her back, I held her away at arm's length and struggled to look at her. "Rachel, how many people are here?"

Her body shook with sobs and she blinked rapidly against the tears when she answered, "What?"

"How many people are in this building. We need to make sure we get them all before we get out of here."

"Um, I don't . . . Trent said there were thirteen—"

"Who's Trent?"

She turned to look over at the man and Mason. "He's— Mason, no!" she yelled when Mason hit him over the back of the head with the butt of his gun, his knee in the man's back keeping him on the ground.

Pulling away from where I'd been holding her, she ran to where Mason was now zip-tying his hands together. I watched as she fell to her knees, pushed Mason away, cradled Trent's head in her lap, and continued to run her hands over his head and shoulders as she apologized to him.

I was going to be sick. I stumbled back into the wall, and somehow kept myself vertical as I felt my world shatter around me. What new nightmare had I just landed in?

She kissed him.

She left me for him.

I'd spent over a month searching for her, and worrying about her . . . and within a minute of getting her, she ran from me to another man.

"Oh God. Trent, wake up, please."

He groaned and whispered her name, and she cried out in relief.

"Rachel, get away from him. Now," Mason demanded when I just continued to stand there, staring at them like a bad car accident.

She looked over at Mason, then me, and reached an arm out toward me. "Please release him and call an ambulance. Hurry, he's hurt!"

"What the fuck, Rachel?" Mason looked up at me with a confused expression.

Grinding my teeth, I turned so I couldn't see them anymore and spoke into the empty hall. Trying to get my mind on anything else. "How many others are there?"

"Seven," Trent groaned from the ground. "There were thirteen here, but I took out five last night."

Turning back around, I saw Rachel staring up at me with Trent's head still resting in her hands, on her lap. She was crying silently, and even in the dark I could see the hurt on her face. But her hurt didn't make sense. She wasn't the one that felt betrayed.

"Why did you take them out?" Mason asked, but I couldn't take my eyes from Rachel.

She kept staring at me even as she answered for Trent. "They tried to take me from him and they were going to kill him. He was going to help me escape, he was trying to keep me safe and one of them shot him last night during the fight."

"There were three outside smoking when we came in, two guarding the door to come in here, and two guarding the metal door behind me. They're all unconscious and tied up upstairs. You're sure there are no others?"

"Yes," Trent grunted as he sat up, and away from Rachel.

Mason approached me and whispered so his voice wouldn't carry. "What the fuck is happening right now?"

"I have no idea."

"Do we call a bus?"

I shook my head and shrugged helplessly. "We will when we call everyone else. Let's get him upstairs and away from my god-damn fiancée."

Mason walked in front of me, and grabbing Trent's arms, roughly pulled him up. I had no doubt he was doing that for my benefit.

A pained cry left Trent as Mason yanked him up the stairs, and Rachel yelled, "Mason, stop! He's been shot, and he's not going to hurt anyone. Untie his hands, *please*!"

"Rachel"—I cleared my throat and somehow managed to stop looking at her—"come on, we need to get you out of here."

"Please don't hurt him, he protected me!" I watched her struggle to stand and realized too late that I should have been trying to help her. "You need to do something, they'll kill him when they wake up."

What was I supposed to say? *I'm sorry?* She was breaking my fucking heart.

The door burst open, and Mason came back in.

Giving Mason a look, I nodded toward Rachel and said, "We need to get Rachel out to the truck. Then we'll, uh, we'll call everyone." I was thankful for our years of working together as he reached for Rachel, and began leading her up the stairs. I needed a minute to process everything I'd just seen.

Falling back against the wall, I bent over and rested my hands on my knees as I breathed heavily through my nose. This couldn't be happening. I couldn't lose her now. I'd almost lost her too many times, and too much had happened between us for this to end us. There was no way I was about to let whatever happened to her here, or whatever was going on between her and Trent, take her away from me. I would fight for her. I'd always fight for her.

When I'd collected myself enough, I made my way upstairs. Glancing over at the eight men, my gaze hardened as I saw Trent sitting there, head bent so he was looking at the floor. Bastard didn't even have the decency to look at me as I walked right past him on my way out to the truck.

My heart picked up seeing Rachel, but I tried to control it . . . not knowing where we stood anymore.

Mason walked over to meet me, and stayed facing the building behind me as he spoke to me. "She's just sitting there begging me not to turn him in."

It felt like I'd been punched in the stomach. *Begging Mason not to turn in one of her captors. That's all she's doing? Not thanking Mason for helping rescue her? Not wanting to see me?*

"She's covered in blood"—Mason continued—"and before you go freaking out, I'm almost positive it's his. She looks pretty bruised, but I don't think she's bleeding anywhere."

"Bruised? What the fuck, where is she bruised?"

"Half of her face is practically black and blue, and when I tried helping her into the truck, she almost screamed from where I was touching her arms."

I didn't care if Trent had been the reason behind it or not, I was going to fucking murder him. I started turning, but Mason was right there with a hand pressed to my chest.

"Don't do it, Kash. I know you want to, but don't fuck up your life over this. What the hell is even going on here? I thought for sure she would have been a hell of a lot more excited to see us. She seemed happy for all of fifteen seconds before running back to him."

"I know," I growled, and gave him a warning glare. "I think it's some fucked-up form of Stockholm syndrome."

"Shit." Mason glanced behind him at the building, before looking over my shoulder where the truck was. "Are you okay?"

I looked up at Mason and huffed, but it sounded pained. "I spent a month thinking my fiancée was being tortured and murdered. I thought I would never see her again. And not only did I just watch her kiss another man, within seconds of having her in my arms again, she ran out of them and back to him! Do you *think* I'm fucking okay?"

Mason and I both looked over when a choking sound came from Rachel, now looking at us through the open truck door. "It isn't—it isn't like that! I just . . . Trent was . . . it isn't like that, Kash, I swear!" She dropped her head into her bloodstained hands and started sobbing again.

I mumbled a curse and slowly walked over to her. My hands clenched into fists when I saw the bruising on her face when she looked back up at me. "We're going to call the department and have them come pick up everyone. They're going to want to question you, and I want someone to check your face. Okay?"

"I swear I didn't—it isn't like that! He just took care of me, and I thought we were going to die . . . a-and I'm sorry! All I wanted was to get back to you, he was going to help me find you, you have to believe me."

"Okay, Rachel. It's okay."

"I'm happy to see you, I swear!"

And yet it sounded like she was trying to convince herself rather than me. I dropped my head back so I was facing the sky, and ground my teeth to stop my jaw from shaking. I just needed to be thankful that she was alive. The rest . . . well, the rest we would just have to sort out later. Bringing my head back down, I forced a smile and stepped back, and away from her.

"Stay here while we call the department and inform everyone of what happened today. When this is over, if you want to go back to our home"—I swallowed past the lump in my throat—"then, uh, that's where . . . that's where I'll take you."

"Logan," she choked out, but I had already turned and walked back to where Mason was playing with his phone.

"Do you think you should be upsetting her more right now? Maybe just—"

"Just what, Mase? You're not the one having to go through this shit, so don't tell me how to fucking act right now. Let's just do our jobs." I let out an aggravated groan and rested both hands on top of my head and forced myself not to turn and look at Rachel. "Did you call the department?"

"Yep, before you ever came out of the building. Police and ambulance should be here any minute. Chief and some of the others will be here not long after."

I nodded my head and walked toward the building just so I could get away from Rachel, and Mason's observant eyes.

"Kash," Mason said in clear warning, but I didn't stop.

As soon as I entered the building, I went directly to Trent and bent down so I was closer to his eye level. He finally looked up at me, and his dark eyes were hard as we stared at each other.

"If you put those bruises on my future wife's face"—I growled—"I will pay back every one tenfold."

"I would die before doing that to her."

I saw red. My hands clenched into fists as I yelled, "I'm sure you'll understand why I don't fucking believe you! You've held her here for over a goddamn month, you worthless piece of shit! If I find out that *any* of that torture actually happened, you won't live to see the next day!"

Trent kept his eyes on me but didn't say anything else until after I'd stood and began walking away. "She loves you."

My chest clenched painfully. "You should have reminded yourself of that *before* you kissed her." Turning to look at him, I held his gaze as I said, "She's mine. Do you get that? You can't have her, and if you touch her again, I won't be held responsible for my actions. She belongs. To. Me."

When his eyes fell back to the floor, I turned and left the building. The faint sound of sirens could be heard as I made my way to Mason.

"Mase, I'm going to want to go back with Rachel when they take her in, if they still need you here. Are you cool?"

"Yeah, just— Never mind. Yeah, I'm good."

"No, tell me."

He sighed and looked over my shoulder at the truck before looking back at me. "Just be prepared, all right? She was kidnapped and kept here for over a month, and we don't know what they did in fact do to her."

A short, humorless laugh left me. I'd just been saying the same thing. "Trust me. Mase, I know that. Be prepared for what?"

He chewed on his bottom lip for a moment before blowing out a ragged breath. "Anything, Kash. She might not be the same Rachel anymore. Even with everything that already happened, you just have to be there for her, and hope that she's still in there."

God, I hope like hell my Rachel is still there . . . somewhere. I shut my eyes tight against the tears pricking the backs of them and locked my jaw. It wasn't until the ambulance and two patrol cars were on the scene that I finally opened my eyes again and made my way back to the truck.

"You ready, Rachel?"

Her jaw trembled when she looked up at me, and it broke me to watch her eyes fill with tears again. She opened her mouth, but only nodded when nothing came out.

"All right, let's get you to the station then."

AS WAS EXPECTED, I wasn't allowed in the room as they questioned all the men we'd arrested or Rachel on everything that had happened from the actual kidnapping, to the month that she'd been gone. At least Chief had let me stay in the observation room to Rachel's room so I could watch.

I hadn't decided if I was glad I'd stayed to listen, or not.

After finding out Trent was the one to physically kidnap her, and keep her locked in that fucking small room with the mattress in it, my jealousy turned into pure rage, and it took everything for me to not hunt down the room he was in and finally do what I'd been wanting to. After listening to Rachel countlessly remind the detectives interviewing her that Trent had been protecting her, taking care of her, and trying to help her escape, I just wanted to throw up again.

She talked about him like he was a hero. She described him as being tortured emotionally, and being forced to do everything. *"But, oh no! He isn't a bad person!"* And apparently I wasn't the only one thinking it . . . because Detective Byson asked her if she'd ever heard of Stockholm syndrome.

"What? No! I mean, yes, I've heard of it; but no. I don't have that, he was just good to me. He was just protecting me and keeping me safe, and it's something I appreciated, that's all."

I wanted to scream. I wanted to remind her that he'd taken her from me. That he'd kept her from me and had me believing she was being tortured. I wanted to know why she'd let him kiss her. I just wanted to fucking throw something. That must be why they didn't have tables or chairs in the observation room. And I completely stopped breathing when Byson asked his next question.

"Rachel, did you and Mr. Trent Cruz have any form of a sexual relationship while you were in captivity?"

"N-no! No! He— No! We just . . . No!" She licked her lips quickly and turned to face the one-way mirror.

I stared into her blue eyes through the glass for a few seconds before I turned and walked out the door. There was so much pain radiating through my chest, it felt like I couldn't breathe. I'd been prepared for her to be hurt. I'd been prepared for her to have some things to work through if we got her out okay. I hadn't been ready for this.

18

Rachel

AFTER FOUR HOURS AT THE STATION, and another three and a half hours in a hospital receiving a sexual assault examination and checking the bruising to the front of my body to make sure there were no broken bones, I was released and allowed to go home.

Logan hadn't spoken a word to me since before we'd arrived at the station, and now we were standing in our living room just staring at each other.

I'd envisioned being with him again so many times while I'd been in that room with Trent. Each one had us rushing to each other, kissing each other like we needed the other to breathe, and different variations of him making love to me, and us finally getting married. Not one of them had been like this, not one of them had made me sick to my stomach with guilt that I didn't know if

I should have or not. And not one of them involved me wishing Trent were still here with me.

Despite the questions from the detectives, I wasn't in love with Trent. Even though I'd been adamant that we hadn't had a sexual relationship, I wasn't sure how to describe our kisses in the final half hour; or the fact that I knew that he wanted me without making it seem like the kidnapping could have been something it wasn't. So I'd stumbled over my words, and in turn had received the sexual assault exam, which I'd rather not go through again.

I wasn't in love with Trent, and I didn't have Stockholm syndrome. I just understood him in a way no one else ever had. I hadn't known about the torture, though I'm sure Trent had, but I still knew he'd had no part in it, even if no one else believed me. And trying to clear his name just made it look worse for my "relationship" with him.

I could only imagine that was part of the reason Logan was staring at me like he wasn't sure he could speak without crying or punching something.

"Logan—"

"Why don't you, um"—he cleared his throat and looked up at the ceiling—"why don't you go shower? I'll order some food."

"Logan, please—"

"Do you want anything in particular?"

My jaw started trembling and I blinked back more tears before I shook my head. Of course I wanted something, just not food. I wanted to never have been kidnapped. I wanted my fiancé to look at me like he was still in love with me, instead of looking like I'd betrayed him by going along with the hand I'd been dealt.

I turned before the tears began falling and quickly made my way to the shower. The route was familiar, but at the same time, so foreign. It felt like I should be clinging to Trent's shirt, like I should be watching out for any of the others to suddenly pop out of the shadows and grab me. It felt wrong to be in the bathroom alone with no one keeping guard. But I knew I needed to get used to my normal.

Or, well, what my normal *used* to be.

I mechanically went through the motions of getting clean and scrubbing every particle of Trent's dried blood off me while trying not to think about whose blood it was, or how it had gotten on me in the first place. Twice while in the shower, I'd lost the battle with trying to keep my cries silent, and the last time my legs had given out from the exhaustion of the day . . . of the last thirty-six days.

I wasn't sure I even knew what I was crying for anymore. It's funny how when in the situation, in the moment, those bits and pieces didn't seem like that big of a deal, or seemed like something I could easily handle. Then once it was all over, it was like a tidal wave had just crashed down on me and I was standing there confused, not knowing what to do, or how to act, or what to say anymore. All I knew was the exhaustion, and the terror, and the grief. All I could do was sit there for countless minutes until the water was cold and my tears were long gone before I could finally turn the water off and pull myself up.

In the same robotlike state, I dried myself off, brushed my hair and teeth, and went about finding my own pajamas. I stood there just staring at them, letting my fingers run over the material on my body, and wondering if I would ever be able to go back to wearing Logan's clothes in bed again. Or if men's shirts had been ruined for me forever.

Forcing my mind away from the direction it had been headed,

I purposefully didn't look in the mirror on my way out of the bathroom, not wanting to see the bruises on my body again. I walked down the hall and had almost reached the living room when I heard his harsh voice.

"No, Mom . . . no— What wedding, Mom?— There's not going to be a wedding— Because she's not the same Rachel anymore, that's why!"

Even though my throat was raw from the crying, and my eyes could produce no more tears, one hand flew to my mouth to quiet any cry that could force its way out. The other hand flew to my chest, which felt like it was splitting in two.

"You think I don't know that?— No, don't put me on speaker— What, Dad?—I *know*! I fucking know that! But you guys didn't see her reaction to me today. You didn't see her reaction to the guy that took her from our goddamn house! You didn't watch her kiss him or stumble over her answers about her relationship with him. You weren't there for it, okay?— No, don't come see her right now— Because, she . . ."

I finally figured out how to make my legs move again and turned to go back to the bedroom. What do you say to something like that? What do you do? How do you handle all the confusion and emotional pain, and then find out that some of your worst nightmares are coming true . . . because of you? I crawled onto the bed and didn't even bother covering myself with the comforter. I just gripped at my chest and prayed the pain of losing everything would go away soon.

It didn't.

And sleep didn't come easy.

I lay there awake for hours, watching the glow from the sun behind the curtains eventually fade to darkness. I heard Logan come to check on me once, but it sounded like he hadn't gotten past the doorway before stopping, and after a few seconds, turning and leaving. When I finally did fall asleep, I did it alone, and woke the same.

The fact that being alone went so much deeper than physical, made the pain intensify.

I missed Trent and was terrified for him. I needed my fiancé. I wanted my life to go back to normal.

I knew I wouldn't get the first back, and hated that I wasn't sure about the others.

Kash

I GROANED, and my eyes blinked open when the persistent knocking finally woke me. Putting my feet on the floor, I pushed off the couch and stretched my sore body from sleeping on the deceptively comfortable-looking couch. Checking the peephole, I let out a harsh breath and hung my head as I unlocked and opened the door.

"You have a key, Mason."

"Yeah, but I didn't want to use it if you were actually spending time with your *fiancée,* now that *your fiancée* is back from a fucking traumatic experience that *your fiancée* just went through. You know, because she's your *fiancée* and all."

"Say *fiancée* one more time." I squinted my eyes at him. "Mom and Dad call you?"

He huffed roughly through his nose and pushed me back so he could fit in through the door. "Duh. You look like shit, so I'm guessing I'm not interrupting anything."

"Wow, thank you. Would you like to insult me some more before I kick you out of my—"

"The couch?" he interrupted. "You slept on the couch? Please tell me that was by her request."

Knowing he wouldn't leave until he felt like it, I walked back over to my makeshift bed and sat down. "No, it wasn't. I haven't talked to her since we got back here."

"And why is that?"

"Because she went to sleep after her shower. What did you want me to do? Wake her up so we could talk about her time away? About Trent?" I snarled and rubbed at my jaw.

"Yeah, sure, why the hell not? Why not ask her how she's doing, ask if she's fucking okay!"

Looking behind me, I listened for sounds from her and, when I didn't get any, turned back to Mason. "She's still sleeping, keep it down. And I'm sure she's not okay, she was kidnapped and held for over a month. Who would be okay after that?"

"So then talk to her about it!"

"I can't, Mase, okay? I can't."

He paced back and forth in the living room and finally stopped directly in front of me. "Why? Why can't you? She *needs* you. I saw how she acted yesterday too, I watched the entire interview last night. I also know the sexual assault exam came back negative! Maybe he really was trying to help her, and she clung to that. Did you *ever* think about that?"

"Why would he after taking her?"

"Ask her yourself, since Chief told me you didn't stay for the entire interview. But think about it, Kash . . . We were in gangs and helped some girls escape too. Did that never once cross your mind yesterday?"

I wanted to argue that we hadn't kissed them. But we'd always had to do whatever was necessary to make our story believable for the gang we were in. My eyes shot up to Mason's, and he gave a sad laugh as he crossed his arms over his chest.

"God, you're so dense sometimes. I believe Rachel's story, I don't think he was an undercover, but I wouldn't doubt for a second that he didn't want to be in Juarez's gang. I'll admit, seeing her with him was weird, but you need to think about the whole situation. I don't know what it is about her, but you seem to forget *everything* when it comes to her."

"What the hell are you talking about, Mason?"

He started ticking off points on his fingers. "We think she's been raped and you automatically want to kill anyone that's come near her before we even know for sure that it happened. The guy that raped her, and that she was terrified of, forces her to leave you . . . and you just automatically believe that she was really lying to you the entire time and wanted to be with him. A guy that has protected her in captivity kisses her right before they thought they were entering a suicide mission, and without a second thought you think she didn't *want* to be rescued any-more?"

I really need to stop telling Mom and Dad what I'm thinking. They always fucking tell Mason.

"She's been *missing* for thirty-six days and underwent some pretty shitty things from what I heard in the interview, and she goes to bed early and you take that as a cue to sleep on the couch?"

I groaned into my hands and sagged into the back of the couch. "Mase—"

"You know I love you like a brother. You know I trust you

with my life. You're one of the smartest guys I know, and not just when it comes to our job. But when it comes to your *future wife* you are dumb as shit."

"Tell me, why is it that you're the dumbest guy I know, and you're always the one trying to show me how stupid I'm being?"

A cocky smirk crossed Mason's face and he shrugged before turning toward the front door. "It's because I'm fucking awesome, bro. Go make sure she's okay."

"I can't get the sight of them kissing out of my head," I admitted.

"There's a lot of shit we will never get out of our heads, Kash. Don't let this one ruin the best thing you've ever had." He opened the front door and looked back at me one more time. "You should really watch the entire interview. What we saw yesterday wasn't a normal occurrence for them."

I watched as he walked out the front door, and I leaned forward, putting my elbows on my knees, and my head in my hands. I knew he was right. It didn't make any of this easier though.

Mason had taken this case about as hard as I had, and he'd seen every part of it just the same as me . . . but it wasn't the same for him. He wasn't in love with Rachel, he hadn't been planning his wedding and about to marry her, he hadn't had to watch his fiancée kiss her kidnapper.

So different.

Still, I knew I had reacted the wrong way yesterday. I should have tried to understand, I should have just been there for her. I should have sat down and listened to her side when detectives weren't interviewing her. And I should have fucking held her last night. She was finally back and I didn't even try to be near her. *I'm such a dick.*

Standing quickly, I walked down the hall, toward the closed bedroom door. I raised my arm to knock before I realized how fucking ridiculous that was and just opened the door. The bed was empty, so I walked into the bathroom and called out her name. When I didn't get a response and didn't find her in the bathroom or the closet, fear surged through my veins and I ran back into the bedroom calling after her.

"Rachel! Rach!" *This isn't fucking happening.* "Rachel!"

I'd just started to turn to run back to the living room in search of my phone to call 9-1-1 when I saw the paper and ring sitting on the nightstand. My stomach dropped and I stared at the nightstand for a few moments before I could force myself over to it. Grabbing Rachel's engagement ring, I fisted my hand around it and tried to make sense of the words on the paper.

I understand, and I don't blame you. I'm sorry.

"Understand what?" I whispered to the empty room.

The sound of pounding feet on the hardwood had me turning just as Rachel entered the room.

"Where the hell were you?" I yelled across the small space.

She flinched back into the wall near the doorjamb and her eyes darted around the room as her mouth opened and shut. "I-I-I, um . . ."

"Rachel, you can't disappear like that after what we just went through, okay? Fuck!" I stalked over to her and for the first time in over a month, I brought my mouth down onto hers. "I thought—Jesus Christ, I thought you were gone again," I choked out and started to kiss her but stopped abruptly when I realized she was cringing into the wall. "What's wrong? Am I hurting you?" I took a step back but kept the hand that wasn't clenched around the ring on her waist.

She kept her eyes on the ground, and I watched as her chest rose and fell roughly before she finally shook her head.

My eyes fell over the bruised parts of her body that I could see, and I wondered again how she'd come to get those. I hadn't stayed for that part of the interview yesterday. Like Mason, I knew the sexual assault exam showed nothing, but why was she shaking . . . *Oh my God. I'm scaring her. My fiancée is scared of me . . . after being kidnapped and held captive for over a month, she's scared of me. Son of a bitch.*

Strike one.

"Rachel," I said softly, making sure to keep my voice low and even. "Am I scaring you?"

Her eyes darted up to mine quickly, but long enough for me to see the moisture gathering in them.

"Damn it," I whispered, soft enough that I'm not sure she even heard me. "I'm sorry, I didn't mean to scare you. I'm sorry for yelling at you, I was just fucking terrified when I walked in here and couldn't find you," I explained to her as I slowly brought her body closer to mine. "Please don't be scared of me, I honestly don't think I could deal with knowing that *I* am what scares you after everything you've been through."

"I just—I just didn't want to be in a bedroom anymore. I'm sorry. I went outside to write, you were still asleep, and I didn't think you would go looking for me . . . I just wanted to be outside."

Slipping the ring into the pocket of my jeans, I cupped her face, lowered my forehead onto hers, and watched the few tears slip down her cheeks. "Shh, no it's okay. Don't cry, Rachel. I'm sorry, I shouldn't have yelled." *Jesus, of course she wants to be out-*

side, she was in a room for thirty-six days! "Let's go back outside, we'll talk out there, all right?"

She swallowed audibly and nodded her head as I pulled her away from the wall. When she didn't make an attempt to go back down the hall, I grabbed her hand and started leading her down it. I didn't understand why she kept walking directly behind me instead of beside me, and I shot her a confused look when she grabbed onto the back of my shirt with her free hand, but she wasn't even looking at me. She was staring down at the ground.

I opened my mouth to ask what she was doing, when a flash from yesterday hit me hard. The way she'd been following Trent down the hall as Mason and I waited in the rooms. *I heard her say in the interview that he would take her to a bathroom that was at the other end of the building. Is this how she always walked with him?* Stopping suddenly, I turned to her and noted that she looked calmer now than she had since we first found her yesterday. But I couldn't let her do this; this wasn't normal.

"Rachel, does this feel right to you?"

Her eyebrows scrunched together as I loosely grabbed the hand holding on to my shirt. "What?"

"Does this feel right to you? Normal . . . walking like this, holding on to my shirt?"

"What? No, I—" Her eyes widened and she quickly released my shirt before taking a step back. "I'm sorry, I didn't realize I—"

"Don't apologize, Rachel. You have absolutely nothing to apologize for, okay?" Bringing her back to me, I made lazy circles on her back and waited until she was looking up at me. "Is that how you had to walk with him?"

Rachel's eyes turned pleading. "Yes, but it was only because he needed to make sure no one took me! He didn't do it—"

"It's fine," I assured her. "I'm just making sense of it, but we're going to fix it, okay? You're going to walk the rest of the way in front of me without any physical contact from me. You already went through the hall a few times alone, and you know this hall well. No one is going to come after you in it, there's no one here but you and me."

Instead of the tears or fear I had been expecting, her eyebrows slammed down and her mouth formed a tight line before she sneered, "Don't treat me like I need to be fixed, Logan! Don't talk to me like I'm going to fall apart. Don't act like you know how to make it all okay again. You have no idea what happened there, and you are the last person I need treating me like I'm a broken child. I know how to walk down a fucking hallway without touching someone, it was just instinct!"

She pushed past me, and my head dropped as my shoulders sagged in defeat. Bringing my hand up to the back of my neck, I rubbed over it and squeezed it hard once before turning to follow her.

Strike two.

At the very least, I should be happy that Rachel still had her fire. It may be buried deep under confusion and . . . whatever else she was feeling. But it's there. And I was determined to uncover the rest of it.

19

Kash

I FOUND RACHEL sitting out on the porch in her favorite chair with her arms crossed under her chest, and her knees bent with her feet on the cushion of the chair. With a deep breath in, I made my way to the chair near her and automatically grabbed her ankle to bring her feet onto my lap.

My eyes shot up when she quickly pulled her leg back, but there was no lingering anger in her action. She had this anxious look about her, as if she wasn't comfortable with me taking her out of the position she was in. Without a word, I sat back and decided against asking what was so essential about staying like that.

"Where's Trip?"

I tried not to roll my eyes at her attempt at pushing aside the awkward tension that had just formed between us, and cleared my throat. "He's at Mason's. He came and picked him up before we got home yesterday. We both felt it would be better to not have any distractions between you and me for a while." *And then I'd gone and slept on the couch.*

Rachel pursed her lips and started involuntarily picking at her nail polish. I started to ask her how she'd gotten it while she was gone but decided I might not want to know.

"Do you feel better being out here?"

She nodded mindlessly for half a minute before clearing her throat. "I was thinking earlier how funny it was. Trent's room and mine felt safe there. Like if we weren't in one of them, anything could go wrong. I hated the walks to and from them, and once we were back in one, I could finally breathe again. But now, all bedrooms just seem like a cage."

I had to shut my eyes and breathe in and out through my nose for a few seconds before I could look back up at her. Every time I thought about him with her, and every time she talked about him, was like tearing my soul open all over again. I played Mason's words over and over in my mind and waited until I knew I could speak without gritting out the words.

"Do you want to tell me about what happened? Tell me about him?"

"Why?" she asked on a pained laugh. "I know what you think, it's all over your face what you think I feel for him . . ." She trailed off before whispering, "What you think happened."

"I'm giving you a chance to talk about him without feeling like it's an interrogation instead of an interview."

Her head turned quickly to face me, and the same anger from earlier was back and covering a deep ache. "Or maybe it's because you're looking for a more concrete reason to tell everyone else the wedding is off?"

"I don't want the wedding to be off."

"Oh, no?"

"Of course not." Digging into my pocket, I pulled her ring out and leaned forward so my elbows were resting on my knees. "I told you to never take this one off," I murmured. "What did the note mean? What do you understand?"

"I understand your wanting to call the wedding off. I'm sure you're right, I'm sure I'm not the same Rachel anymore."

I looked up so I could see her face and watched as she turned her head away and brushed at her cheeks. "What?"

"So I won't put you in the position of having to break up with me . . . I won't make you be seen as the man that broke up with his fiancée the day after she was rescued."

"Rachel, I'm not breaking up with you. I don't want to call off the wedding, why are you saying all—"

"I heard you talking to your parents last night, Logan! Don't lie to me."

"I— Shit." I groaned and sat back in my chair. "I *don't* want to call off the wedding. I'm sorry you heard that conversation, but, Rachel, I was mad and confused and thought you were in love with that guy!"

"Trent. His name. Is. Trent."

"I know what his name is, Rachel, please try to see it from my side. I reacted the wrong way, I wasn't thinking about you, and I'm sorry about that. I lost my shit when I saw you kissing him and when you immediately left me for him, and then to find out later that *he* was the one to steal you from our damn house? None of it made sense to me, and it killed me to watch you not know what to say to Byson when he asked if you'd had a sexual relationship with him. I was hurt, and I was pissed, and I was so fucking jealous I couldn't see straight. So last night I was just lashing out because I was too scared to find out what really happened between you two. I was wrong. I know that. I'm so damn sorry you heard that conversation, but that isn't what I want, that isn't how I feel; and I'm ready to listen to you now."

I took in her closed-off posture and after fumbling for a moment, put the ring on the table near us, closest to her. Rachel stared at the ring for a long time before looking back at me. Those blue eyes of hers were so guarded I had no idea what she was thinking or feeling, and I hated it.

"This ring belongs to you, and the only place I want it is on your left hand . . . and hopefully someday if you'll still have me, I want it accompanied by another ring. Like before, I won't push you, but this is yours. If you decide to put it on again, Rachel, you better understand what I'm saying this time. I don't want you taking that ring off."

She didn't move toward the ring, and she didn't say anything. She just stayed in the same position, staring at me.

"You were still wearing your ring when we found you. So, tell me something," I said softly, "while you were gone, were you hoping to escape, or to be found . . . and did you ever think about us and our future together?"

"Of course I did." She sounded like I'd insulted her with my question. Thankfully, after turning away from me, she continued. "I never gave up hope until the day before you came for me. Trent said you . . . all of you . . . stopped looking for me. That you hadn't been looking for me for a week. I figured you thought I was dead. That was the first time I ever felt like there was no hope. Every day before that I thought about you, thought about how long it probably was until we were supposed to get married. What you were telling people." She paused and chewed on her bottom lip for a second before rushing out, "I wrote to you."

"What do you mean?"

"Trent bought me a journal. I wrote to you the same way I write to my parents. I never stopped thinking about you, or us." When she looked at me again, her eyes were glassy, and it was taking all my willpower to stay in my chair and not take her in my arms. "Did you?" she asked suddenly.

"Did I what?"

"Did you stop looking for me?"

I shifted forward again and brought my hands close to where her feet rested flat on the seat cushion. "Not the way you're thinking. I was almost positive I knew where you were. Enough that Mason agreed to go in with me and attempt to rescue you if you were there. I had been taken off the case immediately because I was too close to it. So I did my own investigating. I looked all over the streets and used every resource I had until I got a lockdown on the building. By that time, the department had already figured out from the tests they did on the hair from your brushes, that at the very least, the hair they sent wasn't yours. Just like the blood wasn't even human. So they had to begin assuming all the 'evidence' was false, and they stopped responding to the men who took you when they called.

"Only problem is that it could have gone two ways: one, they would go crazy trying to get the department's attention and mess up enough that the department could find them. Or two, they would get so frustrated with the department that they would actually do something to you. From what Mason said, the department was banking on the fact that since they gave you a month before they said they would kill you, and they stopped responding to them right before a month was up, it would make them crazy wondering why the department stopped looking for you all of a sudden in the last hour. The department assumed I still knew what was happening and would find out soon that they had stopped looking for you and would flip, so they began watching me like a hawk. I couldn't do anything right away, but every day that passed was killing me. And then I found out about the building you were in. So Mason and I finally started the process of figuring out how to get you back. But we needed to be careful with our jobs, losing them would have been the least of our worries for a while if we would have just rushed in. That took another few days."

"Are you going to lose your job?"

"No. Because, technically, we could say we were finishing up an old job. And we did find you. We might get a few days' suspension, but nothing serious." Keeping my eyes on her face, I slowly moved my hands up her feet to her ankles, and back down. Her body stilled, but she didn't move away from me again, so I continued the path. "I don't know what they told you while you were there, but did Byson explain *why* you were taken?"

"Not really. He didn't say much that made sense. He asked if I was ever tortured and asked if there were any other girls there, that the department had been sent evidence of me being tortured. As for where I was kept, a few of the guys at the house let it slip one of the last nights that some guy named Romero would want Trent 'out' because he'd turned on the rest of the guys. I ended up guessing that Trent was in a gang, and after trying to find out who Romero was, I more or less guessed that he was in prison and was calling the shots. But I still don't know who Romero is or why I was taken."

"It was my fault you were taken, Rachel."

A brief smile crossed her face and her eyes darted over to mine for a second. "Well, you *are* the one that works in the gang unit. I kind of figured that too, but that wasn't until the same moment when I knew for sure that you would find me . . . only to find out less than a minute later that you had already stopped looking for me."

"You remember the last gang Mason and I infiltrated?"

She nodded and thought for a second. "Juarez."

"Right, and he'd put that hit on us as insurance because he thought we were cops, which is why we had to go undercover in Texas. Juarez and his boys from the meth house are still in prison, as are the two men that were hired to take Mase and me out. Apparently *Romero* Juarez has two houses for his gang. Mase and I weren't in with him long enough to be trusted to even know about the other house, which is made up of the men you were with."

Rachel looked shocked. I believed her when she said she hadn't known why she was taken, but I still didn't understand why this Trent guy never told her *why* he was keeping her if he was supposed to be helping her.

"They wanted their brothers out and, more importantly, the head of their 'family.' They were using you to do that, and to get back at me and Mason. From what you said yesterday, you didn't see the destruction in our bedroom from when they took you. But on one of the walls in red spray paint were the words 'Did you think we would forget?' and the gang's symbol. As soon as I saw that I knew *why* you were taken. I just didn't know who had you, and how to get you back. They didn't want money, just the members out of jail. Which is obviously something the department couldn't do and why it took so long to get you. We just had to hope we found you before they—well, before they did what they threatened to."

"What they threatened to . . . I—" Rachel shook her head rapidly before dropping her face into her hands. "I just don't know."

"Don't know what, Rach?"

"This is—well, from your side it seems like a completely different kidnapping. Like I feel like I have no connection with it at all, none of it triggers anything. I never *saw* any of that. I never saw any of the 'torture' that you apparently were receiving evidence of. I didn't know they were in contact with you. It was just . . . nothing, basically. Just a whole lot of nothing. Being confused about why I was there and why they would take me. Confused about Trent being so nice and making himself so uncomfortable to make sure I was safe. And just day after day of absolutely nothing but sitting on the mattress, being given meals, and writing in my journal.

"Yours sounds terrifying . . . not that I wasn't scared. I was always so scared. But mine sounds like nothing compared to what you were thinking I went through. I was really just kept in a room, and I was taken care of. There was never any danger . . . up until the end."

Scooting my chair closer so I could cup the back of her neck, I licked my lips and struggled to find the words. "Rachel, you have no—you don't understand—fuck. Seeing you yesterday. Seeing you alive, seeing you completely whole and well was the biggest relief of my life. You have no idea how damn happy I am, how happy everyone at the department is, that you weren't tortured. But don't downplay what you went through. No one should have to go through what you did, and I still hate that you went through a minute of it, let alone over a month. You may not have been tortured, but that's just a blessing right now. It doesn't change what still happened."

She took a shuddering breath in and held it for a while before releasing it and resting her chin on her knees. Her eyes were glassy, but no tears were falling. I hated that she didn't look happier to be home. I hated that she didn't want to be closer to me. I just hated this whole damn thing.

"Tell me about . . . tell me about him, Rachel. I won't ask questions like the detectives did yesterday, just tell me about your time with him."

"I know you don't want to hear about him," she huffed. "You're just going to be more pissed off hearing his name. Every time I say it I see the way your eyes harden."

There was no point in denying that. And I really didn't want to hear about him. But she looked so lost, the only way I knew how to help her was to get her to talk. If she didn't, she was going to shut down and start shielding against me. I wasn't about to go through that with her again.

Not giving her the option to pull away, I grabbed both ankles and sat back in my chair before placing her feet on my lap. She looked down at her feet, but didn't move them and didn't say anything.

"Tell me all of it, start from the beginning. Don't leave anything out for my benefit, Rachel, really, I want to hear it all."

HOURS LATER, we'd moved back into the house so I could make us lunch. Rachel never once stopped talking as I cooked, and only took brief breaks when she was chewing. A couple hours in,

I started trying to remember why I'd originally hated Trent when I realized I was thankful that he had gone out of his way to make sure no one touched her. Staying in the room and bathroom with her had pissed me off at first, but I understood.

It wasn't until a few hours after we'd finished eating that I had to use every ounce of self-control so I wouldn't lash out for what Rachel saw one night in the bathroom, and for the *two* kisses they had shared. Rachel explained both kisses as: "We thought we were about to die, we didn't know what we were about to walk out of that room and into. He'd taken care of me, killed his 'brothers' for me, put himself in danger for me and was about to willingly do it again." All I could think of as she'd explained the kisses was, *You were still engaged*!

I couldn't imagine kissing another woman in any situation, let alone that one. Rachel must have seen that thought repeating itself, because she looked directly into my eyes and whispered, "You weren't there for all of it. So don't judge me, because there is no way you could understand why it happened, or why I let it happen."

When she was done with her story, she started picking at the bottom of her shirt and refused to look at me again; and I just didn't know what to say.

So I didn't say anything.

We sat there silently for another hour as she looked at everything but me, and I couldn't take my eyes off her.

I wasn't sure if I was happy I knew now, or not. At least some of the images I had been visualizing had been put to rest. If she said that was all that happened between them on a romantic or sexual level, then I believed her . . . completely. But that didn't make what *had* happened any easier.

I knew that Rachel believed she didn't have romantic feelings for Trent . . . but there was something. I could see even as she told me about her time when she was gone, the way she talked about him changed. Scared of him, to confused about him, to grateful for him, to viewing him as friend, to viewing him as something else entirely. Only problem was she didn't even realize that final change; and I didn't have a name for it.

From what she had said, she'd wanted to get out of there and get back to me, and Trent was going to help her. And after watching the way she continued to avoid eye contact or slowly inch away from me, I stopped wondering why she would be doing that after so long apart if she wasn't actually in love with Trent.

Because I knew the reason now.

Just like I'd envisioned a reunion with her that was completely different from the one we'd had. She'd been dreaming of me rescuing her and taking her away from it all. And instead, I'd let my jealousy get in the way and had been a bastard to her the entire first day after the supposed bad guy had just done everything to save her.

Strike. Three.

Rachel

I COULDN'T FIGURE OUT WHAT TO SAY or what to feel when I finally finished rehashing everything I could think of from my time with Trent.

Now I was sitting here, trying to sort through all the emotions that were coursing through me. I knew the members of his gang would kill Trent the second they had the chance, and I was feeling guilty and terrified for when that time came . . . it felt like I was already grieving his loss. I'd promised him I wouldn't let him go down for everything, and in the end, I hadn't been able to do a thing about it. I wanted him back; I wanted him safe and away from the other members of his gang. I wished more than anything that he could have gotten a start at a new life instead of being sent to prison, where he was likely to die for what he'd done for me. But through all of that—through all of those emotions—they didn't compare to what I was feeling for the man sitting across from me.

I was so confused. I had no idea what he was thinking or feeling for me after the conversation I'd heard yesterday afternoon. I'd always known he was quick to react on his emotions, it was one of the reasons I loved him. But everything about yesterday and today was so beyond what I thought it would be, and what *was* us, that I just felt like I didn't know anything anymore.

So I was grieving, but it wasn't just for Trent and what was to come for him, it was also for the relationship that I was afraid was now over after everything Logan and I had been through.

When more than an hour had passed since I'd finished talking, and he still hadn't said a word, I stood up to take a shower.

"What can I do, Rachel?" he asked to my back. "Tell me what to do for you and I'll do it. Tell me how to help you and it'll be done."

My lips tilted up in a forced, helpless smile even though he couldn't see me, and I kept my back to him as I said, "If I had any idea what to do to make that month go away, or to fix us, I would. But I don't, I don't even know if there *is* anything either of us can do."

Without waiting for a response, I walked to the back of the

house and through the bedroom to the bathroom. Stripping down after the steam from the shower started filling up the room, I stepped in and let the hot water soothe my aching body, and hide my unrelenting tears.

Logan never came to check on me, though I stayed in long enough again that the water ran cold. But when I was in new pajamas and was walking out of the bathroom again, something on the bed caught my eye.

My engagement ring was on top of the same piece of paper I had left it on this morning, sitting in the middle of the bed.

I sat on the edge and reached for the paper, letting the ring slide off it onto the comforter.

> *I understand, and I don't blame you. I'm sorry.*
> *I'm here. Always. And I'm never giving up on us. I love you.*
> *"So fall when you're ready, babe . . ."*

Somehow, impossibly, more tears filled my eyes, and I pressed the paper to my chest as I fell back onto the bed. Grabbing my engagement ring, I held it above me and stared at it through blurred eyes as I replayed yesterday, then replayed the first and second times Logan sang "Fall into Me" by Brantley Gilbert to me. It was after our first time together, and then again as he danced with me in my kitchen last fall on the anniversary of my parents' death.

I loved him. I loved the man that was waiting for me somewhere in the house. I loved the way he loved me, and I loved all his faults. Including his quick reactions based solely on emotions rather than on facts.

But the events of the last month wouldn't just go away. Just like the horrific night with Blake hadn't gone away overnight. Logan was right about one thing, I was sure of it. I wasn't the same Rachel as before, and I didn't know how to get her back. Because this time, it wasn't just the events that had changed me . . . it was also Trent, and he had changed Logan too.

Logan didn't understand my relationship with Trent, and I wasn't sure if he understood now that I wasn't in love with him. But for Logan, there was still that level of unease and suspicion when it came to Trent, and that needed to be addressed, just as much as I needed to work my way through all that had happened before Logan and I could move forward.

Sitting back up, I opened the drawer of my nightstand and kept both the note and ring in my left hand, suspended over it, as I thought of the past . . . the future . . . and most importantly, the present. What happened here and now could change everything.

Letting the note fall, I shut the drawer and stood to leave the room.

20

Kash

SLIPPING THE CHAIN holding the badge over my head, I pulled on an old Henley shirt and made sure it covered my duty weapon resting in the holster on my belt. Grabbing my tactical boots, I put them on and ran a hand through my hair as I walked out of the bedroom.

It was weird. Getting ready for work whenever Rach was home usually consisted of me trying to get ready, and her doing everything to make sure I had fewer clothes on ten minutes later than when I'd begun. Now that she was back, I hadn't expected it to go back to that immediately. But she shut herself in the closet when she changed and always seemed to walk out of the bedroom whenever I was doing the same. And it'd been close to three weeks since she'd come home.

I stopped near the end of the hall and leaned a shoulder against the wall as I watched her. She was sitting on the far end of one of the couches, her legs up in that way that she always seemed to sit now, and was staring off into the backyard. Her journal was resting in between her knees and her chest, a pen in her hand like she'd forgotten she was writing again.

This happened a lot now too. She wrote more than she used to, and even when she wasn't writing, there were times when she would suddenly stop whatever she was doing and just stare off . . . usually outdoors. I didn't ask what she was thinking about, or what she was remembering, because it wasn't exactly hard to figure out. I just usually tried to let her be alone in her thoughts during those times.

With all that said, though, she was getting better all the time, and I was so damn proud of her. After that second day home, when she'd walked into the living room with her engagement ring back on, we'd slowly been working on everything. Neither of us mentioned the fact that she put it on, but I'm positive I hadn't stopped smiling like a lunatic for hours after.

We'd worked on her fear and anxiety, as well as my jealousy issues and insecurities over Trent. But most of all, we'd just worked on being *us* again. She hadn't cried since her second shower, as far as I knew; and after a long talk about how she'd felt like she didn't know the man who'd come to rescue her . . . she slowly went back to calling me Kash again. As I'd seen that second day, my bitchy Rachel was still there, and her attitude was slowly coming out more and more. I'd gone back to treating her like I always had from day one, and she'd gone back to teasing and fighting with me again, as well as smiling a little more every day.

Though she didn't ask about him, she knew that I'd made sure Trent was put in an isolation cell so that no one could get to him except for the guards, and I knew she only didn't mention him for my benefit. Because every night, in her sleep, she'd whisper his name. Sometimes her voice was laced with fear or agony, and sometimes it was as if he were standing right there . . . but it never failed. Though we were working on us, and I knew without a doubt that she loved me, there was always that nagging thought of what her real thoughts of him were. Even still, Mason and I had been working for the last few weeks on getting him moved somewhere else for his safety, but since Rachel didn't bring him up, I wasn't sure how to bring that up to her . . . especially when there was the chance we wouldn't succeed.

I held her every night in our bed, and took any opportunity to kiss the top of her head, forehead, cheeks, and neck . . . but we still hadn't kissed since that second morning. There were lingering touches from her, brushes here and there; and when I would hold her in my arms, her eyes would search mine as her fingers gently trailed over my face and through my hair. It was the sweetest form of agony I'd ever endured.

I pushed off the wall, and Trip lifted his head as he watched me make my way toward him and Rachel. He'd come back home a few days ago and hadn't left Rachel's side since. Scratching his head when I got close, I tried not to shake my own when I got directly next to Rachel and she still hadn't realized I was here.

She jumped a little when I cupped one of her cheeks in my hands but smiled and pressed her fingers gently into my chest when she looked up at me.

"Gotta go to work, Sour Patch."

Her lips twitched, and her fingers trailed up the side of my neck and into my hair. "Be safe."

I leaned in and kissed her neck, and then closer to her ear before whispering, "Always. I love you, Rachel."

"Love you too."

I'd barely gotten out the door before my phone was blaring the department's ringtone. Looking down, I saw CHIEF on the screen and double-checked the time to make sure I wasn't running late before answering.

"Yes, sir?"

"You headed toward the office, or do you have something that has you going straight to the streets?"

"I believe Gates and I are both going into the office first. There isn't much we had planned out today."

"Good, can you come see me as soon as you get in? I have something I need to talk to you about."

I paused just a few feet from the driveway and squeezed my eyes tightly shut. "Both of us?"

"Just you."

Shit. "Uh, of course. I'm leaving right now."

"See you soon."

I threw my leg over my Harley and tried not to overthink what I could be called in for. I'd gone against the department to find Rachel, and Mason and I had both already had three meetings with Chief and some of the detectives who had worked the case regarding that. Everyone had agreed that we wouldn't be suspended or punished, but that still didn't ease the fear of being called in to talk to Chief.

As soon as I was sitting in front of him, the fear left and was replaced by confusion when he placed a journal in an evidence bag on the desk.

"This was recovered from the building where they had been holding your fiancée."

Rachel's mention of writing to me floated through my mind, and I gripped the arms of the chair so I wouldn't grab for it.

"It's up to you if you tell her that we had to go through every entry in order to gain more information about the situation, but there's nothing here for us. Nothing more than what she told the detectives when they interviewed her, and most are letters to loved ones about her fears. So I'm handing it over to you. She wrote a lot to you, but you know your fiancée, so it's your call on whether you think you should read it or not. As well as if you should give it back to her. She might not want to have that reminder."

Of course I want to fucking read it. "Thank you, Chief. I appreciate it. Was there anything else you needed to speak to me about?"

"One last thing now that we're alone, Ryan. Completely off the record, and I'll deny it if you repeat it."

My lips twitched and I crossed my arms over my chest. Chief's off-the-record-speeches were usually him venting about someone in the department, or his in-laws coming for a visit. And for the most part, they were funny as shit. The rest of the tension in my body melted away and I relaxed into the chair as I waited for him to begin.

"I don't blame you for what you did. If it had been my wife, or any of my kids, I would have done whatever it took to find them and get them back. The moment you got into the police department, I made the decision to pull you off patrol and put you in the worst situations imaginable by having you as an undercover narcotics officer. The things you and Gates had to go through there, and what you had to do to survive with those people, has made you both the incredible detectives you are today. Unfortunately for me, and some of our other detectives, it made it so that you don't feel the need to follow the law sometimes. They don't understand, because they've all had to follow the law, but to be honest, we can't ask for much else after what the both of you did for us over the course of those years. I guess I just want you to know that I think you did what you had to as a man. As one of my officers, I will always stand behind you for what you've done for our department, and our city."

Completely unexpected. Mason and I had gotten off free, but Chief still hadn't looked happy with either one of us during our previous meetings. I sat there speechless until Chief stood and offered out his hand. "Thank you, sir. I appreciate that."

"All right now, there's already too much of a bro-mance in this office as it is, I don't need you getting all mushy on me too. Get your ass out of here and go get some work done."

"Yes, sir. And thank you for this." I raised the bagged journal in the air and slipped out the door.

Mason was already at his desk when I got there, and after filling him in, I sat at my own and tried to get some work done. But hours later, even after I'd moved the journal to a drawer so it wouldn't be there in plain sight to tempt me, it was all I could think about. I looked over at Mason throwing a baseball above his head over and over again and finally opened the drawer.

"Jesus, about damn time. I couldn't concentrate thinking about that thing."

Looking up at Mase, I glared at him as he continued to throw the ball up. "*You* couldn't concentrate? How do you think *I* felt?"

"I don't know, but we really don't have a reason to go on the streets unless there's a call for something today. I'm just in here catching up on shit, and since all I can think about is that journal, crack it open and read it to me."

"Mase, I'm not reading you Rachel's journal."

"Well I don't want to hear her love letters to you. Just read me the rest."

Like her entries to her parents? Uh, no. "If there's anything like that, I'll read it to you."

I went through the entire journal, and let Mason read over my shoulder through the parts that I thought of as the "captive entries." Each day she had pages where she wrote to her parents and me, and then pages of everything that had happened during the day. What she ate, what she drank, what she and Trent talked about. Like I said, captive entries.

Over three-quarters of the way through the journal, one of her entries to her parents suddenly stopped, and there was nothing after it. I sat back in my chair and folded my hands behind my head.

"Is there more for me to read?" Mason asked as he scooted his chair over to me.

"No, it's done. It just cut off."

We watched as the last quarter of the journal's pages slowly fluttered over to the other side from the weight of the rest of the pages, and I lurched forward in my chair at the same time Mason harshly whispered, "Shit, is that blood?"

"What the hell?" I scanned through the last ten or so pages, which had smears of blood all over them, and came to a stop when I got to the last page. "Oh my God."

"What? What's on— Oh damn . . ." He trailed off when he saw the top of the page.

I read over the words on the last page and hung my head when Mason eventually took the journal from me so he could read the entire last page too.

"Are you going to show her?"

I rubbed at the back of my neck and looked over at him before shrugging. "I have to. I can't keep that from her. She would hate me if she found out later."

He nodded and tossed the closed journal on my desk. "I agree. Shit, I hope this doesn't hurt the progress you've both had though."

"Me too." I breathed out heavily. This could change every-thing. "Me too."

Rachel

MY EYES KEPT DRIFTING SHUT as Trip and I watched TV on the couch while we waited for Kash to come home. I'd spent almost the entire day outside, writing in my journal, and hadn't noticed how much time had gone by until I realized it was dark outside. After a shower and quick snack, I'd curled up on the couch and hadn't moved since.

I knew I needed to start living my life again—having an entire day slip by without realizing it had been proof—but I was so used to doing nothing that it was hard to think of doing something as simple as going out for coffee with Maddie. And, to be honest, a small part of me was terrified to leave the house. It was a ridicu-lous fear, seeing how I'd been taken from home, but at least here I didn't feel so vulnerable. Out in the open, anyone could see me. I needed to change that, though. I couldn't let fears of what had happened dictate the rest of my life, just like I hadn't let what happened with Blake define me or how I lived in the months after.

The sound of Kash's Harley echoed in the cul-de-sac, and Trip jumped off the couch to wait by the door for him to come in. I sat up when I heard him unlock the door, and the smile fell from my face when I noticed his careful expression.

"Hey, Rach. You have a good day?"

"I did. Are you okay? Something bad happen at work?"

"No, work was pretty calm. But I do need to talk to you."

My body instantly tensed up as I waited for what was coming next. We'd been doing so well these last three weeks, so what was wrong now? Did this have to do with why he still refused to actually kiss me? Was I not getting better fast enough for him?

"Stop overthinking, I can see you freaking out already. I got called in to talk to Chief today, and I'm fine. My job is still safe, but he gave me something . . . and I'm about to give it to you."

"Uh, okay?" That so hadn't been where I thought that was about to go. I pulled my legs up on the couch to rest my chin on my knees, and waited until he got comfortable next to me.

"If you don't want to see this, let me know, and I'll make sure you don't see it again. But, uh, well, they recovered this from your room at the house." He held out the journal Trent had bought me, and my throat constricted as I reached out for it. "Before I give it back to you, I need you to know that I read it. I read the entire thing. Are you okay with that?"

"Yes, yeah of course I am. A lot of it was to you anyway, that's fine." I grabbed for it again, and he grabbed my hand instead, holding the journal away from me. I looked up at him, my face scrunched in confusion. "Why—"

"There's something else. Something I'm positive you didn't know about, and something I almost didn't see myself. I read it also, and if you want to read it alone, I understand. Just know that I'm here for you, and you can talk to me about whatever you need to after reading it . . . okay?"

"I don't . . . I don't understand. Okay? I guess?" *Why does he look so unsure of himself all of a sudden?*

"Trent wrote you something in the back, Rachel. Do you want to read it?"

Trent wrote to me. He wrote to me! Not a day had gone by that I hadn't thought about him, and what may be happening to him. And not a day had gone by that I hadn't thanked God for him . . . for keeping me safe. Despite our last day together, and my confusion about my feelings for him, I still knew without a doubt that I wasn't, and never had been, in love with him. He was my friend, and I owed him my life. I was still dealing with the guilt that he'd done all he'd promised, and I couldn't keep my promises to him, but I knew that would take time to get past.

Looking up at Kash, I finally nodded my head and grabbed for the journal again. "I want to, but don't leave me alone."

"I won't, sweetheart."

My chest ached when the blood-smeared pages came into view as Kash flipped to the last page in the journal while it sat in my hands. *This had to have been done that last night . . . why hadn't he told me?* Looking up at Kash, I saw his eyes were on me and were full of nothing but understanding as he waited patiently for me. No jealousy. No insecurity. Just compassion as I gripped his hand like a lifeline and looked back down onto the page.

Rachel—

Is it twisted that I want to thank you for the time I've had with you? You've been nothing short of amazing throughout all of this, and I'm thankful for every moment. I know I've avoided answering you before, but I want to tell you why I stole you away in the first place.

It had nothing to do with you, but everything to do with the men you're associated with. They're good men, never doubt that; but by doing their job, and putting assholes like the leaders of my crew in prison, they put their lives on the line. And when you came into the picture, it put you in my hands.

We were going to use you as bait to get the leaders out, and it was my job to watch you . . . and eventually take you. Watching over you once you were here in this house had never been part of the plan, but after the four months of watching you day in and day out, I couldn't leave you to fend for yourself here. As you've come to find out, I would do anything to keep you safe, and I won't stop until I get you out of here.

What will happen after tonight, I'm already prepared for and know I deserve. But I want . . . no, <u>need</u> you to know, I never wanted this life. I would have done anything to stay away from it, and even more to get out of it. Sometimes we just don't have a choice.

Because of who I am, and what I've done, I never thought I was meant to find love. Thank you for unintentionally showing me how wrong I was. Even though your heart belongs to him, loving you—even in secret—has changed my life. And if I die tomorrow, I'll consider myself lucky to be able to die loving you.

Trent Cruz

I read his words three times before I finally shut the journal and fell into Kash's arms. No tears came, but there was a soul-deep ache for my friend.

I hated the way he viewed himself, and his self-worth. As I had so many times over the last couple weeks, I wished he'd had another chance at life, one far away from all he had ever known. But to continue wishing he'd been given that chance wouldn't change a thing. Everything in me wanted to visit him, and slap him across the face with the journal before throwing my arms around him, and hugging him tight. But with all that Kash and I were working toward right now, visiting Trent would just set us back. Maybe one day Kash and I would be in a place where I could visit Trent, but that time wasn't now. I needed to keep moving on with my life with Kash, and, for now, I just needed to be thankful for everything Trent had done for me.

"You okay?"

I breathed in the cinnamon scent that clung to Kash from the gum he was always chewing, and fell deeper into his chest. "I will be."

Kissing the top of my head, he leaned back so he was lying against the arm of the couch and I was on top of him, as he had so many times before, and waited a few minutes before asking, "Did you want to talk about it?"

"There's not a lot to say. I feel bad for him, but know there's nothing I can do. If anyone in that house was tortured, it was him. He hated who he was, and what he had become; he honestly didn't see a way to get out of it, though. He has very dark eyes, but they're really descriptive. It wasn't hard to see how the years in the gang tormented him every day. All I've wanted for him was for that torture to go away."

"Like he said in the letter, sometimes they don't have a choice, Rachel. I don't know why he was in it in the first place, but sometimes you're recruited whether you want to be or not. Sometimes it's about your blood family, and sometimes it's because of a crime you've done. But to get out, Rach, it's practically impossible to get out."

I stilled against his chest, and he hurried to continue.

"I'm not telling you to upset you more. I'm just letting you know he was probably living the way he was in order to stay alive. From what you've told me, and from his letter, I'm sure you're right, sweetheart. I'm sure he's not a bad person deep down."

"He really isn't," I unnecessarily argued in Trent's defense.

Kash's lips pressed down against my head, and he kept them there as he said, "I know. How could he be? He kept you safe and was trying to bring you back to me."

I looked up into his gray eyes and searched them before asking, "So you believe me now? You don't hate him anymore?"

"Well, he *did* admit in that letter that he was in love with you. You can't expect me to really be okay with any man loving you." His mouth curled up on one side in a smirk before his expression went back to serious. "But I do respect him, and I am thankful for him. It's hard, knowing that he took you and he was the cause of that month from hell. Knowing that he was most likely forced into gang life, and that he *was* forced into doing what he did, I understand that all too well. Mason and I had to do a lot we aren't proud of. There are some things that you still don't know, and if you ever want to, I'll tell you. But you have to be prepared for what you might find out . . . We had to live with them, and live like them. So because of that time in my life, I understand him in a sense, but only to an extent.

"What Mason and I did was for the betterment of the city, and while we had to do bad things, we were doing it with the knowledge that those men were all about to go away for a very long time and wouldn't be able to hurt anyone else again. With Trent, he didn't have the satisfaction in the end that he was still helping people, until he met you. So I guess to answer your question, no, I don't hate him. I can't hate him because I understand him too well. There are some things that I wish hadn't happened, but they did, and we're moving on from them."

I let my fingers run over the muscles of his chest and shoulders before making their way up to hold his face in my hands. I couldn't figure out if I wanted to smile or cry because I was so in love with this man, and so thankful for him. Instead I just continued to stare at him and finally whispered, "There are times when you know exactly what to say, and your words leave me speechless."

"I've been known to make good speeches on Wednesdays."

I huffed and grabbed a chunk of his hair before pulling on it. "Way to kill the mood, and it's Thursday, you ass."

His face remained serious as he said, "I've been known to make good speeches on Thursdays."

Rolling my eyes, I started to push off the couch, but his arms caged in around my back and brought me back onto his chest.

"There are still times when I stop dead in my tracks when I see you, and wonder how you're mine. You're beautiful; and your fire for life, and strength after everything you've been through, amazes me. So if anyone leaves the other speechless, it's you."

My heart pounded in my chest and a smile broke across my face. I couldn't have contained it even if I wanted to. "I love you, Logan Kash Ryan, and I'm so thankful for you."

"Ditto, Sour Patch."

I closed my eyes, shook my head, and laughed softly at his breathy words. Funny how I still hated that nickname, but my heart fluttered every time he said it. I hadn't forgotten the longing to hear him say it again while I was with Trent, because I knew hearing him say it meant seeing him again. And I knew that no matter how ridiculous it was, I would never complain about it again.

"Rachel, open your eyes."

As soon as my eyes fell on his, he sat up and pressed his lips to mine for the first time since my second morning back home. A high-pitched moan rose up the back of my throat before I relaxed into his body and returned the long-awaited kiss that he'd saved for the perfect moment.

His lips moved slowly against mine, and soon his tongue was parting my mouth and teasing my own. A collective sigh filled the silent space between us, and his full lips tilted up in a smile before he captured my mouth again. I moved my legs so I was straddling his hips, and dug my knees into the couch as I deepened the kiss. My hands wove their way through his messy hair to hold his face to mine, and his hands on my back trailed down my body until they landed on my hips to press our bodies closer together.

Kash placed openmouthed kisses down my jaw and throat, and I let my head fall back as I rocked against him. Goose bumps covered my skin and the softest of moans sounded in my chest at the friction I'd been craving. I rocked over where he was straining against his jeans, and my eyes rolled back when he gently bit down on my throat.

"Kash . . ."

He released my hips and grabbed my cheeks to bring my lips

down to his again, and I sat up and reached in between us, grabbing at the buckle on his belt. I'd just gotten it undone, and was grabbing for the button when his hands wrapped around my wrists and moved them above our heads.

"Why—"

"Just this for now." He let go of my hands and pushed me back an inch so he could look in my eyes. "Trust me, I want every part of you. But with what we've had to overcome the last few weeks, I'm not going to rush that. Just like we didn't rush anything else."

Some small part of me could understand what he was saying, but I was wearing the thinnest cotton shorts known to man, and with each ragged breath in, I was slowly losing the last bit of control I had.

"Rachel, I'm saying the words . . . but if you don't get off me soon, I'm not going to be following through with them."

I looked directly into his eyes and ground my body against his, and the sexiest growl I've ever heard from him left his lips. "Then don't follow through."

"Sonofabitch," he whispered through gritted teeth and his fingers flexed against the skin between my shirt and shorts. "Rach, no. I— Shit." He sat us up and gently pushed me back so I was no longer on his lap. "Rachel, you still shut yourself in the closet when you change; and when I start to do the same, you leave the room. I don't want you to force yourself to change that now, but I know you're not ready yet, and that's okay."

Sitting back, I pulled my knees up to my chest and stopped immediately after my head began shaking. *Oh God, I do shut the door.* "I just, I never had privacy . . ."

"Rachel, I get it. It's fine, but just trust me to know when you're ready again, okay?"

Looking back into his stormy gray eyes, I gave him a small smile and nodded. "All right."

He kissed me hard and rested his forehead against mine. "But now I need to go take a *really* cold shower. So I'll be back . . . in a while."

I laughed and snuck in another kiss before pushing him away. "Go, I'll make pancakes."

He stopped midstep and turned to face me. "You're perfect."

"I know."

His eyes slowly ran over the length of my body when I stretched out on the couch, and I watched as his eyes got hooded, an unmistakable desire hitting them.

"Shower, Kash."

"Right . . . uh, I'll be back."

I waited for a few minutes before letting my fingers run over the hardwood until they hit the used journal. Picking it up, I opened the cover and carefully worked back the binding until I felt the paper hidden inside. I never had gotten around to telling Kash about this in my entries to him. By the time I'd felt like I was in danger again, I couldn't get to my journal. Unfolding the paper, I let my eyes fall over the tear-stained letter before shutting the journal, placing it on the coffee table, and leaving the note on top.

Day 1 with journal

Kash—

If you've found this, and I'm with you, then you know that I love you, and let me take this time to remind you that I will love you with everything that I am for the rest of our lives. I hope that

*by now I'm getting tired of hearing the name Sour Patch again,
but, please, don't ever stop calling me that. No matter how much
I say I hate it, it reminds me of when we first met, and I love those
memories.*

*I hope we're already fighting again. Couples are afraid to fight
with each other, but fighting with you is one of the things I miss
the most. You drive me crazy, and I know you push my buttons
on purpose, but you also don't put up with my bullshit, and that's
one of the many reasons I fell in love with you.*

*Knowing you, I'm probably making you pancakes as you read
this. And I guarantee you I'm already tired of those, but I'll continue to make them as long as I can continue eating your green
Sour Patch Kids.*

*But . . . if you're finding this, and I'm gone, please know that
I loved you fiercely up until the very end. I know you did everything to try and find me, don't blame yourself for any of this,
because I don't blame you. Take care of Trip, and take care of
yourself. Don't be afraid to fall in love again, I can't stand to think
of you spending the rest of your life alone. Love her as much as
you've loved me, and I pray the woman knows how lucky she is
to have a man like you by her side.*

*. . . I know you, Kash; you come in and save the day at the last
minute . . . so I'll be here, waiting for you at the "last minute."
But no matter what happens, Logan Kash Ryan, you're still my
hero.*

> *I love you.*
> *Always.*
> *—Rachel*

21

Rachel

I WAS MIXING THE BATTER for pancakes when Kash strode back into the living room. He smiled devilishly at me as his eyes slid over to the coffee table and then did a double take. Looking back over to me with a raised brow, I answered his silent question the same way. I simply shrugged, dropped my eyes, and kept stirring. When I heard the sound of rustling paper, I looked up under my eyelashes and held my breath as he read my first—and what I'd been afraid would end up being my last—letter to him.

So many different emotions played over his face as he read it. His lips tilted up in a soft smile at first, and slowly grew larger until he huffed a laugh and his eyes flicked up to me quickly. But just as soon as they were back, all humor left his handsome face, and his forehead tightened seconds before he began sucking on his lip ring. Suddenly his mouth popped open and he slowly looked back up at me, his gray eyes glassy with tears. With a slight shake of his head, he forced his eyes back down to the paper and finished reading the letter.

I knew when he had finished, because even though his head was somewhat bent over the letter, his eyes weren't focused on the paper. He stood there for what felt like hours before he let the letter fall from his fingers to the table and walked over to me.

Reaching over, he unplugged the griddle and grabbed the batter before turning to put it in the fridge.

"Let me make this, you need to eat."

"I'll live." His voice was low and rough as he reached for my hand and towed me to the bedroom. He called for Trip to follow us and waited until he was in the room before shutting the door and taking me to the bed. Sitting me down on the edge of it, he began pacing back and forth with his hands on his hips.

"I'd kept it hidden in the binding, do you—"

"Rachel," he said, cutting me off. Abruptly he'd stopped pacing and placed a hand on each side of me, his face directly in front of me. "I refuse to take care of myself alone. You take care of me, and I'll take care of you, and together we'll take care of Trip."

"Okay . . ."

"And don't *ever* tell me again to love another woman the way I have loved you, and will always love you. There is no way you could have expected me to move on after you."

"You say that now, but you don't know how you would have felt in a few years."

He grabbed my face in his hands and his voice shook as he shouted, "I don't give a shit! I know I don't know how I would feel in that situation, there's no way to know that. But I know that no matter what happens in our lives, if you were taken from me for good, there would never be anyone else like you. There would never be anyone else I could love the way I love you."

"Kash, okay. I'm sorry," I whispered and brushed the tips of my fingers against the angry set of his face. Something in my touch broke him, because a pained cry burst from his chest at the same time heavy tears fell down his cheeks.

He dropped to his knees on the floor and pressed his head against my stomach, his hands gripping my back as he cried into my lap. "I've come too close to losing you too many times," he forced out. "I will do *anything* to keep you by my side for the rest of my life." Looking up at me, I felt helpless staring back at his broken expression. "Knowing that you even had to consider me moving on with someone else because you might die, *kills* me. I hate that you went through that, and I hate that you prepared yourself for that."

"Okay, but I'm—" My voice gave out and I had to clear my throat. "I'm here, we're together."

"I'm not letting you go, Rachel, for anything. It's you and me. Always, got it?"

I nodded, unable to respond, and his head dropped back against my stomach as another sob ripped through him. I'd only ever seen Kash begin to cry twice. Usually when he was upset, he got angry. So to see him break like this was absolutely breaking my heart. I kept one hand holding his head in my lap, and ran the other over his back. The muscles bunched and shuddered beneath my fingertips as he let everything out.

As he let everything *go*.

I could only imagine that this went so much deeper than what had been written in the letter, and what it had signified. This was all the lies, this was Blake, this was the months apart, and this was the torture that Kash had gone through while I'd been kidnapped.

Kash eventually climbed onto the bed with me, and he pulled me close after his tears had subsided and his breathing had evened out. For countless minutes after, we lay there, staring into each other's eyes . . . not saying anything. One of his hands cupped my cheek as dark gray eyes tried to convey a pain to me that I just couldn't understand.

I didn't know all that Kash had been through in his time as an undercover. I didn't know what it was like to be the one *looking* for your significant other . . . just as he didn't know what it was like to lose both your parents, be tortured by a man you'd grown up with, or be the one that was waiting to be found. Our pains and fears were so different that I didn't know if we would ever fully understand the depth of the pain that the other had experienced. And yet, at the same time, I knew him, and he knew me . . . we knew when the other was terrified, or upset, and we would always be there for each other to help the other through whatever was happening at that time.

So although I couldn't understand the grief he'd gone through that had caused this breakdown, I was here for him as he worked through it, just the same as he'd always had been there for me.

I KNOCKED ON THE LARGE DOOR and fumbled with the armful of food as I waited for Marcy to open the door. It was the Fourth of July, and while all of Kash's family was going to be coming to his parents' house, Kash wouldn't be here until later tonight. He and Mason were on call today and had been called in two hours ago . . . surprise, surprise. I needed him here; I hadn't seen his extended family since before I'd been taken. And while I hadn't had an issue with any member of his family, I hadn't felt comfortable with them . . . but that could have probably had something to do with the fact that everyone seemed to keep bringing up my mom and dad. I'd ended up breaking down that night and was afraid of questions that might come up today.

After the emotionally draining night we'd had last night with Kash's breakdown, I didn't think I was up for one of my own. And then Kash had been so weird today . . . like he was worried about something. The way he'd kissed me right before he'd left for work had left me feeling uneasy, but I'd finally decided he was probably just as worried about me going to this party without him as I was.

"Hi, sweet girl!" Marcy said when she opened the door. "Oh, let me help you with all that. Gosh, we could have made a few trips out to the car, you didn't have to bring it all in at once."

I transferred some of the bags and food into her arms, and kicked the door shut behind me as I followed her inside.

"It's so good to see you getting out more, and I'm glad you wanted to come over early! You know I love our girl time."

My chin was holding some of the boxes down, so I had to wait until I reached the counter to answer her. But as soon as I relieved my arms of everything with a large exhale, I turned to hug Marcy and took a deep breath. "I know, it's like I was still keeping myself locked up by not leaving the house." I began taking things out of the bags and setting them on the counter, or putting them away in the fridge and freezer. "Hey, Marcy, I was wanting to talk to you about something."

She stopped what she was doing and eyed me curiously for a moment. "Is it something we should be sitting down for . . . or maybe not setting up for the party tonight?"

I laughed awkwardly and tossed the package of paper plates I was holding down on the counter. "Neither . . . I think. I'm not sure." Rolling my eyes, I leaned on the counter on my forearms and just started talking. "Kash and I were supposed to have gotten married a week ago tomorrow. Neither of us said a word about it when the day came and went, because at the time, well we were working through a lot at the time. And I think for both of us, it was hard thinking that it was another thing that had changed in our lives, or wasn't going the way we had planned, because of what happened."

"He told us you overheard the conversation the night you came back. I hope you don't think he doesn't want to marry you, Rachel. He was confused and hurt, but he—"

"No, I don't think he *doesn't* want to marry me. I mean, I did . . . but, I don't anymore." I pressed the tips of my fingers into my temple and shook my head. "He and I already went through that, I understand all that now. But what I'm getting at today . . . is that I was kind of hoping you would help me. I think he's waiting for me. Waiting for me to be ready, waiting for me to bring it up, just waiting for me to let him know I'm ready to move forward with our lives again."

Marcy's lips kept tilting up like she was trying to contain her smile, but she wasn't saying anything yet.

"Will you help me think of a fun way to tell him I'm ready?"

"Yes! Yes, yes, of course I will!"

"Okay!" I straightened up and drummed my hands on the granite countertop. "I want some ideas from you, but I was wondering . . . while I was gone, did you ever go pick up my wedding dress, and do you have it here?"

Marcy's face lit up with a massive smile before she turned and took off, leaving the kitchen.

I'll take that as a yes to both.

We spent the next few hours thinking up ideas and taking pictures, running back to the store to use the one-hour print, and then back to my house to set them up. Kash wouldn't be going back there between then and the party anyway, so he wouldn't see it until we got home that night.

By the time we got back to Richard and Marcy's, we were running around, trying to set up for the party and getting all the food ready. I had so much adrenaline running through me that the setup seemed to fly by, and by the time Kash's extended family began showing up, I was already wanting it to be over. I was anxious to get Kash back to our place and see his reaction.

After an hour and a half of the party and Kash's fun-loving family—which had been graciously avoiding asking questions about my time away—my desire to get back home and my need to see Kash's reaction . . . all faded away.

Kash walked into the living room, and after searching for me, he walked over to me with purpose, and the most scorching gaze I've ever seen from him as his eyes raked slowly over my body. Wrapping an arm around my waist, he pulled me close and pressed his lips firmly to mine for long seconds before giving me another quick kiss and leaning back.

"Well, hi," I said breathily. For a second I wondered if he *had* gone back to the house and had already seen everything. But I still felt light-headed from what should have been a simple kiss, so I focused on breathing normally and the feel of his heart racing beneath my palm.

He toyed with his lip ring as he studied me. "I have something for you, sweetheart."

"Do you now?"

"I do. You wanna come outside with me for a minute?"

I eyed him and asked softly, "Do you really have something for me outside, or is this your attempt to save me from your thousands of cousins?"

A loud, awkward laugh left him, and he kissed my forehead as he grabbed my hand. "Uh . . . you just need to see this."

Vague. I let him lead me outside and smiled when I saw Mason standing out on the front lawn. "Wow, you're giving me Mason? I'm pretty sure this is the best gift ever."

Kash stopped walking and growled, and Mason burst out laughing. Elbowing Kash's side, I urged him to keep walking, and rolled my eyes when he wouldn't. "Oh, you know I'm joking. Show me whatever it is you brought me out here for."

"Mase?" Kash prompted softly.

Mason pulled out his phone and made a call. As he did, Kash turned me toward him and brought me in for a lingering kiss.

"If you need anything, we'll be right inside, okay?"

I pulled back and looked back and forth between him and Mason. Both wore matching looks of understanding mixed with fear. "Wait, what? Why are you leaving?"

"Trust me on this," he crooned and ran a soothing hand up and down my back. "I need you to know, Rachel. No matter what happens, I just want you to be happy."

"Happy? Kash, what's going on?"

"Just know that I'll always love you."

As soon as he released me, Mason picked me up in a big hug before setting me back down and following Kash into the house. Leaving me out in the dark alone. There were dozens of people just inside the house, and tons of other houses on the street, but I suddenly felt very alone and terrified.

I didn't understand Kash's cryptic words. And now I was second-guessing the way he'd been acting this morning before he'd left.

My body stilled when I heard someone walking up the grass behind me, and when I turned to see who they'd left me with, I understood why Kash had taken me away from everyone. Because as soon as I saw him, I burst into tears and ran up to him, launching myself at his large frame.

Trent caught me easily, and held me close to him for long minutes before releasing me.

"What are you doing here?" I asked through my tears and grabbed his arm. I needed to know that he was actually here, that I wasn't dreaming all this. "How did you get out of prison?"

"With your testimony, and with the help of your fiancé, his partner, and their chief, the charges against me were dropped."

A sob broke free from my throat, and I slapped a hand over my mouth as I continued to cry. Trent reached forward and cupped my cheeks in his hands, his thumbs brushing away tears. "Are you serious?" I finally managed to ask.

"Yeah, Rach, I am."

"I'm so happy for you! This is all I wanted for you . . . to have another chance at life." Throwing myself into his arms again, I wrapped my arms around his waist and cried into his chest. "God, Trent, I'm so happy for you. I've missed you." Remembering last night, I stepped back and tried to glare at him. It didn't hold. "I wish I had my journal, I really wanted to slap you with it."

His eyebrows pinched together, and he laughed softly. "Why?"

"I read your letter, Trent." Understanding flashed through his eyes, and I continued. "I hate that you view yourself like that. You deserve everything, you *have* to know that. You deserve an amazing life, you deserve an amazing woman. And now you get to experience all that!"

Trent licked his lips, and his dark eyes searched my face, before looking up at the house. "That's something I'm supposed to talk to you about, Rachel." With a deep breath, he turned and pointed at a black SUV parked on the street. "That car is about to take me to my new life. I don't know where I'm going, but Kash arranged for me to be completely protected when I got out."

I frowned as I tried to understand what he was saying. "You're going into witness protection?" I asked on a whisper. When he nodded, I felt like crying again. "Why can't you stay here?"

"It's not safe for me here, and you know that."

I did know that. But now that he was out, I wasn't ready for him to be gone . . . I knew when he left this time, there would be no seeing him again. I wasn't ready for that.

"I shouldn't have been allowed to come see you at all, but that was another thing Kash arranged." Taking my hand, he pulled me close and looked at me for a long moment before speaking again. "Rachel, he's giving you the choice to go with me."

My brow furrowed, and I shook my head in confusion. "I don't—like Kash and me go with you?" When Trent shook his head slowly, I grasped what he was saying . . . and my chest tore open. "Just me," I stated. It was no longer a question.

Some small part of me hated that Kash was still questioning my feelings. My mind kept screaming, *He just said last night he wouldn't let me go for anything!* But, if I was being honest with myself, I knew that wasn't what this was . . . he was making sure *I* knew what I wanted . . . and giving me the option to have that.

I loved him. I loved how selfless he was.

"Trent, I will never forget you, and I will never forget everything you did for me. I owe you everything. I know how you feel for me; to be honest, I've had an idea since before I got out of that house. And I'm so sorry if I ever led you to believe anything different, but I love Kash. I'll always love Kash."

Trent cleared his throat, and looked away quickly when his dark eyes filled with pain.

"I hate that after finally knowing you're safe from those men, you're going to be leaving me. But I've only ever viewed you as a friend, and protector. I'm sorry."

"I know. I knew even when I kissed you that your heart belonged to him. I've never loved anyone until I met you, Rachel, and I don't think I'll ever get over you."

"You'll find someone, I know you will. You have so much to give to someone, and whoever she ends up being, she will be incredibly lucky to have you."

He watched me for a few seconds with a sad smile as he cupped one side of my face. "I'll never forget you."

More tears fell down my cheeks as I admitted, "I'll never forget you either, Trent Cruz."

With a kiss to my forehead, he released me and took a few steps back and looked over at the dark SUV. A few seconds later, it started up and pulled into the driveway, and soon Kash and Mason were joining us.

Turning to look at my fiancé, I noticed the tears in his eyes as he stepped up to me. "No matter what you decide, I'll always love you. I just want you to be happy."

Grabbing his hand, I stepped close and placed a hand over his racing heart. "You are what makes me happy. I can't live a life that you're not in, Kash. I've already tried it once before, it didn't work."

A deep exhale left him, and he pulled me close to his body.

"Thank you," Trent's deep voice sounded behind us, and I turned to see him holding out his hand, which Kash shook. "For everything. What you did means more to me than you could possibly know. So . . . just, thank you."

Kash nodded and released his hand. "Take care of yourself."

After Trent and Mason exchanged a similar good-bye, he turned back to me, and much like I had earlier, I launched myself at him. Hugging him tight once, I stepped back and wiped away tears.

"Never forget you, Rachel," he said again, and I gave him a shaky smile.

"I'll miss you."

And then he was turning and walking toward the SUV, and driving out of my life forever. My chest ached at a different kind of loss for Trent than the one I'd been dreading, but I was so happy for him.

Once the taillights had faded, I turned to Kash and punched his shoulder. "You can't get rid of me that easy! Don't you understand that I love—"

His lips cut me off, and I moaned into his mouth as we shared a kiss to rival every other one we've ever shared.

"I had to give you the choice," he whispered when we pulled away, our breathing ragged.

"I know, and I love you that much more for it. But it's you, Kash. Like I told Trent, it will *always* be you."

He kissed me thoroughly again and repeated his words from last night. "It's you and me, Rach. Always."

"Always," I agreed.

Kash

MASON STOPPED TALKING and nudged my arm before nodding toward Rachel. Turning my head, I looked down at her lying in between my legs asleep. One of her arms was hanging over my leg, and her body was still turned toward Mason from when they'd been talking.

After everything that had gone down tonight, she was still here . . . with me.

Mason and I had been working on getting Trent into witness protection for almost two weeks. Because of his background, and his involvement with Rachel's kidnapping, it took time to get his charges dropped so we could move forward. But I'd known for a few days now that it could happen at any time. I'd wondered how to tell Rachel, and a part of me was afraid of how she'd react if she knew I'd done it all behind her back and Trent was already gone, but then Chief had given me the journal.

Before Rachel had been taken, I'd vowed to always look for signs that she was struggling with something . . . anything. It wasn't hard to know she'd been hurting since she came back, and after reading Trent's letter to her, I'd known what I had to do. As much as it killed me to think of Rachel choosing him, and as much as we'd progressed, I knew he was constantly on her mind. And though I didn't doubt her feelings for me, I couldn't deny that there was something for him too. It was the last thing I wanted, but if it was what she needed, I'd known I had to be strong for both of us . . . and let her go.

I'd almost changed my mind after reading Rachel's letter to me, though. I'd woken up early this morning and watched her while she slept, and was trying to convince myself that I would gladly take her anger if it meant keeping her. But then I'd gotten the call that Trent was getting out, and going to be leaving today, and I knew in that moment that just because I wanted her for myself, didn't mean I could take away her option to choose.

Mason had had to stop me from walking back outside the entire time Trent and Rachel were out there, and when he'd gotten the call from the detective that would be taking him to a waiting jet, everything switched. I wasn't ready to know what her answer was, but Mason had practically shoved me out of the house and walked me down the lawn to go talk with them.

I'd been afraid her constant thinking about him had been a sign that even with her denying them, she had stronger feelings for Trent than maybe she even knew. It wasn't until I asked her not long after he left that she told me she knew he would die in jail, and she'd been struggling with the guilt that she couldn't help Trent like he'd helped her.

Ever since, Rachel hadn't left my side, and this was the most I'd seen her smile in the three weeks since I'd gotten her back. And I was so damn glad for it.

I smiled at Mason and bent to kiss the top of Rachel's head. "You ready to call it a night?" I asked Mason quietly.

"Yeah, it's late." Just as I began to move, he asked, "Did you think we'd be here?"

"What do you mean?"

"A little over a year ago we were in a bare apartment in Texas, and you were telling me not to go bang the hot neighbor because it would mess with the case. I'd called your bullshit that day. I told you if either of us had to be careful, it was you. And now, here we are. Back in Florida, you're engaged to Rachel; Candice will be here in a week, and we'll be in the same place we've always been."

I laughed at the memory, but something close to terror still slid through my veins at how right Mason and I had both been. Our jobs had been dangerous, for Rachel. We'd been proven right too many times already on that. I wrapped my arms around her waist and pulled her body closer to mine when Mason repeated himself.

"So that day, did you think we'd be here?"

"You know, I think even then I did. I knew there was something different about her from that first moment. I knew it, and you could see it too. I couldn't see *this* at that time . . . but I think I knew we would be here."

"I'm happy for you, man. You deserve this. You deserve her."

The corners of my mouth tilted up in a smile and I looked back over at him. "Thanks, Mase."

He just nodded before clearing his throat. "Let's get her to a bed, yeah?"

"Yeah." I pressed my lips to Rachel's neck and spoke softly in her ear as I let my fingers trail up and down her arms. "Wake up, Sour Patch. Time to go home."

She groaned and turned in my arms, but went right back to sleep.

"Rachel, come on, babe. Let me take you home."

Her only response was to nod her head and let it drop into

my chest. I laughed and scooped her up before getting my legs beneath me, and standing with her in my arms.

"See you tomorrow?" I asked Mason. At his nod, I walked over to where my parents were talking with some of their friends and said good night before getting Rachel into my truck.

About halfway home, Rachel slowly started waking up.

"Where we going?" she mumbled.

"We're going home, you fell asleep after all the fireworks."

"Hmm . . . yeah. Where's my Jeep?"

"Still at my parents. We'll go get it tomorrow."

"Yeah . . . 'kay."

I smiled and squeezed her knee. She just groaned and swatted at my hand.

"Oh my God!" she yelled suddenly, and sat straight up.

"What?" I'd been slowing for a red light but slammed on the breaks at her outburst.

"I have something for you at home! I almost forgot!"

"You . . . Jesus Christ, Rach! I thought we were about to get hit or I was about to run over someone!"

"Well, get over it! We didn't. Come on light, turn green, go, go, go, come on we have to get home!" She bounced up and down in her seat and looked at the empty streets around us.

"Fuck, swear to God you're going to be the death of me."

She stopped bouncing and turned to face me. Her dark blue eyes narrowed as she crossed her arms. "Keep being an asshole and you won't get it."

I couldn't help it. A massive smile crossed my face. I put the car in park, unclicked her seat belt, and pulled her across the seat to me. "There's my fiery girl. You're such a cute little monster when you wake up."

"I will cut you."

"I said *cute*."

"I hate you."

"Liar." I kissed her hard and trailed my hand in between her thighs, smiling more when her gasp filled the cab of my truck. She opened her legs wider and I moved my hand up her shorts; and just as my fingers touched the edge of her underwear, I removed my hand and pushed her back into her seat. "Put your seat belt on, the light's green."

"Kash!" she gritted as she angrily yanked at her seat belt.

I smiled and put the car in drive before taking off again. "There's a word . . . I'm having trouble remembering it right now. Oh, right. *Frustration* . . . Enjoy that."

She looked back at the road for a second, turned her body toward me, and released her seat belt. "Maybe you should learn to enjoy frustration." Leaning over, she grabbed for the buckle on my belt and I grabbed her wrists in one of my hands.

"I don't think so. This doesn't go both ways, Sour Patch."

"It's about to."

"Don't make me handcuff you." When she didn't make another move toward me and didn't say anything, I glanced over at her and I swear to God my jeans shrunk when I saw the heat in her eyes and the way she was torturing her bottom lip. "Shit. Put your seat belt back on."

We need to get home. Now.

I pressed harder on the gas and forced myself to focus on the road rather than imagining Rachel cuffed. *Jesus. Drive, Kash!* By the time we got home, I didn't have the patience to wait for her to get out of her own door. As soon as she had her seat belt off, I grabbed her and dragged her across the seat. Bending low, I pressed my shoulder into her stomach and lifted her out, kicking the door shut behind me.

"Your shoulders are still super uncomfortable!" She laughed, but didn't make any other complaints as I unlocked the door and walked inside with her. "Okay, now put me down and go let Trip inside."

I set her on the ground but slammed her body back to mine and captured her lips with my own. A soft needy sound rose up in her throat, and she gripped my shirt in her hands, trying to bring our bodies even closer together.

"Kash," she moaned.

"Go get in the bedroom. I'll be right behind you."

She took off for the back of the house after I released her, and I locked the front door before going to the back to let Trip inside and feed him. Taking off my badge, gun, holster, and belt, I laid them on the breakfast table before putting the handcuffs in my back pocket and heading down the hall. I pulled my shirt off my body and let it fall to the ground, and awkwardly tore off my boots and socks without stopping my advance.

Turning the corner in the hall, I stopped dead when I saw things hanging from the ceiling between the bedroom doorway and me.

"What the hell?"

Flipping on the hall light, I walked closer to the pictures hanging and slowly turning from the air blowing through the vents in the ceiling. As I grabbed the first one, my eyes widened and my breathing quickened.

It was a picture of an August calendar, and Rachel's engagement ring was circling August 23. Next to her ring, on that day, was a question mark.

Stepping quickly to the next picture, I stopped it from spinning and looked at the words *I LOVE YOU ALWAYS* in Scrabble tiles. In between the YOU and ALWAYS was a green Sour Patch Kid.

Letting go, I walked to the last picture and stopped it from spinning. It was the upper left half of Rachel's back, and she was looking behind her, and down. Most of her back was bare, but she looked like she was wearing a dress. I flipped the picture over and read the words I had seen as the picture spun.

I'M READY FOR YOU TO SEE THE REST OF THIS DRESS. I'M READY FOR FOREVER WITH YOU. YOU'VE TAKEN MY HEART; CAN I TAKE YOUR LAST NAME?

Walking into the bedroom I turned and found her worrying her bottom lip as she leaned against the wall. Her blue eyes bounced between mine, and as she took in my expression, her face relaxed and a soft smile spread across her face. Stepping up to her, I cupped her cheeks and kissed her softly twice.

"You're back."

Her brow scrunched together, and she opened her mouth to respond before it shut and her eyes widened. "I'm sorry it took so long."

"You have nothing to be sorry for, you took exactly how long you needed. I'm just so damn glad I have you back again," I told her as I kissed her again. I pressed my knee between her legs and swallowed her soft whimper.

"Was I just proposed to?" I asked teasingly.

She laughed loudly and pushed against my stomach. "No. I just—I don't know, I wanted . . ."

"You don't have to explain, Rachel. I got it, and August twenty-third sounds perfect."

"Yeah?" she asked, her eyes brightening.

"Yeah, and I can't wait to see the rest of that dress either." I released her cheeks and slowly lifted her arms above her head, grasping her wrists in one of my hands before pinning them to the wall. "But I'm going to love taking it off you even more." Trailing my lips along her neck, I loved how her head rolled to the side when my teeth grazed the soft skin there. "Every night while you were gone"—I whispered along her jaw—"I dreamed about you coming back to me. I dreamed about taking you in my arms, and pressing your body to mine. About moving against you . . . with you."

Wrapping my other arm around her waist, I turned us and walked toward the bed. Just before her legs hit the mattress, I stopped walking and slowly took off her clothes, bra, and underwear. Her hands fell to my jeans, but I didn't let her get past unbuttoning them before I pushed her back and lowered her onto the bed. I watched as she sensually crawled toward the center, and lay back, waiting for me. She was so damn beautiful.

Crawling over her, I covered her body with mine and gave her the faintest of kisses before going back to teasing her. "I dreamed of the way you would look as you fell apart beneath me." I smiled and kissed her collarbone when a shiver worked its way through her body. "The way you would tremble around me. How you would gasp out my name as you came." I gently raked my teeth over one nipple and looked up to see her watching me, her blue eyes full of want.

"But most of all," I said as I brought myself back up so I could look directly in her eyes. "I dreamed that when I woke up the next morning, you would be there." She brought a hand up to cup my cheek, and I kissed her lips softly once before asking, "Can I love you, Rachel?"

"Please," she begged and wrapped her long legs around my back, bringing me down to rest against her.

I moved against her twice and smiled when a breathy exhale left her, and her head fell back onto the mattress. I loved seeing her like this, and I'd missed it. With a kiss to her throat, I slowly made my way down her body and ran my fingers along her folds to her opening before leaning forward and tasting her again for the first time in way too long.

"Kash, oh God," she whispered, her body already writhing against the bed.

She came fast, and hard, as I worked her with one hand and tortured her relentlessly with my tongue. I hadn't had enough, but I needed her—needed her around me, needed to be moving inside her. I shed my jeans and boxers quickly and positioned myself over her again. She grabbed the back of my neck and met my mouth hungrily as I lowered myself to her. I groaned and stopped moving completely when I was finally inside her, just to enjoy the feel of her again. And when I moved . . . Christ, I didn't know how long I was going to be able to last.

Kissing her hard once, I began teasing her mouth with my tongue and about died when she bit down on my lip ring and smiled coyly as she gave it a little tug. Fuck, I'd missed that.

"I don't like it when you tease," she whispered when she released the metal, and I couldn't help but smile.

"Liar."

But I didn't have the patience for teasing her any more than I already had. Keeping one hand firmly fisted in her hair, I lifted myself higher with the other and quickened my pace. Her eyes fluttered shut and a needy moan sounded in the back of her throat seconds before she urged me to go harder.

"I need you to go with me," I said into her ear as I reached down between us and began teasing her sensitive bud.

"Oh God—"

"With me, Rach."

I locked my jaw and pushed into her harder as she tightened around me until I felt her shudder and come undone, causing me to fall over the edge with her. A low growl tore from my chest as my thrusts slowed to a stop and I shakily lowered myself onto her body. Kissing her softly, I rolled us to the side and let out a labored breath.

"Christ."

"Ditto," she said breathily and kissed my bare chest.

I laughed softly and put my fingers under her chin, raising her head back so I could look into her dark blue eyes. "In a little over a month, you *will* be my wife. This time . . . nothing is stopping us. I'm going to marry you, I'm going to make you mine, and I'm going to keep you by my side for the rest of my life."

She took a deep breath in through her nose, and a smile crossed her face when she released it. "I can't wait, Logan. I'm so ready for my life with you. I just hope it's really boring compared to this first year."

I laughed hard and kissed her forehead. "Me too, Sour Patch. Me too."

22

Rachel

IT'S FUNNY, the things that used to seem so big—so hard to deal with—suddenly seemed like nothing more than having a bad hair day. The situations that threatened to ruin my life now seemed like nothing more than stubbing my toe on the coffee table. The events that seemed impossible to get through without my parents, all seemed as easy as stepping over a microscopic hurdle.

I was ready for anything. I was prepared for whatever difficult or unexpected situations might arise for Kash and me, or our families. I trusted Kash to take care of us, and was finally opening up to the family that I *did* have. My parents were gone, that would always be hard . . . I would always wish they were here. But I had to give my future in-laws and Candice's family the chance to be there for me in their place.

As soon as I saw Candice and Maddie walk into the café, I closed my journal and put it away in my bag. Kash had surprised me with Candice almost a week after Trent had gone into witness protection, and it couldn't have been more perfectly timed. She'd been able to help plan the wedding, and when she wasn't with Mason, we were spending almost all our time together.

I was glad Maddie and Candice were getting along now. There was a little over a week left until the wedding, and it had been tense between Candice and Maddie when they first met. Maddie wasn't exactly thrilled that Candice was one of her brother's fuck buddies. Who could blame her, though?

"Hey, Rach!" Candice bounced her way over to me and hugged me hard. "Guessing you've been here a while, since you were writing when we walked in?"

I nodded and hugged Maddie after Candice handed me off. "Just an hour or two . . . or four."

"Mason said you've been writing a lot more since you came back."

"Wait"—I shot Candice a confused look—"how would Mason know that I've been writ— Oh . . ."

"Kash," we all said together and shrugged.

"It was worse at first, I'd gotten so used to having nothing really to do all day except write, so it was hard to get off that. But I'm getting back to a point where it's normal. Well, uh, for me anyway. I just had a lot to say today."

Maddie raised an eyebrow and crossed her arms over her chest as Candice's green eyes widened. "Oh really? Do tell!"

I laughed and sat back down in my chair. "Nothing to tell, just all the wedding stuff with it being a week away. I figured with your parents, Eli, and his fiancée, Paisley, coming in a couple days, I wouldn't have a lot of time to write then. So I'm getting it out now."

Candice frowned. "Well, that was boring."

Maddie laughed out loud before covering her mouth and looking around. "Uh . . . I'm gonna go get some coffee. Want anything?"

"I'm coming with," Candice said as she picked up her purse, which she'd dropped on the chair earlier. "Rach?"

"No, I'm good." When Candice eyed me curiously, I lifted an arm out to the side before letting it flop back onto my lap. "What? I already had something earlier. I'm good. I won't sleep if I have anything else."

"Whatevs." She turned, and the ever-present bounce in her step was even more prominent than usual as she made her way to where Maddie was in line.

I wanted to tell her she didn't need any more caffeine or she'd turn into a squirrel on speed, but that would probably just make her get an extra shot of espresso in her drink. So I kept my mouth shut.

"You okay, Rachel?" Maddie asked when they sat down at the table again. "You look like something's bothering you."

"No, I'm fine."

Candice snorted and crossed her legs as she took a sip of her drink. "*Fine. Good.* Keep using those words, Rachie, see if I start believing you."

"But I really am!" I said on a laugh. "I'm having a great morning, I'm excited to see everyone, I'm ready for this week to be over so I can get married. I really am fine."

She studied me for a few moments before pointing at me with her coffee cup. "Are you and Kash okay? Are you having sex regularly?"

Maddie made a gagging noise and my lips twitched as I fought back a smile.

"Yeah, we're fi—"

"Don't say that word!" Candice nearly shrieked in the café.

The three of us looked around at the people giving us odd looks, and I nodded awkwardly at the old woman closest to us, who no doubt had heard Candice's questions.

"Okay, Candice, we're incredible. Is that better?"

She didn't reply to my question before asking her next one. "And the sex?"

"Oh God," Maddie said, and made another gagging sound.

"Uh, Candice, that's *so* not your business . . . but I know you love sharing yours. So how are you and Mason doing in bed?"

"Shit." Maddie didn't need to fake the gag that time. She looked like she was about to throw up what little she'd already drank. "Can we stop talking about them? Just . . . gross."

"She's being weird," Candice hissed to Maddie.

"Yeah, caught that. Don't need to talk about my brother and Kash right in front of me, though. Jesus, let's just get to what we were going to talk to her about."

I raised an eyebrow and waited.

"Oh, yeah!" Candice set down her cup and did her little happy clap. "Totally forgot. Rachel, which one of us do you love more?"

"Uh . . ."

"That's not fair, you've known her longer."

Candice looked at Maddie with an expectant expression. "Exactly."

"What is this about?" I asked.

"We've been fighting over who gets to babysit Trip while you and Kash are on your honeymoon," Maddie responded. "I think

I should get to, since I'm the one who led you to him. Technically I led Kash, and then you. But, you know."

"And *I* think *I* should get to, since I don't actually live here and won't be able to see him whenever I want, once I go back to California. Well, and because I've known you forever." Candice sat back in her chair and crossed her arms like she knew she'd won.

"Hmm, both valid arguments," I mused.

"What? Hers didn't even make sense!" Candice said at the same time Maddie laughed. "She's using her time of knowing you as her argument. So not fair."

"I was being sarcastic. Both those arguments sucked," I said and drummed my fingers on the table. "You both sounded ridiculous, but why don't you both babysit him? One day at Mason's, the next at Maddie's."

"Well—" Candice began, but I cut her off.

"We're not even really going anywhere. We'll still be in town, and it's only two days. So this way you each have a day, and we'll pick him up from Maddie's on our way home."

"I guess that works." Maddie sniffed as though she wasn't happy with it.

"I don't see how neither of you came up with that before. You really thought you had to have me choose who got him for that time?"

Despite Maddie's hate for Candice the first few weeks, they were just alike. Well, if you didn't count Maddie being Candice's opposite in looks. Their personalities were the same, and as I sat there watching them defend their arguments to each other, I realized that must have been why Maddie and I had gotten along so well when I first moved here.

My phone vibrated and I looked down at it.

> KASH:
> *I'm home, where's my Sour Patch?*

> *Café with Maddie and Candice. I'm coming home now.*

"I'm tired, guys. I think I'm going to go home and take a nap."

Candice gasped and Maddie snapped before pointing at me. "I knew there was something wrong."

I paused from putting my phone in my purse and eyed them curiously. "Meaning . . . ?"

"You're tired," Candice answered for her.

"Yeah, and . . . ?"

"So there was something wrong. You weren't normal Rachie."

I laughed and stood up. "You're both just crazy today. Maybe I'm being perfectly normal, and there's something wrong with you." Before they could say anything, I blew a loud, ridiculous kiss toward them and hurried to the door. "Love you two, see you later."

I sped the entire way home and practically ran into the house. Launching myself at Kash, I kissed him hard and wrapped my legs around his waist as he laughed against my mouth.

"Well, hello. I missed you too."

I smiled and kissed him again. "Take me to bed, babe."

He pulled back to study my face. "Bed? It's four in the afternoon. Do you still feel sick from this morning?"

Curling my hands around the back of his neck, I pressed against him harder and watched his gray eyes become hooded. Grinning to myself when he began walking us toward the bedroom, I thought about Candice and Maddie as I said, "Nope. I'm just fine."

Kash

I HANDED BOTH ELI AND MASON A BEER, and my eyes scanned the crowded house, looking for my fiancée. We were getting married tomorrow, and instead of having a normal rehearsal dinner, Rachel had wanted my entire family here so they could spend time getting to know the Jenkins family. I knew it was a good idea, but I'd found out right after the rehearsal that the girls were stealing Rachel from me tonight and having a girls' night at Maddie's apartment so I couldn't see her at all before the ceremony tomorrow. And now I was wishing this wasn't as big as it was, because other than a few chaste kisses, she and I hadn't gotten to talk since before the rehearsal.

My eyes finally fell on her, and I tried to rein in the caveman instinct that rose up inside me. She was holding Shea again. I swear to God there was something about that woman holding a baby that just set my blood on fire and made me want to get her pregnant immediately. I hadn't brought up the baby topic since the night we'd fought about it before Rachel had been taken. With how upset she'd gotten, I'd been afraid to, but God, the more I saw her holding my cousin's daughter, the more I wanted this for us.

I knew we were both still young. Rachel was twenty-two and I was twenty-six, but not only did I have a career that constantly reminded me of how fragile life was . . . my entire time with Rachel had been one giant reminder that everything you knew could be gone in a second.

Seeing death as often as Mason and I did already made us both the kind of guys that didn't wait for what we knew we wanted . . . and a family with Rachel wasn't an exception. But until she was at a place where she wanted a family too, I would keep my mouth shut about it.

Rachel laughed at something Eli's fiancée, Paisley, was saying to the group of girls; and like I had just a few seconds ago, she began scanning the room. As soon as her eyes met mine, her body relaxed and she smiled softly.

I said I'd keep my mouth shut. But when had I ever been the kind of guy to make sure Rachel wasn't pushed out of her comfort zone?

Lifting the beer up to my lips, I raised my eyebrows and let my eyes slide over to Shea before meeting Rachel's again. She just shook her head at me, but that smile never left her face, and her eyes didn't leave mine until Mrs. Jenkins captured her attention.

Well. That hadn't been the *"fuck you, Kash"* I'd been expecting.

Eli called my name, and I reluctantly dragged my eyes from Rachel to look at him. "Come talk to me," he said softly and walked toward the back door.

"Dude," Mason said, and put a hand on my chest to stop me from walking. "This is where he kills you. Don't go out there."

"What? Mase, you're so fucking dumb."

"I'm not joking, give me a minute, I'll go around the front and to the side. I'll be waiting just in case he tries anything. The dude hates both of us."

I snorted and took another long pull of my beer. "I wonder why, Mason? You're having sex with his sister, and I'm sleeping with someone he views as a sister. There's no way he doesn't know that. Rachel lives with me, and Candice has been living with you;

and neither of you are worried about how public you are with it. At least I'm in love with, and about to marry, the sister that I'm sleeping with. You're just fucking Candice because you're bored."

"Don't make it seem like he hates me more! Homeboy is staying in my apartment tonight. I want to be able to sleep without being afraid he's going to kill me."

I rolled my eyes and pushed past him.

"He has to hate you more, you didn't even ask him if you could marry Rachel."

I turned and threw my arms out. "I asked Candice and Eli's dad, George! Well, I asked him before I asked her to marry me the second time."

Mason pointed his beer bottle at me and I shook my head.

"So fucking dumb, Mase."

Walking to the door, I turned and made sure Rachel was still distracted with all the women in the corner before slipping outside and finding Eli. He stayed silent as I walked over to him and still didn't say anything for another minute after I was in front of him.

Maybe I should have had Mason wait on the side of the house.

"Uh, what's going on, man?"

Rachel had told me about how Eli had helped her through the time after her parents had died. I remember her telling me how he had this quiet intensity that soothed her. But right now, I had to wonder how it soothed her, because I was noticing the quiet intensity . . . and it was scaring the shit out of me.

"You know I love Rachel just the same as I do Candice. I've grown up having her there, she's always been a part of the family, just like Candice was a part of hers before her parents died."

I nodded and waited for him to continue.

"There was so much that happened in her life, and no matter how much she'll tell you about it, you'll never be able to fully understand what she went through. But she's so damn strong, I've always been in awe of her and the way she's made it through some of the shittiest situations. I have no doubt that a lesser woman wouldn't have made it through what Rachel has in the last year. Sometimes I wish that she wasn't as strong, that she would need to come back to California so that I could make sure she was okay there. But then she wouldn't be Rachel, and she wouldn't have you.

"I wanted to hate you when she was kidnapped. I just needed someone to blame, like I'd blamed Blake for all that happened last year. But I know I can't, I know you did everything you could to find her. When Mason, Candice, and I all talked last year while the two of you were separated, I found out a lot about how you blamed yourself; and I can only imagine you did the same this time. Despite the reasoning for their taking her, it wasn't your fault, and I hope you know that. I want to say I'm sorry for the way I treated you, and above all, I want to thank you for bringing her back."

"I, uh, well I'm glad to know you don't blame me or hate me, but you don't have to thank me. You know I would do anything for her."

He took a long drink from his beer and wiped the back of his hand across his mouth. "I do kind of hate you. You've taken one of my sisters away from us and all the way across the United States . . . but there is no other guy I would trust with her life, and with her heart."

Before I could respond, I felt, before I heard, Mason coming up behind me. "Mason . . ."

Eli eyed me, clearly confused, and his eyes widened when he must have finally seen Mason.

"Years of undercover work together," I answered Eli's unspoken question. "We couldn't sneak up on each other if we tried."

"Ahh . . . him I don't like."

"What the hell did I do?" Mason asked as he joined us.

Eli looked up at him, and even though he was a good head shorter than Mason, I fully understood why Mason looked like he wanted to go hide again.

"Stay away from my sister," Eli said in clear warning before walking toward the house.

"Is he for real?" Mason asked.

I just shrugged and drained my beer. "You should totally sleep with one eye open tonight."

"Son of a bitch," Mason groaned and followed me back into the house.

23

Rachel

I TOOK DEEP BREATHS IN AND OUT as I studied myself in the mirror. I wasn't nervous about the lifelong commitment I was about to make. I wasn't worried that Kash was getting cold feet. I just felt like I was going to hurl.

The parents had already come in and given hugs before going to take their seats, and Candice and Maddie were behind me in light gray dresses, talking animatedly as they checked each other's hair. We'd spent the morning relaxing at Maddie's apartment and watching movies as Mason's mom did our hair. Then we'd run over to the hotel where Kash and I were going to be staying the next three nights, and checked in before leaving our bags in the room, so he and I could go straight there after the reception without having to worry about anything.

The day had been nice, and easy, and just what I'd needed. But right now, I needed a bathroom. I needed a toilet, and I needed the girls to leave the room.

"Easy," a deep voice commanded when I turned to find the bathroom. Eli's hands gripped my wrists, and his thumbs pushed into the pulse point on each one. "Breathe in and out."

I let the intensity that always seemed to roll off Eli pour over me, and surprisingly, the whole thumbs-on-the-inside-of-my-wrists was really helping.

"Good girl, keep breathing. Deep breaths," he said, and suddenly he was at my ear. "You okay, sis?"

"I'm good, just got a little light-headed there for a minute."

"You sure you weren't about to take off out of here? You need to get away, just tell me. You don't have to do this if you don't want to."

I laughed shakily as more of the nausea left me. "No, nothing like that, Eli. I'm ready for this . . . so ready. I really just felt sick for a second."

"Are you okay now?"

"Yeah, much better. Thank you."

He kissed my forehead and stepped back. "Let me see if I can go find a Sprite or something around here. But you should get dressed soon. It's supposed to start in ten minutes. Unless, you know, you need to run."

"Eli, no." I pushed him back and smiled at him. "I would love the drink, but not an escape."

"All right, I'm just making sure." He winked and slipped out the door.

He was back in no time, and I sipped at the carbonated drink slowly to help with the last of my uneasy stomach. As I did that,

I stepped out of the loose clothes I'd been wearing, and Candice and Maddie helped me get ready.

I loved the lingerie we'd found a few weeks ago, and I couldn't wait to see Kash's reaction to it. I just didn't know if I was going to last in the white corset that was covered in lace if my nausea came back. We'd just gotten on my favorite part of the lingerie when there was a knock at the door.

"Is Rachel decent?"

"No!" we all shouted back at Eli.

"Okay, then someone catch this, I'm not going to look where I throw."

"Wait! What are you throwing?" Maddie shrieked and turned toward the door just in time to catch the package sailing through the air.

"Crackers."

"Why crackers?"

"Rachel said she didn't feel good. Make her eat those," he said, and then shut the door.

Maddie eyed me through the mirror, and I'm sure Candice would have been doing the same if her face wasn't near my butt at the moment. "You don't feel good?"

"I just got a little queasy earlier, I'm feeling better, but those will help." Oh Lord how those would help. "It's just nerves."

She handed me the little package and I quickly opened it up and popped the first one in my mouth just as Candice jumped up.

"Okay, it looks perfect!"

I turned in the mirror and smiled at my underwear. "So cute," I said through a mouthful of cracker.

It was a white thong with a thick band of see-through material, ruffled on each side of the band, and a mix of cotton and lace for the rest. But the best part was the satin bow that covered anything that shouldn't be seen. Thong or not, I still wanted it covered.

The girls made me finish the crackers before they helped me put on my dress, and as soon as I saw the completed look, with my hair in a low bun off to the side just as Maddie had done it in the dress shop, an overwhelming feeling of peace settled over me.

My mom would have loved to see me like this, my dad would have been proud of the man I had chosen. And now, I couldn't wait to get to that ceremony so I could finally become his wife.

"Naked or not, we're coming in," Mason said as the door flung open.

"Mason!" Candice and Maddie scolded him, but he just shrugged.

"You look beautiful, Rach," Eli said and pulled me close to whisper in my ear. "And I really don't like that guy."

"He's harmless, I promise."

"Uh-huh." He gave Mason a look as he stepped back, and Mason stepped in to get his hug.

"For real, the dude hates me!" Mason hissed at me, and I couldn't help but laugh. "But you look gorgeous, Kash is gonna die when he sees you."

"Thanks, Mase."

I watched Eli and Mason leave with Maddie and Candice, and then turned to see Candice's dad, George, tearing up.

"No, no! Don't cry. Because if you cry, then I'm going to cry, and I so can't cry right now, George!"

"I know, I'm not crying. It's just dust or something." He wiped at his eyes and held his arms out for me. "So proud of you, baby girl. Your mom and dad would've been too."

I hugged him hard before releasing him. "I know they would have."

He blinked a few times before turning away. "Damn dust."

"Yeah . . . damn dust," I said and fanned at my face so the tears gathering in my eyes wouldn't spill over.

"Come on, let's go do this before the dust ruins my makeup."

My head jerked back and I looked at him before busting out laughing. "Oh yeah, *your* makeup would definitely be all over the place."

Putting my arm in the crook of his, I let him lead me out of the room, and we waited until it was our turn to walk down the aisle. The second my eyes found Kash standing at the end of it, my body warmed and my heart took off. He was standing there in black slacks, a light gray button-up shirt with the sleeves rolled up to his forearms, and a black suit vest. He looked amazing, but what I couldn't take my eyes off was the huge smile that spread across his face as he watched us walk toward him.

The second my hand touched his, I took what felt like my first real breath since we'd left the dinner last night.

I was where I belonged. He was my home. And I was so ready to marry him.

Kash

PUSHING RACHEL UP AGAINST THE DOOR to our hotel suite, I captured her mouth with mine before making my way down her neck as I searched for the key in my pocket. Once I found it, I fumbled with sliding it in the lock twice before giving up and kissing her again. She laughed against my lips and grabbed the keycard out of my hand, and turned her body around so she could attempt to get us in the room.

I wrapped my arms around her waist and pulled her against my chest as I made a trail of openmouthed kisses across her shoulder and up the back of her neck. A soft giggle bubbled up from her chest but quickly cut off when I grabbed her hips and pressed my hard-on against her. She shivered in my arms and her head dropped back onto my shoulder just as the light turned green and the door unlocked. I quickly pushed us inside and let the door slam shut behind us as I hurried her to the bed, my hands going to the zipper on her dress as we walked. It'd been getting to the point where I would have taken my wife right there in the hall, not caring about anyone that may have seen us.

As soon as the zipper stopped its downward path, I stopped ours toward the bed and pulled away from Rachel so I could watch the dress fall from her body. The material pooled around her bare feet, and I took my time letting my eyes reverse the path the dress had just taken. I groaned when I saw her lingerie.

"Rachel Ryan, you're trying to kill me before we can consummate this marriage."

"I love that name."

"Not as much as I do."

Turning her around to unhook the top, I stopped breathing for heated moments as my hands gripped her hips and slid down her ass.

"This"—I nibbled on her earlobe and ran my fingers over the see-through, barely there material—"is the fucking sexiest thing I've ever seen."

White lace and a ribbon. Who knew?

"Kash," she said on a breath and pressed herself against me. "If you don't take it off soon, I will."

"So impatient," I teased, but even as I did, my hands went to the dozens of hooks on the top. With each unclasped hook, I placed a kiss on her shoulder, the back of her neck, the sensitive spot behind her ear . . . and with each one, her knees shook a little more.

When I was finished, I tossed the material aside before pressing her back to my chest again. Grabbing her chin, I tilted her head back and up so I could capture her mouth with mine as I palmed her heavy breasts. She groaned into my mouth and arched her back as her hands covered mine. She slowly removed my hands and guided them down her waist to rest against her stomach, and released me to run her hands through my hair.

Letting the tips of my fingers trail over her stomach and across her hips, I brought them down to the barely there underwear and let my thumbs run inside the band. Taking a step away from her, my lips curved up in a smile at her disappointed groan, but I just pushed her closer to the bed and pressed a hand down at the top of her back. Realization hit her blue eyes, and she bit down on her bottom lip as she rested her forearms on the bed.

I ran my hands over her bare ass again before grabbing the filmy material and slowly sliding it off her hips, down her thighs, and to the ground. She stepped out of her underwear, and I kissed my way back up her legs, biting softly on the back of her thigh just before I stood.

She was so fucking beautiful—so perfect—and she was finally mine.

I'd just barely begun teasing her, and was sliding one finger inside her when she suddenly turned and sat on the bed, facing me. Her hands reached the top of my pants and made quick work of unbuttoning and unzipping them, before dragging them, and my boxers, down. She grabbed my length in her hands, running them up and down a few times before she brought that sweet as sin mouth to me.

I groaned, and my hand automatically flew to her head, but I forced it to stay relaxed instead of gripping her hair. I tried to watch her as she built me up faster than I ever have before, but my head kept dropping back, my eyes rolling to the back of my head as she teased me with her lips and tongue, and her hand continued to work me. She moaned around me, and I about lost it right then when I looked back down and saw her touching herself too. Holy shit.

Pushing her away from me felt like an impossible task, but I needed to. I'd planned this whole night out in my head, I was going to go slow with her, I was going to spend hours worshipping her body. But as the night had progressed, we'd both gotten needier, and there'd been no way to start slow once we were finally here. But I wasn't about to do this.

A confused look crossed her face when I grabbed the hand she was using on herself and moved it away. "This is my job, sweetheart."

"Okay, but I wasn't done with you," she argued and started to reach for me again, but I stopped her hands.

I quickly took off the suit-vest and shirt, and threw them across the room as I kicked off my shoes and stepped out of my pants. "Rachel," I said and laid her down on the bed before crawling on top of her. "I know you weren't, and Christ, that was the hottest thing I've ever seen you do," I told her and pulled her toward the center of the bed. "But the first time we get off as a married couple, isn't about to be in your mouth, and you're sure as shit not about to do it yourself."

She opened her mouth to respond, but I thrust inside of her, and all that came out was a throaty mix of pleasure and pain. I rocked against her faster and harder, and my head dropped to the crook of her neck, a low growl emanating from my chest when her nails dug into my back. I'd always loved the noises she made whenever we were together, but the sounds she was making now had me gripping the comforter and pushing into her harder as she began tightening around me. I clenched my teeth as I held off my own orgasm, but the second her body began trembling around me, I let go with a roar I'd tried to suppress by biting down on her shoulder.

We were both breathing hard as I slowed my movements inside her, and after I pulled out, I collapsed onto my back, pulling her onto my chest. Neither of us said anything as we lay there. I don't know what it'd been, if it was the fact that Rachel was finally mine, if it was the erotic noises she'd been making, or if it was something more . . . but that had been the most intense sexual experience we'd ever had. And all I could do, now that it was over, was lie there and hold her close to me.

"I have something to give you," she said, breaking the silence sometime later.

Tilting her head back, I kissed her lips softly and pulled back to look in her eyes. "What else could you give me? You've given me you, I don't need anything else."

She smiled and her blue eyes glossed with tears. The look on her face and in her eyes contradicted her next words. "You're such a cheesy nerd."

"Then why are you about to cry?" I sat up on the bed and pulled her with me. "What's wrong?"

"Nothing," she assured me and fanned at her eyes. "I'm just being ridiculous again. I'm happy . . . happy we're here, happy we're married, happy that . . . I'm just happy."

I laughed softly, but unease still gripped at my chest when a lone tear slipped down her cheek. "Rachel . . ."

"No, really, I'm fine." She laughed and wiped at her cheek. "God, I feel stupid. But I really do have something for you. Will you wait here?"

My eyebrows pulled together as I studied her face. "Depends on where you're going."

"I'm just going into the bathroom, I'll be right back, I swear." She grabbed my face in both her hands and kissed me soundly before pulling away from me and hopping off the bed.

I watched as she grabbed a large purse that had already been in the room and ran into the bathroom. It felt wrong to sit here and not go after her. I had no idea why she'd started to cry. Had I hurt her?

When a couple minutes had passed, and she hadn't come back into the room, I slid off the bed and walked to where I'd left my clothes. Grabbing my boxer briefs, I pulled them on, and was about to head to the bathroom when the door opened and she walked out. She had on a pair of lacy black underwear, and a matching bra, but I couldn't focus on her body for long.

She was worrying her bottom lip and had her hands behind her as she took slow steps toward me.

"Rachel?"

"I told you to wait there."

I looked back at the bed, then back to her. "I was worried about you. We get married and have mind-blowing sex, and then you start to cry and lock yourself in the bathroom."

With a deadpan expression, she shook her head. "You're making it out like I was really upset. I told you I was fine, I was just being ridiculous."

"Rach—"

"Now sit back down on the bed." When I didn't move, she widened her eyes at me. "Sit, or I'm not giving this to you."

"Fine, I'm sitting."

She took a deep breath in, and her eyes began watering again as the most beautiful smile crossed her face.

And I was so damn lost.

"This is my wedding present to you," she said and handed me a thick, black envelope.

I took it from her hand, and kept my eyes on her face as long as I could before finally glancing down at the card. *What the hell?* There were stickers of Thing 1 and Thing 2 from *The Cat in the Hat* on the front of the envelope. I turned it around to open it, and read the words in silver lettering: "*Will be here March 2015.*"

What . . . is this supposed to be like Disney on Ice? Is there a Dr. Seuss on Ice now too? Did she get us tickets or something? That's just . . . odd. Keep smiling. Keep smiling. I so wasn't smiling. I was confused as hell. I flicked a glance at her, and the beautifully heartbreaking expression she still wore made me even more confused as I opened the envelope and pulled out the small stack of pictures, and pieces of paper.

The first was a piece of paper that said: "*I hope you still want this . . .*" I slid it to the bottom of the pile and my heart skipped a beat before taking off when I saw the picture of Rachel holding my cousin's little baby, Shea.

My body felt hot and cold at the same time as I breathed deeply in and out while I sat there, staring at the picture. From the look of Shea's outfit, this had been taken on the Fourth of July, before I'd gotten there. Rachel looked beautiful holding her. She always looked beautiful, but I loved seeing her with Shea. And right now, I was doing everything to force myself not to think of this becoming my reality. *This could be about to go in a different direction, and I'm just jumping to the conclusion I've been wanting.*

With a shaky hand, I put the picture on the bottom of the pile, quickly followed by the paper that said: ". . . *because* this *is happening.*"

The next picture was of Rachel's upper body. She had a tight shirt on, and had flipped the bottom of the shirt up so her torso was showing. The same beautiful smile I was seeing on her face now would easily keep my attention on this picture if she hadn't been holding up her index and middle finger directly in front of her stomach.

I'd stopped breathing. That hot and cold feeling was getting more intense as the silence filled the air with a terrifying excitement. I looked up to see Rachel freely crying, her hands covering her mouth as her bright blue eyes still showed her happiness as she stared at me. Waiting for my reaction. But I couldn't figure out how to react, this had to be a dream. I'd wanted this; she hadn't. She wouldn't be this excited right now . . . right? Was this a trick, was I still not understanding what all this meant?

Somehow, even though I was sitting, I felt my legs weaken and knew I would have ended up on the floor just then if I'd been standing. My whole body felt weak, and at the same time, it felt like I was on top of the damn world.

My eyes left her face and hit her flat stomach. I tried to put the two together, whether I was still trying to understand what she was telling me, or if I was trying to confirm what I was sure I already knew . . . I really don't know. I gently brought one hand up to her stomach, and a flash of Rachel moving my hands to her stomach just half an hour ago as I'd been undressing her hit me. A huff left me as I realized she had been telling me even then.

"Rachel—" I shook my head in disbelief and looked up at her, a smile pulling at my lips.

"You missed one," she said and reached for the stack in my hand. Taking it from me, she removed the top picture and put it on the bottom before handing me back the pile. "There they"— she choked on a sob—"there they are."

"Oh my God." Any air that was left in my lungs left in a hard rush, and time stopped as I looked at the ultrasound picture. Two dark circles in the middle of a gray screen, and a little peanut shape in each circle. "This? These . . . they're . . . oh my God."

She laughed through her tears and pulled the pile from my hands to set it on the nightstand. Crawling on the bed to straddle my lap, she cupped my face in her hands and brought her forehead down to mine.

"This isn't a joke? This is for real? You're—we're . . . we're having twins? You're pregnant?" She'd barely had time to nod before I crushed my mouth to hers and kissed her like I needed her in order to breathe. "I love you . . . fuck, Rachel. I love you so damn much."

"I know, I know, I love you too," she said when I released her mouth again.

"When did this happen? How long have you known? How far along are you? Are you—are you okay? I know you didn't want this, but you seem so—"

She placed the tips of her fingers on my lips to stop my questions, and a knowing smile lit up her face again. I grabbed her wrist, kissed her fingers, and dropped her hand so I could run my knuckles over her stomach.

"I'm barely over nine weeks now, I just found out a week ago. With how everything happened after I came back, I wasn't paying attention, so I hadn't even noticed I'd missed a period. But I hadn't gotten back on my birth control from being gone, and when I tried, my doctor wanted to see me first. I saw her last Friday, and she asked about how long I'd been off it, why I'd been off it, and if you and I had been together since then. When she asked when my last cycle was, I couldn't remember one after the time when I'd been kidnapped, so she did a test to check before she put me on birth control again. It came back positive, and since I'd known it'd been a while from my last cycle, she did an ultrasound to measure the baby. And then there ended up being two . . ."

Tears started falling rapidly down Rachel's cheeks, but never once did her smile leave her face.

"She figured I was around eight weeks, and I picked up the journal Trent had bought me on my way to meet Candice and Maddie. It took a while, but I finally figured out the dates of when everything was, and after checking I'm guessing it happened the night of the Fourth of July. My doctor had been right, I was a little over eight weeks that day."

I shook my head and laughed softly as I glanced down at her flat stomach. "I still can't believe this. And you're okay? You seem happy."

"Being kidnapped and not knowing if I would ever see you again changed the way I thought about a lot of things. Including having children. It still would have been ideal if we could've had some time of just being us before all this happened, but I'm not scared of being a mom anymore. I'm not scared of going through all of this without my mom. We have so many people that are there for us, and I know they'll help." She kissed my lips softly and smiled against them. "And having you still look at me like you wanted to rip my clothes off in front of everyone when I was holding Shea the other night helped."

"Well, what can I say? You look good with a baby."

Rachel laughed loudly. "We'll see if you still feel that way when I'm the size of a whale."

"I will," I assured her.

"What about you? Are you okay? You still want this, now that it's going to be a reality?"

"More than anything," I told her as I pressed my lips to hers again.

Leaning back until I was lying on the bed, I rolled us over and hovered over her body. She dragged her hands through my hair and giggled when I bent low and kissed her stomach over and over.

"What does it feel like?"

"Nothing," she said on a laugh as her fingertips continued to trail across my head.

"You haven't really been sick, have you? I remember that day last week, but I can't think of anything else." I felt shitty for not noticing, if she had been. I should have picked up on this, shouldn't I?

"Not really. There's been times here and there, but from the horror stories I've heard, I don't have it bad at all."

I nodded and kissed her stomach again before reaching over to the nightstand. Grabbing the ultrasound picture, I laid it down on the bottom of her stomach and hopped off the bed, looking for my pants. After I found them, and took my phone out of the pocket, I walked back over to Rachel and opened up the camera app.

"What are you doing?"

"Letting everyone know about my present."

That soft smile was back, before her eyes went wide in horror. "No! I'm in my bra and underwear!"

"Calm down, Sour Patch. I'm not about to let anyone see the rest of you. You're mine, not theirs."

All that you could see in the picture was her torso and the ultrasound picture. As soon as she gave me the okay, I set up a text to go to Mason, Candice, Maddie, Eli, and all our parents. Above the picture I typed out: MY WEDDING PRESENT, and underneath, I did a twist on Rachel's words from the envelope: BABY RYAN 1 AND BABY RYAN 2 WILL BE HERE IN MARCH.

Once the message went through, I turned both our phones on silent and put them in my bag.

"What are you doing? You know they're all going to call us."

"Exactly," I said as I climbed on top of her again and moved the ultrasound picture to a safe place. "But right now it's our wedding night, and I'm not done celebrating with just you."

Epilogue

Two and a half years later . . .

Rachel

"Babe, do you have Kennedy?" I called as I went from room to room with Kira.

There is no way to keep track of twins that are running all over the place while you're trying to get ready to go somewhere. I swear, if she is getting in Trip's food again . . .

"Kash! Do you know—"

"Where this beautiful monster is?" he asked as he rounded the corner with Kennedy in his arms. She was missing her shirt.

I stopped and blew out a thankful breath that at least she was only missing an article of clothing instead of being completely naked, or covered in baby powder again like last time.

"Where's her shirt?"

He shrugged and held her up to blow a raspberry on her stomach. "I don't know. I was hoping you knew."

"I don't." I looked at Kira in my arms and shook my head as I smiled at her. "Your sister is crazy, absolutely crazy!"

Kira just smiled and set her head down on my shoulder as we began walking through the house, looking for Kennedy's shirt.

"Your daddy better be happy at least one of you is calm."

"What? Kennedy's just having a little fun."

I shot him a look. "She can't keep her clothes on. Are you going to keep saying that when she's sixteen and still doing the same thing?"

His face fell into a look of pure horror. "Oh no. No, no, no. That's it. You're going to homeschool them. Both of them! And they're not allowed near boys until they're thirty. And . . . and . . . and from now on, they only wear dresses. Ugly ones that are three sizes too big."

I laughed and leaned in to kiss Kennedy's big smile. "You take after your daddy. The crazies."

"I'm so serious, Rach. They're never allowed out in public without me."

"Yeah, okay."

"Don't act like that! You're the one that said she was going to be taking her clothes off when she was sixteen."

I rolled my eyes and pointed at the discarded shirt on the ground so he could bend down to pick it up. "She's not even two, calm down. I was just saying that so I could make a point. And I'm not homeschooling them, or making them wear ugly clothes, so you can work at getting over that right now."

He set Kennedy down and pulled her shirt back on before pointing at it. "You keep this on. Always. Even if boys tell you to take it off when you're older. You don't listen to—" He cut off and hung his head when Kennedy zoomed away again with Trip chasing after her.

"You'll have a lot of time to tell her that when she's older . . . when she'll understand it."

Looking up, he made a face at me before leaning forward and grabbing my hips. "I'm so glad you're going to be a boy," he said to my large stomach, and placed a kiss on it. Standing up, he pulled me as close as my stomach would allow and kissed me thoroughly until the shrill laugh of Kennedy filled the air.

"Naked baby." I pointed as she ran through the living room and into the kitchen. "You catch her and I'll finish getting Kira ready?"

"Oh, so *you* get the easy one tonight? Why?"

"Uh, yeah . . . because I'm Rachel."

Kash smiled and kissed me hard once more. "The last time we had this conversation, it ended in you slapping me. So I'm just gonna keep my mouth shut."

"Good choice."

He winked and took off after our crazy daughter. "Kennedy, clothes stay on, baby girl."

Once I had Kira ready, and we got Kennedy to keep her clothes on, we got all of us in the car to head over to Richard and Marcy's for their New Year's Eve party. Mason and his family were all going to be there along with some family friends, and I was ready for the time to hang out with everyone . . . and to have extra eyes to make sure Kennedy kept her clothes on.

We'd gone to California for Christmas, and while I wouldn't suggest flying with two toddlers, it was so worth it to see my family again. Candice was still being Candice. I'd figured she'd start settling down after college, but she didn't show any signs of stopping anytime soon. She was working at a physical therapy place, and loved her job . . . as well as half the men she worked with. But she was happy, she was enjoying her life the way she wanted to, and I was happy for her.

For the first time, I'd taken Kash and the girls to my parents' graves. I still wrote to them daily whenever the girls went down for a nap, and writing to them was still something that made me feel closer to them. But I'd wanted my family to be able to talk to them too. Not that the girls really said much that made sense yet, but I was happy we'd all gone, and knew it was something we would do when we visited California again.

Kash grabbed my hand, and pulled it toward him to kiss the inside of my palm when we were a couple minutes from his parents'. I smiled over at him and curled my hand around his to squeeze it, and his eyes flashed on my pale blue nails. Kissing them, he smirked at me before bringing our hands down to rest on the center console.

"I wonder what color he'll send this time."

I didn't have to look at his eyes to know there was no lingering doubt there. After Kash had given me the option to leave with Trent, and we'd talked about everything I'd been feeling, he seemed to understand how I viewed Trent. Nothing more than my protector, and friend. A month after Trent had left, I knew for sure that Kash was finally okay with him.

Every month, on the fourth, a small package was delivered to Kash at the police department. And every month, I was waiting anxiously for him to come home with it. It was always a bottle of nail polish with a card that only ever said two words. "I'm fine." The only time it ever changed was on the Fourth of July. Along with the polish, there would be a new journal for me, and somewhere in the middle would be a letter from him giving me more insight into his new life, without ever giving away his name, location, or job.

That first month, Kash had been confused but had finally pieced it together by the time his shift was ending. He'd read my journal from when I'd been kidnapped, and remembered everything Trent had bought me, and was honestly appreciative that Trent was—in a weird way—letting me know he was safe. I wished there was a way for me to thank him, but there was never a return address, and every month it was somehow sent from a different state. Besides, he was already risking a lot; it could put him in danger if we tried to get in touch with him. So I would be happy with my monthly gift from him. At least Kash and I could be happy for him and his new life, based on the two letters.

With a soft smile, I squeezed Kash's hand and said, "Few more days and we'll find out, I guess."

After putting the car in park, Kash looked at me seriously and whispered, "I've got fifty on orange."

"Silver," I whispered back. "And you're on."

He laughed and kissed me swiftly before getting out of the car. After we got Kennedy and Kira out of the car, we made our way inside the house, and everyone rushed over to take the girls.

"Oh, we haven't seen you in so long!" Marcy crooned at Kennedy as Richard took Kira.

"Mom, it's been a week and a half."

She leveled her signature glare at Kash, before smiling and raining kisses all over Kennedy's face. "Don't start with me, Logan. A week and a half is a long time to go without my favorite girls."

"Rachel!" Maddie screamed, and ran toward me.

Kash stepped in front of me and blocked my stomach. "Calm down, turbo."

Maddie rolled her eyes and pushed him aside as she bounced up and down on her toes, her left hand going in front of her face as she squealed.

"Oh my God! Congratulations!" I grabbed her hand and looked at the ring on her finger before pulling her in for a hug. "When did he ask?"

"Christmas!"

"Congrats, and nice rock, Aaron," I teased as I pulled Maddie's new fiancé in for a hug.

Like I hadn't known. I'd gone with him to pick out the ring.

"She loves it. Thank you," Aaron whispered into my ear, and I winked when he pulled back.

I listened to Maddie tell me all the details of the proposal as I accepted hugs from her parents and other family friends. After we'd said hello to everyone, Kash pulled me into his chest and ran his hands over my swollen belly, and I continued talking to Maddie as he talked to Aaron.

Maddie and I had grown incredibly close over the last couple years, and I was so happy to see her with Aaron. Too many guys had burned her before. Aaron had swooped in at the perfect time, and was beyond perfect for her. He was the biggest sweetheart I'd ever met; and though he seemed pretty calm for Maddie's over-excited personality, they balanced each other really well.

"Where's my brother?" she suddenly asked.

Kash shrugged. "I don't know, he said he'd be here. But I haven't seen him since before we left for California."

"I haven't seen him since before Aaron and I got engaged. He keeps saying he's busy, I want to show him my ring!"

Looking up at my husband, I nudged his stomach with my elbow. "Call him, babe."

Keeping one hand on my stomach, he pulled out his phone and brought up Mason's number.

Kash and Mason were still in the gang unit, and things were going as well as they could in that field. Mason was at our house more often than not and loved playing "Uncle Mase" to the girls. Like Candice, Kash and I had been hoping he'd settle down soon . . . but girls came and went from his apartment just as often as they always had.

"Mason's bringing a girl," Kash spoke directly into my ear so no one else could hear us.

Apparently I'd spoken too soon.

"Like . . . ?"

"Like a girlfriend."

"No way!" I hissed and looked up at him. Kash looked just as surprised as I felt.

A shriek filled the living room and I turned to see Kennedy running as fast as her little toddler legs would carry her.

"Jesus," I whispered and pointed. "Naked baby."

Kash laughed and kissed the back of my neck. "You are home-schooling the girls."

"Whatever you say, Kash." I winked and watched him take off after Kennedy.

Marcy walked up next to me and handed me Kennedy's forgotten clothes. "How do you keep that girl in these?"

"We haven't figured out a way yet. Where's Kira?"

"Sleeping in Rich's arms."

I turned until I spotted them, and smiled at my daughter and father-in-law. They were so cute together.

"Okay, well, I'm going to help Kash with Kennedy, be right back."

Taking the clothes from her, I walked through the halls until I heard Kennedy's belly laugh and found Kash blowing more raspberries on her stomach.

"I caught the monster."

"Your mom collected all her clothes."

After we got her dressed again, I lifted her onto my hip and walked out toward the living room. Marcy was waiting at the entrance of the hall and made grabby hands at Kennedy.

"Come back to Ya Ya, sweet girl, let's go hang out with Poppi and Kira."

Handing her over to Marcy, I giggled when Kash pulled us back into the hall and pressed us close as his mouth teased the sensitive spot behind my ear.

"I don't think so, mister."

"I can't help it . . . this is the one time we're not chasing after our girls and someone else is watching them. And, fuck, Rachel, you look so hot. Swear to God I'm keeping you pregnant all the time. We're going to have a football team."

I laughed and elbowed his stomach. "Whatever."

"Don't 'whatever' me, Sour Patch. You know you're sexy as hell."

I rolled my eyes and turned to kiss him before whispering against his lips, "Liar."

"Never."

He captured my lips and I moaned into his mouth when his tongue caressed mine.

"Naked baby!" Maddie called and I let my forehead drop onto Kash's chest.

"Homeschooling those girls, woman." He kissed me again before taking off after a squealing Kennedy.

I walked to the front of the hall and scooped up a tired-looking Kira as I enjoyed the view.

Maddie and Aaron were talking quietly in a corner. Close friends were gathered in clumps around the living room and kitchen—some talking to their group, others laughing at the circus that was my family. Richard and Mr. Gates were wiping back tears as they laughed over Mrs. Gates, Marcy, and Kash chasing after Kennedy and looking for her clothes. Soon Mason and this mystery girl would be here, and she would get the crash course in meeting everyone while we all individually interrogated her.

I loved my family, and I loved our life. Kash and I had gone through rough times at the beginning, but life was good and I prayed it would stay that way. There was never a dull moment— there were plenty of laughs, and plenty of happy and sad tears. He and I still fought like there was no tomorrow, and pancakes were made a few times a week . . . but we loved each other fiercely, and we helped each other through everything. Most importantly, there were never any lies.

Acknowledgments

As ALWAYS, a huge thank-you to my husband, Cory! You keep me sane, you don't make fun of me when I start crying, or screaming, about whatever my characters are doing. (Don't worry, I know you think I'm crazy, but I love that you hide those thoughts and just smile, like my reactions are completely normal!) And if it weren't for you, I'm pretty sure we would have starved by now. You're amazing, I love you!

A big, big thank-you to my editor, Tessa Woodward, and my agent, Kevan Lyon. You two mean the world to me, and I don't know what I would do if I didn't have you to talk to about my crazy—and sometimes really horrible—ideas for my books. Kevan, I love that you gag over Kash's lip ring, and, Tessa, I love that you stop me from trashing my books.

Kelly Elliott, um, I just love you. Plain and simple. What would I do without our weekly lunches? I love that I'm usually crying throughout most of our lunch from laughing so hard, and

I love that we rush to claim a name for one of our characters! Like I said, I just love you.

Amanda Stone! I love my Sef! There's no one else I can sit on the phone with for hours while talking about nothing . . . or just not talking at all, and I love that I can sit there and whine about something I just wrote, and you just tell me to get over it. I will always make sure you approve my posts before I post them. I will always make you pick out my teasers, even if you haven't read the book yet. And I will always send you snapshots of songs that we've listened to a thousand times, just to make you want to listen to it again. Love yewwww.

Jennifer L. Armentrout a.k.a. J Lynn (a.k.a. JL Armentrout when I start mixing your names together! Ha!). I love you and your hilariousness. I love our conversations and appreciate how honest you are with me when it comes to my work. You have no idea how much I love that you aren't afraid to tell me if something is awful, or demand that a certain character should get his own book. Watch out for the zombies in your backyard!

A.L. Jackson, Kristen Proby, and Rebecca Shea, thank you all for our daily sprints, which keep me motivated, and always start my writing day off with a bang! I love all of you! Kishes!

To all the authors, bloggers, and readers that support me, promote me, and pimp out cover reveals and teasers . . . I love you all so so much. You have no idea how much I appreciate each and every one of you!

Want more Molly McAdams?

Turn the page for an exciting
peek at *Capturing Peace*.

Available in e-book.

Prologue

Reagan

ALL THE AIR left my body in a hard rush. It felt like my stomach was on fire and simultaneously dropping . . . it felt like my heart was being torn from my chest.

No. No, I must have heard him wrong. He didn't just say that to me.

"W-what? Austin, what did you say?" My voice came out barely above a whisper.

Austin looked around us, the set of his face was hard, and so unlike anything I'd ever seen from him. You usually never saw him doing anything other than smiling. He was the quarterback of the Varsity football team, he was one of the most popular guys in our school. Everyone loved him and his easy-going—somewhat cocky—attitude. I loved him . . . he loved me. I knew he did, he couldn't be doing this to me.

Leaning in, his blue eyes darted around us again one last time before he whispered, "I said get rid of it."

One hand flew to my mouth to muffle the shocked cry that had just left me, the other went to my stomach. "No, don't say that to me." Tears streamed quickly down my face. I'd been afraid when I'd first realized I was pregnant; I kept telling myself all Austin needed was some time to get used to the idea. "I know we're young, but we can do this together, I know we can."

"Reagan, I'm not about to have a mother fucking kid at sixteen. Get rid of it."

My head shook back and forth slowly. "Austin—"

"I'm not gonna let you ruin both our futures. We have two and a half years of high school left, they were already scouting me this last season, Ray. Do you know how rare that is for a sophomore? Get. Rid. Of it."

"No!" I shouted and slapped at his hands when he reached for my arms. "No! I can't—I can't believe you'd even ask me to do something like that. I know it's scary, baby, I'm terrified. But we'll get through it together, I *need* you. I can't go through this alone."

"Reagan . . . I'm not asking you. I'm telling you. Get rid of it, or we're done."

Another choked sob tore through me, and my hands dropped down to my stomach.

"Jesus, will you stop?" he hissed, and pulled my hands back so they were at my side. "Everyone can hear you, and when you do shit like that, they're gonna figure out what's happening."

It was the end of the last day before winter break, there were only a handful of people still at the school, and none of them were near us. I'd been trying to figure out how to tell Austin, and hoped that he'd help me find a way to tell my parents over break. Hoped that the couple weeks from school we could spend figuring out a way to get through this together.

I'd been wrong.

I stood there, staring at his hardened features for a few minutes before backing away from his grasp. "I can't rid of the baby. I won't."

"You're screwing with your future, Ray, think about that. That thing,"—his nostrils flared, and lips curled as the word left him—"is not a damn baby yet. Last chance . . . I'm not going to tell you again."

He called our baby a thing. A thing!

I didn't know how far along I was since I didn't pay attention to my cycles that were never on time anyway. Something my family doctor said probably had to do with my dancing and cheerleading. I hadn't had any morning sickness; and it hadn't been until my cheer skirt stopped fitting, and the captain of our team told me I should start eating less, that I'd even thought I could be pregnant. By the time I'd gotten over the denial, gained the courage to even buy and take a test—or five—and gotten over the denial again, I was already sporting a small bump on my otherwise flat and toned stomach. A bump proving there was a life growing inside me . . . not a *thing*.

Squaring my shoulders, I ignored the tears still falling and my quivering chin, and looked directly into Austin's blue eyes. "I'm keeping the baby."

A look of shock crossed his face for all of two seconds before he was glaring at me again. "Just remember . . . you're the one that threw us away. You're the one ruining your life. Try to bring me down with you, and I'll say that thing isn't mine."

Locking my jaw, I refused to give him the satisfaction of seeing how much this was killing me. How much I wanted to beg him not to do this. Well, more than I'd already shown. I knew he was hoping his ultimatum would change my mind, and nothing could at this point.

His eyes searched mine for a few more seconds before he straightened with a huff. "Fuck it. Goodbye, Reagan."

I watched him walk away toward the parking lot, his head turning to each side to see who'd witnessed our conversation. Once his shiny black Camaro peeled out of the lot, I finally unlocked my knees and somehow made my way to my car.

I didn't remember the drive back to my house. I didn't remember climbing the stairs to my room. The next thing I knew, I was in my bathroom with my shirt pulled up, my yoga pants pushed down a little, and my hands were gently running over my stomach when a gasp sounded behind me.

My head snapped up before I whirled around to see my mom standing there. Even through my blurred vision from the tears, I could see her standing there, her head shaking back and forth, her hands over her mouth.

"No . . . Reagan, no!"

I burst into strained sobs, unable to try and brush it off as something else. My boyfriend of the last sixteen months had just broken my heart. He'd called our baby a thing. I'd been stressing over hiding my bump with loose-fitting clothing for almost a month now. I'd barely turned sixteen and was having a baby.

All the emotions crashed down on me, and no matter how much I wanted to deny it, I needed my mom right now.

"M-mom." I somehow managed to say through the near-hyperventilating crying.

"No. What have you done?" she shrieked as she backed away from me.

"Mom, please!"

I'd followed her into my bedroom, and our heads turned

toward my door when heavy footsteps sounded on the stairs. My older brother burst into my room quickly followed by my dad.

What is he already doing home? He usually isn't home for another few hours.

I panicked when I saw the look of horror cross both their faces. Their eyes glued to my stomach. I quickly pulled my shirt down to cover it, but my arms stayed in front of my little bump, like I was protecting my baby from what was about to happen.

"Daddy," I cried, and started to take a step toward him, but he took one away.

"I'm going to kill him," my brother, Keegan, whispered. "I swear to God I'll kill him."

"What have you done, Reagan?" Mom screamed again.

My chest ached, and the tears somehow—impossibly—fell harder. "Mom, I'm—"

"Tell me you're not pregnant! Damn it, Reagan, tell me!"

Hands gripped my arms just as my knees gave out beneath me. "Stop screaming at her!" Keegan yelled back as he walked me toward my bed. "She's upset enough as it is, you're not helping anything."

When we were sitting, I gripped my brother's hand like a lifeline . . . the only way I could thank him in that moment.

"Did you know this?" Mom turned her attention on Keegan, her voice still shrill. "Did you know this, and you kept it from us?"

"Austin wouldn't be alive if I'd known about this! But you're making this worse, she's probably terrified and you yelling is stressing her out!"

"Don't tell me how to react to this situation! Don't you dare! Get out of the room!"

"Mom, I'm pissed too! I'm forcing myself not to leave this

house because I know I'll go hunt Austin down. But we need to calm down for Reagan! If she's pregnant, this isn't going to help the baby."

Mom gripped my desk like she needed it to stay standing. Even though her voice wavered, she never stopped screaming. "She can't be pregnant . . . Reagan, you can't be pregnant!"

Even though Keegan was trying to calm the room, my dad was the only one that hadn't spoken and not crying. I looked at him, hoping for something from him. Anything. But his eyes were still glued to my stomach. "Dad . . .?"

He slowly looked up at me, his face still showing how horrified he was. "I can't even look at you right now. You're not my daughter."

"Daddy!" I choked out when he turned and left the room.

"Dad!" Keegan barked, his hold on me tightening.

"Why would you let this happen?"

I looked back to my mom when her now-soft voice reached me. Somehow, my heart continued to break even more when I saw the disappointment in her eyes.

"This can't be happening," she said, and then turned to quickly leave my room.

I collapsed into Keegan's arms, and was surprised at the force of my next round of sobs. I hadn't expected my family to be happy, but even my worst fears hadn't been prepared for that. We'd heard the front door slam shut just a few minutes after Mom had left my room, and from her pleas as she called him over and over again, I'd known he left.

"I'm sorry," I mumbled hours later when my tears had run dry. Keegan hadn't once left my side. "I'm so sorry."

He kissed the top of my head and hugged me tighter. "*I'm* sorry,

Ray. I—I can't believe this either, but you know I'm always here for you. They'll come around, they're just shocked right now."

"They hate me."

"No they don't. You just need to wait until they process it." I didn't respond, because I didn't believe him. A few minutes later, he asked, "Does Austin know?"

I nodded my head and told him everything that had happened that afternoon. I didn't cry again, I wasn't sure if I'd ever be able to cry again. My voice was robotic as I replayed the conversation, and I didn't flinch when Keegan's hard voice swore again that he would kill Austin. I knew he wouldn't, but I had no doubt that he would do something.

Keegan held me until I fell asleep on his shoulder from the exhaustion of the day. When I woke, it was dark in my room, but I could still make out my dad's shape as he sat on the edge of my bed, his back to me, one of his hands gripping mine. I didn't move, or give any indication that I'd woken. To be honest, I was afraid of what he'd say to me now.

He hunched in on himself, and his hands tightened around mine. And for the first time in my life, I watched my dad as he cried.

Chapter 1

Six and a half years later . . .

Reagan

BENDING DOWN TO kiss my son's head, I straightened and tip-toed out of his room, shutting the door behind me. Grabbing my phone, I called my mom as I went around the apartment picking up the toys Parker had received for his sixth birthday.

"Hi, sweetheart!"

"Hey, Mom," I huffed as I dropped everything into his toy chest, and let the lid shut. "Parker passed out playing."

Her soft laugh filled the phone. "I bet, today was crazy. Did he have fun?"

"Understatement. 'Fun' is an understatement. Thank you for everything you did to help, he really did have a blast, and he *loved* his presents."

"Good, I'm glad. What are you going to do for the rest of the night? Did you want to come over for brunch tomorrow?"

I smiled as I waited for the next words that would come from her.

"I just hate that you two are so far away."

Laughing, I plopped down on the couch and stretched out. "It's not even a ten minute drive!"

"But you're all alone, and ten minutes is a long time in case of an emergency."

"Mom, I love you, we're fine. I'm just going to watch TV until I'm tired, and, yes, brunch tomorrow sounds great."

There was a beat of silence before she said, "You're always welcome to bring someone, honey."

I suppressed a groan. I knew she was just looking out for Parker and me, but I didn't need—or want—a man in my life.

There hadn't been anyone since Austin had given me an ultimatum of being together, or keeping Parker. There hadn't been a need for a guy. I knew no one would want a child at my age, and I had my family. Even though the first day of my family knowing had been intense—well, really, the first week had been—my family had supported my decision to keep the baby, and had been there for me through everything. Keegan had gone to Austin's that first night and beaten the shit out of him. Austin and his parents hadn't pressed charges when Keegan told his parents about our break up, and Austin hadn't said a word to me since.

I'd continued going to school, and when rumors had started flying about my growing belly, Austin had told all our friends that I'd cheated on him. He'd taken another beating from Keegan for that, but I'd never tried to stop the rumors. Like I'd done in our last minutes together, I'd refused to give him the satisfaction of seeing how much he'd hurt me.

I refused to let *anyone* see how much they were hurting me.

With help from my mom, I'd finished out the rest of high school, and graduated with a 3.9 GPA. Even though my parents encouraged me to go to college, I'd decided against it and had immediately began looking for a job that could support my son and me. I'd started at the bottom of a local business, and had slowly worked my way up over the last six years. Within six months of graduating, Parker and I moved into the apartment we still lived in, and I'd fought my mom on putting him in daycare.

She'd won.

She watched him while I worked, but I paid her just as much as the nicest daycare in the city charged. I wasn't stupid, though, I knew she was "secretly" putting the money in a college account for Parker. But Dad had made me promise I wouldn't let on the fact that I knew, so I'd kept paying her, and Parker had continued going to her house five days a week until he'd gone into Kindergarten this last year.

My life was perfect. My son was healthy and incredibly smart, he and I both had a great relationship with my parents and brother, and I was supporting us well enough that we lived in a great complex and I could give him whatever he wanted. Eh, well, to an extent. But why mess that up by throwing a guy in the picture?

"Mom, I'm not bringing anyone."

"You need a man in your life . . . *Parker* needs a dad."

Damn it. I hated when she involved Parker . . . she knew how that got to me. "He has Keegan and Dad."

"Keegan only comes home every other weekend if he's not deployed."

Keegan had joined the Army after deciding college wasn't for him two years in. I was so proud of him for doing something with his life. "And he's getting out soon, so he'll be around more."

"I know you *can* do this on your own, Reagan. But that doesn't mean you have to or should."

"Dating would be exhausting for me . . . and I don't want to put Parker through that." I chewed on my bottom lip for a second as I debated whether or not I should voice my fears. With a hard breath, I told her the rest quickly. "Austin didn't want him, I wouldn't be able to handle it if I let someone into our life and he decided he didn't want Parker either."

"Reagan," she said, her voice wavering. "They won't all be like him."

"I know, I just—I'm not ready for that possibility. You know? I can take the rejection . . . just not if they reject him."

"I understand, sweetheart. I really do. But I'll never stop praying for the perfect man for you and Parker."

I wanted to tell her that even if he was out there, I probably wouldn't give him the time of day; but the way she was talking broke my heart, so I kept my mouth shut. I knew everyone in my family wanted that for Parker and me, and it's not that I didn't want that for us either. I just couldn't imagine myself taking that leap of faith in someone else. Someone that could potentially ruin us forever.

Coen

"SACO, MAN, YOU can't let her fucking do this to you. It's your fucking kid, she can't just keep him from you."

"What am I supposed to do? Try to get custody of him from my own wife? I've never even seen him before. I was gone through Liv's pregnancy, the delivery, and for the first five months of his life. No judge is going to grant me custody."

"So you're actually going to listen to her? This is bullshit."

"I know, Steele, but I have no choice. I *need* to be able to see my son. I'm already waiting on this realtor to go look at some places. I'll call you when I have news, yeah?"

"Yeah, all right. Sorry this is happening, man, I really am."

"Me too." An exhausted sigh sounded through the phone. "Later."

I pressed END, and looked over at Hudson. "His bitch wife is making him buy them a house before she'll let him meet their son."

"The fuck?" Hudson, said and lowered himself into a chair. "Can she do that?"

I shrugged and tossed my phone onto my dresser. "Apparently, because he's meeting with a realtor."

Our friend, Brody Saco, had gotten out of the Army not even a week ago. He'd been planning on making this a career, but all that had changed when his girl from back home wound up pregnant. He'd married her immediately, and ever since, she'd refused to see him or let him meet their son . . . and it'd been a year since their wedding. I could respect him for taking responsibility, but we all felt bad for him because he was the only one that couldn't see she was just dragging him through the mud.

"What are you doing this weekend?" Hudson asked me, and it was then I noticed he was shoving some clothes in a backpack.

"Got some shoots booked in the area. You heading home?"

He nodded as he continued packing. "Yeah, I missed my

nephew's birthday last weekend, I need to go see him and my sister."

"All right, I'll see you when you get back."

"If you don't feel like coming back to base between your shoots, hit me up, you can stay at my parents place or something."

I laughed and shook my head. "Nah, I'm good. Thanks though."

Hudson stopped at the door, and a knowing look crossed his face. "Try to get some sleep."

"Uh . . . yeah. I'll do that."

He knew better than anyone that wouldn't be happening. I was lucky if I got two hours in a night. If I didn't have photos I could edit during those long hours, I would go insane.

Once he was gone, I made sure everything was charged, and packed up all my equipment before heading out to the studio I had about forty minutes from base. I had a few photo shoots set up for the night—some with friends, and one with a new client. The shoots, along with the editing and wedding I was covering tomorrow, would keep me busy throughout the weekend. Busy was how I liked my life. How I preferred it. It kept me from remembering things I wished I'd never seen.

TWO WEEKS LATER, I walked into the room I'd been sharing with Hudson for the last few years, and stood there staring at everything for a few minutes. Today was bittersweet. It was a day I'd been waiting on for months now, and at the same time, a day I couldn't have prepared for.

I'd been in the Army for almost six years, and like Saco, I'd been prepared to make this a career. But with my photography business taking off and demanding more of my time, I'd had to make a decision. The Army was all I'd known since I turned eighteen, but in the last year, I'd started realizing that photography was more than a hobby; it was my passion.

I hadn't thought I was getting out for another month or so, but I'd gotten the call this morning and had spent the next handful of hours in an office waiting, and then signing my separation papers. Typical "Hurry up and wait", and then, *"Surprise, fucker!"* bullshit for the military. Like I should have expected anything else.

Halfway through throwing everything in my bags, and moving my camera equipment out to my car, Hudson came back.

"Man, with you and Saco gone, it's gonna be boring as shit until I get out of here too."

"Aww, you're gonna miss me? Touched, bro, really am. But I told you, I don't swing that way," I joked with him as I grabbed more of my stuff.

"Fuck off, Steele. You know what I meant. Whatever, though, I'll be out of here soon."

"Are you going to get a place with your girl?"

Hudson fell onto his bed and stretched out. "Probably, it'd just be easier that way. But I don't know if she really wants to move half an hour away. I mean, I know its not far, but her job is close to here, and I need to be close to my sister."

Out of all the things we'd talked about through the years, his sister wasn't one of them. All I knew was if he wasn't sticking around base on the weekends so he could see his girlfriend, he was going home so he could be near his sister and her son. "I've never asked because I figured you'd tell me if you wanted me to know. But what is it with your sister that always has you going home?"

He thought for a few minutes before responding. "Reagan just needs me. She'd never admit that, she's stubborn and independent as shit; but she needs me. We've always been close, but she got pregnant when she was sixteen, and her asshole boyfriend told her to have an abortion or he was leaving her."

"Shit."

"Yeah, obviously he's not in the picture anymore, but all her friends ditched her, and she only had our parents and me on her side after that. She's done well for herself and is an awesome mom, but she thinks she has to do this all alone. Like I said, stubborn and independent. The only guys around her son are my dad and me, and he's six now. He needs male role models in his life, you know?"

"Understand. That sucks for her, though."

My mom had had me when she was a teenager as well, but had given me up for adoption as soon as I'd been born. I'd never resented her, because I'd grown up in a great family . . . and obviously she couldn't have given me that. That didn't stop me from wondering why she hadn't tried. So hearing about Reagan had me impressed with her drive, and I'd never even met her.

"That it does"—Hudson's voice interrupted my thoughts—"so are you moving back home?"

"Ahh, nah. I don't think so. I miss California and all, but I'd miss my studio. I have a lot of clients here that I can keep using, and I'd miss the location. Colorado is a lot nicer to look at and shoot in than where I grew up."

Hudson laughed, "I bet. Well, where you gonna stay? I know you weren't expecting to get out today."

"I'll just crash in my studio until I find a place, no big deal."

"You sure? I can call one of my buddies."

"Appreciate it, man, but for what? So I can *not* sleep on their couch? I have couches in the studio if I need to pass out."

He looked at me for a few moments before saying, "You should really talk to someone. They could help."

I knew he was looking out for me, but I hated when people said shit like that. I didn't need help. "I have nothing to say to anyone, there's no point."

Sensing my unease with the conversation, Hudson held up his hands like he was surrendering and changed the subject. "Well your studio is close to where my family is and where I'll be looking for a place when I get out. So let's grab some beers when you're not busy, all right? Actually, I'm heading home this weekend, want to go out and celebrate your civilian status tonight?"

"Civilian," I huffed and shook my head. "Fuck this is gonna be weird. I don't know if I remember how to be a civilian."

"It'll be easier than you think, I'm sure."

I somehow doubted that. Grabbing the last of my bags, I looked over at him and nodded. "Yeah, let's go out tonight. Call me when you head into the city, I'm gonna take everything to the studio and look at the places around there for a few hours."

"Will do, see you later."

With one last look at the room, I turned and headed out of the barracks to start my new *civilian* life. Jesus Christ that was going to take some getting used to.

Don't Miss NEW BOOKS from your
FAVORITE NEW ADULT AUTHORS

Cora Carmack

LOSING IT A Novel
Available in Paperback and eBook

FAKING IT A Novel
Available in Paperback and eBook

KEEPING HER An Original eNovella
eBook on Sale August 2013

FINDING IT A Novel
Available in Paperback and eBook Fall 2013

Jay Crownover

RULE A Novel
Available in eBook
Available in Paperback Fall 2013

JET A Novel
Available in eBook
Available in Paperback Fall 2013

ROME A Novel
Available in Paperback and eBook Winter 2014

Lisa Desrochers

A LITTLE TOO FAR A Novel
Available in eBook Fall 2013

A LITTLE TOO MUCH A Novel
Available in eBook Fall 2013

A LITTLE TOO HOT A Novel
Available in eBook Winter 2014

Abigail Gibbs

THE DARK HEROINE A Novel
Available in Paperback and eBook

AUTUMN ROSE A Novel
Available in Paperback and eBook Winter 2014

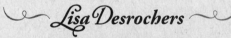